THE Spinster AND I

Also by

Rebecca Connolly

The Arrangements:

An Arrangement of Sorts

Married to the Marquess

Secrets of a Spinster

The Dangers of Doing Good

The Burdens of a Bachelor

A Bride Worth Taking

A Wager Worth Making

A Gerrard Family Christmas

The London League:

The Lady and the Gent

A Rogue About Town

Coming Soon

Spinster and Spice

THE Spinster AND I

REBECCA CONNOLLY

Phase Publishing, LLC

Seattle

Phase Publishing, LLC first paperback edition
November 2018

ISBN 978-1-943048-70-0
Library of Congress Control Number 2018961299

Cataloging-in-Publication Data on file.

Acknowledgements

To Steph, who shares my love for a good love story, who loves the shy girl romances, and who played a key role in so many of my adventures. No one sings in the car with me like you do, and I'm grateful for all the times people got us confused. *Sláinte!*

And to Claire Foy, my key inspiration for Prue, and one of the most elegant, talented, incandescent actresses of our day. Can we please be friends? Think about it. Get back to me. Thanks much.

Want to hear about future releases and upcoming events for Rebecca Connolly?

Sign up for the monthly Wit and Whimsy at:

www.rebeccaconnolly.com

Prologue
Mayfair, 1815

"Miss Westfall, we have an idea."

Prue turned to look at Miss Lambert and Miss Allen, both hurrying towards her. She wasn't entirely sure why they bothered with haste, it was not as though she was going anywhere. She was perfectly situated in her usual chair, as she always was, and no one would have to work hard to find her even at a ball like this.

No one ever sought to find her anyway, for which she was most grateful.

Imagine having to talk with people for an extended time, or perhaps to even dance with them!

Her face flamed just at the thought of it.

"Oh dear," Miss Lambert simpered as she sat down beside her. "We haven't even told you, and we've embarrassed you already."

Prue shook her head quickly, feeling the ribbons in her hair shift within the too-loose curls. "N-not at a-all." She frowned, her brow puckered, and she gripped the fan in her hands tightly. "F-forgive me, it's n-not you."

Miss Lambert looked sympathetic, no doubt hearing the nervous stammer Prue had never managed to be rid of, even with her mother's scolding.

"You can say that, dear, but it's all over your face."

"We don't mean to be intimidating," Miss Allen agreed from her other side. "We've just had an idea and wanted to include you in it."

Prue looked at the fairer of the cousins in outright bewilderment. "Me?" she asked, too shocked to even stammer.

Miss Allen nodded quickly, smiling almost mischievously. "We've already got Miss Asheley and Miss Wright to join us, and with you, we will have five, which is quite a pretty number."

"For w-what?" Prue inquired, looking between the two.

Miss Asheley was nice enough, but Miss Wright was quite a terrifying creature, being both beautiful and bold without being scandalous. Prue wasn't sure she wanted to be in the same circles with her.

"For a group of spinsters, if you'll forgive the term," Miss Lambert gushed, her cheeks coloring in excitement almost to match the color of her hair. "And if you'll permit me to ask… how well can you write, Miss Westfall?"

Chapter One
Tinley House, 1818

Ladies who play the wallflower have earned themselves quite an unfair reputation in their time, though their existence is quite timeless. Society would label them as plain, tiresome, and occasionally unpleasant. This, more often than not, is untrue. They are quite often good, sweet girls with much to say and much to offer. They just aren't quite sure how to go about it.

-The Spinster Chronicles, 7 December 1817

"Smile, Prudence. Whatever else you do, you must smile."

"I know, Mother."

"No, you don't, or you would do it!" she snapped, fluttering her fan in agitation as she speared Prue with a cold look. "And don't be a mouse. This is a grand opportunity for you, and I will not see you waste it on being a corner-dwelling potted plant."

Prue bit the inside of her cheek and lowered her chin dutifully. It would do no good to respond to that, and her mother would not hear it even if she did. She could agree with her mother and still be scolded for it. She had certainly been scolded for less, and at times without any reason.

Prue never did the right thing, and receiving a scolding had become second nature to her now.

She could only hope and pray that her mother would contain her distaste for her, and her instinct to correct, now that they were more observed than ever. Prue had enough to be getting on with on her own, but to have her mother draw even more attention to them, and in such an unfavorable light, would only make things worse.

Not that it could get much worse than it already was, she supposed.

Her life had been turned upside down only two months ago, and she feverishly wished for her former life once more.

Not this. Anything but this.

Her mother clicked her tongue and fanned herself again as they proceeded down the stairs to the dining room. "I still cannot believe that we are even here, Prudence."

Neither could she, it was so far-fetched, but her mother hadn't said much on the subject, so Prue was only too relieved to hear a similar sentiment at last. "I know," Prue sighed, adjusting her almost blindingly white gloves. "It hardly seems real."

"Indeed," her mother agreed with a brisk nod. "A house party during the Season? What can Mrs. Davies be thinking of? I am amazed that anybody is here at all."

The wave of disappointment should have been fairly commonplace, even expected, and yet Prue felt uncomfortable. She should have known that her mother wouldn't be concerned about the same things that Prue was; she never had been. She would be more concerned about the timing of the house party than the fact that they had been invited to the house party at all.

Prudence Westfall, by all accounts, did not get invited to private events.

Marjorie Westfall did not care about the events her daughter went to unless she was going herself.

They had managed to do quite well in that arrangement, aside from the moments where she had opted on a public shaming for her only child due to some flaw she imagined. Those had become more frequent of late, despite Prue's growing more accommodating, and it had begun to draw more notice.

For a girl used to being neglected, there was nothing more unnerving than attention, and even more so for the negativity of the situation.

But she would gladly have gone back to such days, and to such neglect.

It was unlikely she would ever know such bliss again.

Cursed late Aunt Harriett.

"Ah, dinner," her mother huffed, ruffling the lace at her chest in irritation. "No doubt it will be some sort of stew as though we are in the country, despite being just out of the London neighborhoods."

Prue closed her eyes and felt her palms perspire. Her mother had done nothing but complain since they had arrived at Tinley House this morning, though she was the one who had insisted on accepting the invitation to the house party in the first place. She had further demanded that she come along as chaperone for Prue, showing a matronly concern that had never been in her nature before.

Never once had she asked Prue what she wanted to do, or how she felt about matters, which seemed a backwards way to go about things, as Prue was the one who had inherited.

It was Prue who had a fortune.

It was Prue who was now an heiress.

It was Prue who was now one of the most highly sought-after women in London.

It was Prue.

And Prue did not want any of this.

But as Prue had never managed to find either a voice for herself or the will to stand up for anything, they were here.

Where she could not hide, as she had been doing the past few weeks in London.

Where any of the men in attendance could find her with ease.

And if Mrs. Davies had invited the same number of men as she had of women, as was tasteful, there would be several more than Prue was comfortable with.

Especially considering she was hardly comfortable with one.

Her cheeks flamed at the thought.

"Prudence," her mother chirped at once. "Don't color so! We are going in to dinner, and your impossible habit is going to make you look unsightly before all the rest, and the other girls are far prettier and more accomplished than you. They don't have your fortune, but it is a trial to endure your company, so you must work twice as hard."

Prue nodded obediently, having heard all of this before. Dinner was not terrifying, considering she could occupy herself with eating without putting anybody off. If she were seated next to a young woman, it would be easier, and she knew most of them well enough that polite conversation over a meal, if necessary, would be comfortable enough. She would feel only slightly nervous, and with luck, she'd endure only moderate stammering.

If Mrs. Davies knew anything about Prue at all, which was something of a question in Prue's mind, she would know to do that.

And she would have her mother at the opposite end of the table.

Her mother paused outside of the dining room with a frown. "Do we go into the dining room? Or to a parlor where we are shown in?"

Prue tried her best not to smile. For all her high and mighty ways, her mother did not have the background or pedigree Society demanded and still did not know the ways of things. And she did not listen, as they had been instructed as to the procedure. "I b-believe the parlor, Mother."

That earned her a sharp glare. "No stammering!" her mother barked as she marched past her to the parlor.

"Yes, ma'am," Prue muttered, following behind.

Her mother had never had patience with Prue's shyness and even less for her blushing, but nothing irritated her like Prue's stammering. Her irritation with any of them only made everything worse, until it was all Prue could do to escape for some solitude to breathe.

Breathe in, breathe out. Fear in, fear out.

The pattern was the same as it had been when she was five, and her father had taught it to her. He'd never minded her overwhelming shyness and her nervous stammering; he'd said it was what made her endearing and real. Then he'd pinch her nose, wink, and laugh his growling laugh.

But whenever she got overworked or stammered up a storm, he would take her face in his hands, and repeat the pattern until she was calm.

He had been gone for years, but it was his voice in her head when she needed calm. It never worked as fast without his hands on her face, but she was now very much used to that.

She was always on her own now.

Always.

None of the ladies in the parlor talked with Prue, aside from Mrs. Davies, who had greeted her warmly; but, she wanted Prue to marry her son.

She wanted any of the women here to marry her son.

Given the variety of said women, fortune aside, it appeared she was not very particular.

Prue wondered just what Mr. Charles Davies had to say about the matter, being the potential groom.

Oddly enough, her mother was speaking with several of the other mothers or chaperones and seemed to be getting along rather well with them.

Either they were the most polite women in the world, or the most ridiculous.

Dinner was announced quickly, much to Prue's relief, and they were met by the gentlemen on the way to the dining room. Why they had been separated was as much of a mystery to her as to anyone else. It didn't make any sense, given that they were spending five days in each other's company, and the awkwardness of dinner had to be endured before they could get to the freedom of the dance.

But it was not Prue's house party, which was something of a contradiction in terms, and she was only here to avoid a confrontation with her mother of heretofore unimagined proportions. She would endure what she must, if she must.

Which she must.

Her dinner companions were not interested in speaking with her, and her mother was too far away to notice.

The gentleman across the table, however, stared at Prue far too often. She searched her memory for his name, knowing they had been introduced at one time, but seven Seasons allowed for a great many acquaintances to pass through her mind without any significance.

He had paid her no mind before, but she had far more to offer now.

A great deal more.

Posture perfect as it ever was, Prue managed to keep her eyes downcast almost the entire meal. Her eyes would raise enough to flick around, searching for any familiar faces, and finding none. But Mr. Stared-Too-Much was not the only one looking in her direction, and she felt the slow burn of her skin beginning at her neck.

Soon, it would reach her ears, and then her cheeks, and there was no hope once it was there.

Her tripe earned such focus that any observant individual would think it her favorite meal, which it most certainly was not, but she would swallow anything edible, whether palatable or not, to avoid knowledge of attention on her.

An unsettled stomach was far preferable to an unsettled mind.

The conversation at the table swirled around her, everybody jovial and talkative, laughing and excited about the party and its activities. There was distraction enough that it seemed of little importance to anyone that Prue was not participating in any of the discussions, aside from her staring neighbor across the way.

If she reached for her water with a bit of gusto, she could knock aside the candelabra directly into his face or lap…

But she found her glass in her grasp without any flicker to the flames, and after a small sip, it was returned to its position without incident.

She could never cause a scene, no matter how she imagined it. She would never recover from the shame and guilt of such an event.

She had enough trouble as it was.

"And how are you, Miss Westfall?" Charles Davies suddenly asked from her left.

Prue hadn't known he was beside her. She hadn't paid attention to that, but she certainly had not expected that Mrs. Davies would seat her son directly next to her.

She must have wanted Prue for her son more desperately than previously anticipated.

Prue stalled by taking extra care to chew her already soft potatoes, her cheeks flaming. "T-tolerably w-well, thank y-you."

A strained look suddenly filled his features, but he smiled, all the same, turning back to the more loquacious girl on his other side.

The burning in her face raged on, and her throat suddenly constricted, her embarrassment causing her stomach to churn unpleasantly.

Tangle-tongued little fool. Mr. Davies had only asked how she was, sheer politeness, and yet she had panicked and stammered like a ninny.

She *was* a ninny. And she was desperate for home.

She ate the rest of her meal in silence, refusing to look up even momentarily.

Soon enough, dinner was finished, and they all moved to the ballroom, despite not having enough in their group to fill it. But the room was small and rather cozy for a ballroom, which Lady Hetty Redgrave would have had something to say about if she were here. But spinsters of seventy-some-odd years were not marital candidates for anybody, though it seemed stammering spinsters of five-and-twenty were.

The musicians began to play, and dancing commenced, and Prue fled to a corner where chairs had been set up. Thankfully, there were enough guests in attendance to hide her from her mother, who seemed to be getting along splendidly with Mrs. Davies, much to Prue's horror and chagrin.

Not that there was anything particularly wrong with Mrs. Davies or her son, Charles, but Prue had no intention of being married off for her newfound fortune, especially not to somebody who could not be bothered with her before she had it. The best thing that she could say about Charles Davies was that he had never been cruel to or about her, as far as she knew. He had been much like all the rest of London Society, forgetting that she existed and exuding only minimal patience when recollection returned.

Prue was used to it by now, and more comfortable for the neglect. People had never been comfortable creatures for her, though she had no notion as to why she was so terrified in general. She could not recall ever not being afraid of attention or conversation, and only those who took the time and the care to truly come to know her ever reached a level of comfort for her.

Even her friends in the Spinsters still managed to make her stammer from time to time, depending on what it was they had said. She was easily embarrassed, as they knew full well, and it never stopped them from uttering the extraordinary things they did, but she had learned to adjust to it.

As they had learned to adjust to her.

They took care of her far better and far more tenderly than her mother ever had, and she wished desperately that even one of them had been invited to this melee of a house party with her. Just one of them would have been enough to set her at ease.

But Izzy Lambert did not have affluence enough to be considered a candidate, nor did Grace Morledge, which was surprising as her fortune was more than respectable, and she was beautiful. Charlotte Wright certainly did, but Charlotte tended to take over a place when she was in it, and she would undoubtedly have taken attention away from the other ladies.

Clearly, Mrs. Davies did not want her son to marry someone as headstrong and independent as Charlotte Wright.

Elinor Asheley was too young and too poor, and Lady Edith Leveson… Well, Edith was a young widow with an unclear financial situation, and most of London did not know about her yet.

And then there was Georgie Allen. She had been the leader of the Spinsters, in a way, and the one who had started them all. Yet she had married some weeks ago to Captain Anthony Sterling, who was undoubtedly the only man on earth that did not make Prue exceptionally nervous. He was handsome, kind, charming, well set up, and extraordinarily patient, which he would need to be with a marriage to Georgie.

Prue had very faintly, and very secretly, hoped that she might have been able to marry Tony herself, but it was clear from the start where his interest lay, and she could not have wished for more than that.

She was happy for her friends, as she should be, but she also had been filled with a sense of despair. Who in the world would be as patient with her as Tony?

She had grown accustomed to the idea of being alone for the rest of her life, which would not have been such a trial if her mother had been a different sort. Her future as it was would bind the two of them together for the rest of their days, and Prue would always be corrected and blamed, scolded and despaired of.

That was no future she wanted. Her only escape would have been marriage, and her only dream was to have a quiet, content little house of her own.

But then everything had changed.

Word had reached her scarcely two months ago via a letter from a solicitor that her father's sister, Harriett, who had been something of an heiress despite the lack of prosperity in Prue's family, had died without issue, and had bestowed her entire fortune, and her estate, to Prue. She, who had only known Prue as a child and had not seen her in at least fifteen years, named her niece as beneficiary, effectively ruining the solitude for which Prue longed.

Now her mother was invested in everything Prue did and everywhere she went. Now she was concerned about suitors and status. Now she was making arrangements and alterations to their routine and way of life.

With the change in luck, and considering Prue's age, she ought to have been independent, as she was well into her majority and the fortune was hers and not her mother's, but nothing could have been further from the truth. She was weak and timid, and her mother knew it well. She would lord over her for the rest of time, possibly even over whatever husband Prue managed to secure, if any.

Worse, her mother had been the one to make it known that her daughter was now an heiress, seeing a great opportunity for herself in the change. She told everybody she could, including her beloved sister and niece, who held an even worse opinion of Prue than her mother did. Eliza had not wasted any time letting Prue know precisely what she had thought of that change in situation.

Prue, on the other hand, had not said a single word about it to anyone, including the Spinsters.

She couldn't.

Her worst fears were now coming to pass. She was suddenly receiving callers and being approached by men who had skirted the edges of rooms to escape being trapped in a conversation with her. Not that there was any trap at all, she preferred not to speak to them either, but somehow the message had been confused there. She was grateful that none of her friends had witnessed such a thing, as it had only happened twice before they'd gallivanted off to this ridiculous house party.

It really was silly to have such an event in the middle of the Season, but everyone in attendance was sure to be an excellent candidate for anyone looking.

What else could eligible men and women hope for?

Prue shuddered delicately, returning her focus to the room.

And to the four men approaching her.

Oh no…

Two sat beside her, two stood in front.

She was surrounded.

"Miss Westfall," the one to her right said, taking her hand in his. "You are a vision this evening."

A vision? She wore an old lavender gown, as the ones her mother had commissioned on her behalf hadn't been finished before they left. Her hair was the same sort of simple style she usually favored, which her mother had criticized harshly, and her hand was shaking in her new gloves.

She was a vision of a pathetic creature, and that was all.

And she could not remember his name.

"Th-thank…" she tried, stammering and shaking.

"Radiant," one of the standing ones said. "Quite simply radiant."

"Please say you'll dance the next with me, Miss Westfall," the man to her left gushed. "You are so light on your feet, and I so adore dancing, so I must have the chance."

She glanced over at him, the heat from her neck rising quickly into the rest of her face. She could dance well enough, it was true, but he wouldn't know that. More than that, he'd been trying for Emmaline Hurst two weeks ago, and she could not dance even if it only required her to step from side to side. No one who adored dancing would try for her.

"I…" she began, her throat tightening painfully.

"No, with me, Miss Westfall," the fourth chimed in. "Allow me."

"Might I get you some lemonade, Miss Westfall?"

"Would it be too forward if I had two dances?"

"Do you sing, Miss Westfall? I imagine you to have the voice of an angel."

Well, if they were only going to talk at her and not to her, she would not have to respond, and all of this would require minimal effort from her. That might not be so bad, but it would hardly get them anywhere. And considering all of them were exerting themselves for her particular attention, she was inundated with flattery, praise, and pleadings, none of which ought to have been showered upon her, of all people.

The music ended, and they renewed their requests with fervor.

"Me, Miss Westfall," the first seated man said.

"Oh, please with me, Miss Westfall," Standing One said.

"I insist upon two," Standing Two said.

"The waltz!" Seated Two said. "Can you waltz?"

"Me!"

"Me!"

"Me!"

Blood thundered in Prue's ears, drowning them all out, and yet the noise continued to build. Tremors raced up and down her arms, and hazy dots appeared at the edges of her vision. She needed to get away from them.

Now.

Otherwise, she would faint, and one of them would have the privilege of seeing to her care, and someone would presume an understanding between them, and she would wind up engaged before she came to.

Her breath hitched at the thought, and she practically jumped to her feet.

"Exc-cuse m-me," she frantically stammered, sidestepping the standing pair and running as fast as she could.

Thankfully, there were enough people to hinder anyone from following easily, and she was small enough to dash between other guests, most of whom didn't look twice at her flight. The terrace was at the far edge of the ballroom, and a door was slightly ajar.

She fixed her eyes upon that door as though it were the gates to heaven itself, despite the faint calls of "Miss Westfall!" from behind her. She would not stop for them, not even if her mother had barred the way. She had no thought but running, and running far.

She'd have run all the way back to London if she could have.

Prue shoved the terrace door open and moved instantly to the railing at the edge, praying no one would follow.

"Miss Westfall?"

Prue hiccupped and quickly moved down the small stairs beside her towards the garden, tucking in against the shadows of the terrace and the house itself rather than proceeding into the gardens. She heard footsteps approach and squeezed her eyes shut, praying her impromptu hiding place would be safe enough, and that her panicked breathing would not be as audible as it seemed to her.

"I thought you said she came out here!"

"I thought she did."

"Well, I don't see her, and she didn't… Did she go into the garden?"

There was a moment of silence, then a heaving sigh. "Fine, she must be inside. Flighty little thing, nobody ever mentioned that."

"Well, just try harder, old boy. Patience, remember?"

Their voices faded with their footsteps, and Prue allowed herself to release a very shaky sigh of relief. This was all getting to be too ridiculous, and it had only just begun. She needed the Spinsters here to help her, she needed Tony to guard her, she needed Lady Hetty to ward people off, she needed…

Breathe in, breathe out. Fear in, fear out.

She breathed for as long as she could, and only when her face was cool, and her tremors were gone did she open her eyes. She shook her head and straightened up, slowly moving back towards the stairs.

There were a great many things that she needed, starting with a backbone.

"You'd better come up here now, pet. The grass will be damp, and you won't want to spoil those slippers."

Prue's heart began racing again as she fearfully lifted her eyes towards the balcony and the unknown voice.

Chapter Two

What is given in confidence ought to remain in confidence, and the one confiding ought to take much care with the nature of what they are confiding. Strangers make for very poor confidantes. And friends are even worse.

-The Spinster Chronicles, 17 July 1817

Camden Vale hadn't meant to be disturbed out on the terrace of Tinley House, and he'd had no reason to suspect he would be. A dance after dinner on the first night of a house party? No one would be proceeding out to the terrace for some barely observed private conversations this early.

He couldn't even have said why he'd come to this farce of a house party, as he was neither on the hunt for a wife nor a good candidate for one. But with nothing better to do and no good reason to refuse, he'd come along. Sure enough, there weren't any men of particular sense here, and while he couldn't say much for any of the young ladies, knowing so few of them, he hadn't been particularly encouraged.

House parties, as a general rule, followed the same sort of procedure. He'd attended a few of them as the years had passed, being something of an entertaining figure for those wanting gossip to catch their event in its clutches. Nothing really surprised him about parties or people anymore, and he hardly ever surprised himself, either.

But when a tiny young woman in a pale dress had burst out onto the terrace without seeing him, and then dashed down the stairs and into hiding when Mr. Frist and Mr. Gardiner came in pursuit, he'd been more than surprised. And then he'd gone and shaken his head when Gardiner had asked him if she'd gone into the garden, surprising himself yet again. Why should he help her hide?

Then again, why should he let them find her if she wanted to be hidden?

He did not care very much either way, but it was clear they believed him, and he could only be grateful his expression had been blank enough to hide the truth.

He'd waited a few moments after they had retreated, listening to see what the mystery girl would do, and when it was clear she would do nothing but expel some labored breathing, he'd thought it was best if she knew she was not alone.

"You'd better come up here now, pet," he called softly, keeping his voice as gentle as possible. "The grass will be damp, and you won't want to spoil those slippers."

She yelped and came into sight as she scrambled backwards, the light of the windows spilling onto her slight frame, making her dark hair glint with an almost copper shade. Her gloved hands clasped in front of her mouth, and her wide, pale eyes fixed on him in sheer terror.

And she didn't even know his reputation yet.

Poor thing.

Camden continued leaning against the balustrade, watching her. "I should have told you I was here before this, but…" He gestured dismissively to the ballroom, keeping his eyes on her.

She said nothing in response, and a slow spread of color appeared on the exposed skin of her chest, neck, and face, rather like a sunrise.

It would have been fascinating had she not seemed so utterly paralyzed.

"Come on," he urged, waving his hand. "Come on up here. You can sit on this bench out of the grass. It's all right, you're quite safe from me."

She leaned a little away from him, and he thought she might run off into the gardens. He'd be honor bound to pursue, and that would have terrified her more. Then he'd either be a hero or a villain, if not both. He'd probably wind up having to marry her, and nobody needed that.

Least of all her.

But then she surprised him by walking forward, her eyes lowered as his servants might have done. She paused at the top stair and glanced warily towards the ballroom.

"They're gone," he assured her. "I can see clearly into the room, you can hide again if anyone else comes. Sit there on the bench, and no one will see you but me."

Her eyes flicked in his direction, but never quite raised to meet his, and she dipped her chin, then sank onto the closest bench, sighing and putting a hand to her head.

"I-I'm s-sorry," she half-whispered, stammering weakly. "Exc-cuse m-me. I didn't m-mean to d-disturb you."

Camden found himself smiling at the little creature, who appeared too young to be here, yet he suspected she was nothing of the sort. Her fear and stammering reminded him of his cousin, Molly, when they were children, and he'd always been able to coax Molly out of it.

Why he suddenly felt the desire to try with her, he couldn't have said.

"You didn't disturb me," he assured her, shrugging a shoulder she didn't see. "They did. You didn't even see me."

She shook her head. "I w-wasn't even l-looking. I just h-had to g-get…"

"Away," he finished with a nod. "I completely understand that, given who was chasing you. Unfortunately, I'm not sure I am a better prospect."

Her hand dropped, and she looked up at him, wary once more.

"Why?" he asked, voicing the question her eyes held. "Because I'm one of those men who create gossip the way others collect horses or boots. I don't mean to, but it tends to happen. My reputation is such that sensible women flee before me. I've never quite been sure why."

She sat up slowly, her brow furrowing with disbelief.

"No, it's true," he told her, nodding sagely. "I've seen it." He cocked his head at her a little. "But perhaps you have no sense."

Now her thin brows snapped down in irritation, and he bit back a laugh. "I beg your p-pardon?" she retorted as she turned towards him a little further.

Really, her stammer became less noticeable when she was irritated, and he found that particularly charming. Molly's tended to get worse with anger, or any emotion at all.

"You ran out of a ball into the dead of night without checking if your place of refuge had more dangers in store," he reminded her. "Clearly without sense. Yet now I look at you," he mused, pushing off the balustrade, "you cannot be without sense. So, why don't you fear me?"

She wet her lips hesitantly. "Should I?" she asked.

"Probably," he returned, shrugging. "Your reputation will be ruined should anyone know you spoke with me without a chaperone."

"Are you going to tell?" she demanded. "It w-won't work. No one would believe you'd take up w-with me."

Camden gave the poor, deluded miss a pitying smile. "Child, I'd probably take up with a maid if it suited me." He almost laughed at her frown, then frowned himself. "And what is so wrong with you that I wouldn't take an interest?"

She gave him a dubious look, which he declined to respond to. "D-do you know who I am?"

"Haven't had the pleasure," he replied with a shake of his head. "Though I am wild with curiosity."

Clearly, she thought him nothing of the sort, and she wrinkled up her nose a little. "Prudence Westfall," she managed without a stammer, somehow accomplishing a curtsey from the bench.

He raised a brow and gave a hint of a bow. "Camden Vale. And should your name actually mean anything to me?"

"I s-sta… I s-st…" She growled and slapped the bench. "I have d-difficulty s-speaking when I'm nervous."

He widened his eyes and gaped. "You do?" he whispered in a dramatic, shocked manner. "Why didn't you say so?"

She gave him a bewildered look, then suddenly beamed and burst out laughing, and the surprisingly musical sound caught him somewhere in the vicinity of where his heart ought to have been.

He found himself smiling in earnest as her laughter continued, and she gripped the bench for support. When her laughter started to fade, he moved in her direction.

"So sorry, Miss Westfall, I meant no offense." He gestured to the spot on the terrace rail near her. "May I?"

She nodded, still smiling.

Camden leaned against the rail, watching her a little.

She returned the favor. "You don't have any designs on me at all, do you?"

He chuckled to himself and shook his head. "No, my dear. Not tonight."

"Any other night?" she asked, raising a brow.

He gave her a wry look. "Are you suggesting it, Miss Westfall, or simply curious?"

Her eyes widened again, and her cheeks colored. "C-curious," she stammered rapidly.

Ah, he'd forgotten about her timidity, and he nearly cursed. He didn't need to be the cad with her, it wouldn't amuse anybody and wouldn't help matters.

"To be perfectly frank, Miss Westfall, I'm not nearly as wicked as anybody thinks I am, so I can't even promise that any other night would be filled with designs either. I hope that doesn't offend."

She blinked, and one side of her mouth curved just the slightest.

Why that suddenly pleased him was a mystery, but please him it did.

"In fact, most of what people say about me isn't true," he admitted with a sigh. "It's quite unfair, having a reputation one has not fully earned. Not that there isn't a reason for it, because there is. It's just not true. Well, no, it's mostly true, but not entirely. Certainly not to those extremes, but not entirely honorable."

He was talking himself in circles, rambling as if to make up for her impediment, though he'd started off intending to be amusing.

Now he only looked like an idiot.

Figures.

"You seem confused about your own reputation," Miss Westfall stated rather simply.

Camden snorted at that. "If you'd heard the extent of it, you'd be confused by it, too."

She looked away for a moment, her lip tightening as though she gnawed on the inside. "I'm a Spinster," she said quietly.

"That's all right," he replied as he looked up at the stars. "There are worse things."

She hummed a soft laugh and looked up at him. "I am a spinster, but I mean the other Spinster. With a capital S."

Now *that* was a confession! He'd been reading the Spinster Chronicles with everybody else in London almost since they were first published, but he'd never taken up Society's curiosity with the Spinsters' identities. It wasn't his business, and what was it to him if they wanted to amuse themselves thus?

Plus, he enjoyed the articles and frequently laughed out loud.

"Oh ho," Camden chortled, folding his arms and grinning at her. "That changes things, Miss Prudence Westfall. Which article in the Chronicles do you write?"

Her cheeks colored again but to a lesser extent. "It varies. I've written each of them before."

"And which is your favorite to write?"

"The main one, but I don't get to write it often." She shrugged lightly and drummed her fingers on the stone of the bench. "You c-can say a lot in that one, and I have a lot to say, despite…" She gestured to her throat and mouth quickly. "But everyone else has a lot to say, too."

Camden shook his head a little, smiling at her again. "I'd wager you do have a lot to say, Miss Westfall. Probably far more than anybody else, but I won't judge the others when I don't know them."

She smiled, too. "That's very considerate."

"Not really," he retorted. "I'd judge them plenty if I did know them. I'm a very judgmental person."

"That's a pity."

She said it, but she didn't sound as though she disapproved at all. Interesting creature.

"I know," he sighed. "I really am very poorly behaved as far as gentlemen go. Hardly the sort of person to invite anywhere. I almost never go out in polite society, purely because I do not qualify."

Miss Westfall snorted and covered her mouth, making him smile. "So why…?"

"…Am I at this party?" he finished, even as she jerked to look at him. "I don't know. It's the thing to do, isn't it? No idea how I made the invitation list, but one ought to come when one is invited. I have nothing better to do. And I find myself being very polite to you, which is highly unlike me. I'm hoping it will pass soon, but…" He shrugged and looked her over with probably too much thoroughness. "You would be my sort, you know. If I wanted to behave less than politely."

Astonishingly, she didn't color in the slightest. "And you don't?"

Camden smirked a little. "Put out, are we?"

She frowned so quickly he laughed. "No."

"All right, all right," he chuckled, "I apologize again. Forgive my impertinence."

She ducked her chin in a nod, which he took to be a sign of forgiveness.

"So why are you here, Prudence Westfall?" he inquired, losing his teasing air. "If you're going to flee from interested gentlemen, you've come to the wrong place."

Prudence snorted again, this time with outright derision. "They are not interested in me, Mr. Vale, I can promise you that. They want…" Her brow furrowed, and she looked at him again.

"What?" he asked, feeling suddenly defensive.

"Do you promise that you have no designs on me?" she shot back with an accusing air.

He held up his hands in surrender. "I promise on everything I hold dear, which doesn't amount to much, but there it is."

Her lips quirked as though she would smile but she resisted the impulse. "I have recently inherited quite a large fortune and an estate in Hertfordshire."

"Congratulations."

"No, thank you."

"No?" he laughed. "My dear Prudence, you are an heiress, and that is something worth praising."

She shook her head firmly. "Not for me. I don't want it."

"I'd be happy to take it."

"I'd let you," she admitted softly, no longer looking at him. "I'd let you take it in a heartbeat. I haven't even told my friends I have it. I don't mind having financial security, but as for the rest…"

Then, realization set in, and Camden looked at Prudence in an entirely new light. "You are being hunted."

She nodded with a shudder as color appeared in her cheeks again. "It's t-terrifying," she whispered. "Nobody ever paid attention to me b-before, and I was fine with that. N-now I have more attention than ever before in m-my life, and it's overw-whelming and unsettling, and I s-stammer so m-much anyw-way, and…"

He saw her unraveling before his very eyes, and he didn't need her stammering to tell him that.

"Prudence, it's all right," he soothed in the gentlest voice he could, rather as he used to do with Molly. "Shh, it's all right. Prudence…"

"Prue," she gasped as she clung to the bench again.

"Pardon?" he asked, not sure he'd heard her right or if she'd sneezed.

She swallowed, cleared her throat, and then gave him a straightforward look. "If we're being informal, p-please call me Prue. Only my mother calls me Prudence, and the c-connotation is not favorable."

Camden grinned, not caring that she would see it. "Prue, then. Call me Camden. Or Cam, if you're feeling impish."

She smiled back. "I'm rarely impish."

"Rarely is not never," he pointed out. "I'll bring out that impish side, see if I don't."

Prue shook her head, whether in refusal or in amusement he couldn't tell. "I don't want to be an object of attention," she told him, glancing back towards the ballroom. "Not from anyone who doesn't mean it. Not that anyone does mean it, but it's worse to have this attention. To only be wanted for my fortune…"

"I'm sorry," he heard himself say, finding her sad tone rather moving, even for someone as jaded as him.

He really wasn't as wicked or shocking as anybody said, that much was true, but neither was he anywhere close to a perfect gentleman. He wasn't perfect in any respect, either for good or for evil. Aside from his sister, he wasn't a favorite person to anyone on this earth.

There had been Molly, but now...

Well, she had seen the good in him and flat-out ignored the bad.

He had the sneaking suspicion that Prue would see both, but never judge him for any of it. Her eyes were bright, even if there was torment behind them, and being one so overlooked had undoubtedly given her a clearer vision. Yes, she probably did have much to say in her columns, and if she could trust her voice, she might do so aloud.

"That's the proper sentiment, Camden," she replied as she turned back, folding her hands in her lap and managing a smile.

"You didn't answer the question, Prue." He cleared his throat, curious that someone calling him Camden should make him want to smile. "Why are you here? If you hate your fortune and dislike attention, why come here?"

Her smile faded, and she sighed a bone-weary sigh. "I had no choice."

Camden frowned. "Surely not. If you're old enough to be a spinster, with or without a capital S, you are surely old enough to make your own decisions."

She was shaking her head before he finished. "Have you met me?"

"Only just."

Prue giggled a low, almost throaty giggle. "True, I suppose, but even so... I am hardly independent in nature, despite the age and fortune. My mother insisted we come, now that I am at last a proper marital candidate. Never mind that I stammer, flush, and have all the shyness of five shy girls even on the best days."

"Those must be some very bold shy girls," he mused with a raised brow. "You're quite vivacious at the moment." His eyes sharpened on her mouth suddenly, and while it was a very pretty little mouth, it was also an un-stammering one. "Where did your stammer go, Prue?"

Her eyes met his, and she raised a pristine glove to move a lock of hair. "It always fades in private. Don't flatter yourself."

He scowled suddenly. "I wasn't planning on it, but it's unnerving."

"It shouldn't be. Now I speak almost like anyone else. It means I feel safe."

That made him wince. "I'm not sure that makes me feel any better."

"Are you determined to be a wicked scoundrel?" she asked, almost amused by his offended air.

"Not particularly," he replied, playing out his scene, "but I do have a reputation to uphold."

"A reputation you are unclear on," she pointed out.

He considered that. "True enough, I grant you." He flashed her a quick grin. "Don't tell anyone I make you comfortable."

She shook her head obediently. "I wouldn't dare."

Camden narrowed his eyes playfully, and she looked appropriately innocent.

He chuckled to himself and looked past her into the ballroom. "Well, we can't stay out here forever, Prue. Not alone, at any rate."

She sighed and followed his gaze. "I know. But going b-back in there…" She rolled her eyes and gestured at her mouth again.

A ridiculous, completely mad idea suddenly crossed his mind, and he put a finger to his chin, tapping slowly. "I'm having a thought, Prue Westfall…"

"An appropriate one?" she queried as she brushed at her faded skirts.

"Shockingly, yes," he informed her. He dropped his hand back to fold under his arm. "What would you say to an arrangement?"

Prue looked unconvinced. "I'd ask what sort of arrangement."

"See? You are a sensible girl after all." He nodded in approval. "Very good. I'm bored being here, and you're terrified of being here. What if I agreed to be your partner in this house party?"

"P-partner?" she asked, a strained look coming into her features.

"Nothing untoward," he assured her quickly. "Quite the contrary. What if I was by your side almost the entire time? I could show interest so that the others would be warded off."

She relaxed slightly but frowned all the same. "I don't know that it would s-stop anyone. They come in p-packs."

"Ah ha." He straightened and pointed a finger at her. "You forget I have a reputation."

She did not look remotely convinced. "But how would that help me? I hardly need rumors spreading about me, that might make things worse."

Camden shook his head. "It will be as honorable as my intentions."

"Is that supposed to m-make me feel better?" she asked, smiling at last.

She was teasing him now? His delight knew no bounds!

"What shy creature?" he protested pompously. "I see no such thing!"

"You will," Prue warned, turning serious. "Once we are b-back in there, you will see everything that everybody always s-says."

He made a face. "Yes, but here's the thing, Prue; I've never been very good about listening to anything that anybody says, so that doesn't mean anything to me."

She wanted to laugh, he could see it, but she adamantly refused to. "It's not a pretty sight, Camden. It will require patience, endurance, and…"

"…And my reputation will turn as soft as pudding for exuding all those things," he replied with a dramatic gesture. "Yes, yes, I know. But I am willing to do it all, Prudence Westfall, and you may feel free to shower me with gratitude and kisses at any time."

She scoffed rather loudly, which made him smile.

"I thought not, but one never knows." He looked her over once and nodded. "I think I like you, Miss Prudence Westfall, and I very rarely like anyone genuinely."

Absurdly, she seemed to like that, which showed him that she was not as sensible as she should have been. "Time will tell if I like you, Mr. Camden Vale. I make no promises."

He barked a laugh and bowed to her. "You are the liveliest shy girl I have ever met in my entire life, and it is a rare delight, I can assure you."

"It won't last." She sighed and rose, inhaling slowly, and exhaling much the same. "I don't want to do this," she whispered.

"Saying that isn't going to help anything," he told her softly. "Remember, I am coming to the rescue. However much comfort that will be."

"It will be." She looked over at him, her pale eyes steady and clear. "You might be saving me, Camden Vale. I hope you're prepared for that."

Her tone held much weight, and he suddenly felt the burden of it settling against his chest and stomach. More for the complete lack of stammer in her words, which seemed something of a miraculous thing.

"I am no hero, Miss Westfall," he told her with complete honesty, which was rare for him. "Not the saving sort of man. But I will do my best for your sake."

Prue smiled at him softly, the warmth of sunshine in its curve. "I'll be the one stammering in the corner, red-faced and nearly swooning."

"And I'll be the one riding in with shouts of glory," he assured her. "Though white horses are frowned upon in ballrooms."

She nodded and turned for the ballroom, looking within carefully for her admirers.

"You're safe to go in," he called. "They're on the other side of the room."

She looked over her shoulder, her eyes lowered, and dipped her chin in thanks.

"Prue?"

She paused and waited.

"Do you like to dance?" he asked, smiling to himself.

He saw the corner of her mouth curve, and she raised her eyes to his. "D-don't tell the others, but I love to dance." Her smile grew very briefly, and then she moved into the ballroom, away from him.

Camden Vale, disreputable fellow, and nobody's favorite person, sighed heavily and shook his head. "Camden, old boy, you may have just done something incredibly foolish."

He looked up and focused on the small figure making her way along the outer edge of the room, purposefully drawing as little attention to herself as possible.

"But then," he mused aloud, nodding as he reentered the ballroom himself, "I've always been rather fond of foolish things."

Chapter Three

Sometimes there is just no explaining the nature of people. They may surprise you at every turn and prove your assumptions entirely incorrect. Nothing quite sets us up to fail as much as an assumption. And nothing surprises us more than being mistaken.

-The Spinster Chronicles, 2 March 1818

"Prudence, whatever happened to your slippers?"

Prue glanced down at the slippers and saw the telltale evidence from the night before on the pale fabric of the footwear. "I'm n-not sure, Mother. I n-never walk out of doors in these."

Her mother rolled her eyes dramatically and huffed, adjusting her bodice. "Well, change them, stupid girl, before someone sees them!"

Prue exhaled silently and changed the slippers as quickly as she could. They were still in their rooms, so who would have seen her stained slippers was something of a mystery, unless they were now hiding things from servants, as well.

"Hurry up, Prudence!" her mother insisted as though she were the one who had marriage prospects below. "You never know who may wish to speak with you this morning. I was too distracted last night to mind you. Did you meet anyone of significance?"

Did Camden Vale count as a person of significance? He'd seemed significant last night when she'd been in need, but would that count for anything with her mother? Prue knew nothing about Camden's situation in life, nor had she ever heard of him, but that did not surprise her. Prue had rarely heard of anyone, despite being one of the Spinsters and having Elinor and her endless resources about the men of London in her midst.

But her mother was a gossip. Would she know him?

"Oh, never mind," her mother snapped, mistaking Prue's silence for an inability to speak. "Ridiculous girl, we must go down to breakfast. Let me look at you." She eyed Prue up and down without any sort of warmth. "We desperately need that blue muslin from the shop. You are so washed out, it's a wonder you're alive."

It seemed impertinent and rather pointless to suggest that the dress Prue wore now was nearly the same shade, and that Prue's paleness had not changed from two days ago when she was so dark she looked "like a farmer's wife".

There was just no pleasing her mother, aside from the day she had gained her inheritance.

Prue had never been more terrified of the woman than in that moment when she had hugged her repeatedly.

It had taken her half a day to calm herself after that.

Dutifully, she followed her mother out of their rooms and down the corridor to the stairs, taking great care to descend gracefully for all the guests who could be watching, of which there were none, much to her relief.

Still, her pulse quickened at the thought of the guests. They could be in the breakfast room waiting for her, which would have seemed the most ridiculous idea in creation before all of this. But after she'd returned from the terrace last night, two men had been waiting near the chair she had been occupying before, and neither of them had been in the original group.

Their flattery had started the moment she had arrived, despite saying nothing to them, and their queries for dances soon followed. Never one to be rude, Prue tried her best to answer them, though their volley of words provided her with little opportunity to do so. She'd grown flustered and flushed, stammering so much she could hardly stand to hear herself, and she could see the tension seep into their expressions the more she struggled.

It was bad enough to be the one so vocally handicapped, but to see the impact it had on others made things infinitely worse.

But then Camden had come, as he had promised, and while Prue would never say that her situation was resolved completely or that her difficulties faded, she did feel a strong sense of relief.

Which seemed rather odd now.

She knew almost nothing about him. At all. They hadn't asked any questions beyond what they were doing at this house party. She had no idea what his situation was, what exactly his supposed reputation consisted of, or whether he could be trusted. He had done what he had promised the night before, so it appeared he was a man of his word, despite whatever reputation he possessed.

And surely the Davieses would never have invited someone truly disreputable to their event.

Even so, if they had the opportunity to speak today, she would try her utmost to get some useful information out of him. It wouldn't help her cause at all to find her name so tied up with that of a blackguard.

He didn't *seem* to be a blackguard, but she supposed most blackguards behaved that way.

There were only a few guests in the breakfast room, and all of them were female. Two girls and their chaperones, and one of them seemed rather sour despite having a rather impressive spread on her plate.

Either she was not the sort who enjoyed mornings, or she had behaved in a way that had prompted some kind of scolding.

Prue wished Charlotte was here to investigate that for her. Charlotte had ways and means that she suspected the Home Office would have loved to acquire, and absolutely no reluctance or reticence when it came to personal inquiries. Despite being terrified of Charlotte when she'd first met her, she had, over time, found Charlotte to be fiercely loyal, good-hearted, and quite charming, in her way.

She did take some getting used to, but so did Prue.

"Miss Fairbanks," her mother greeted the sour one, speaking more warmly than she had ever spoken to Prue. "I must say, you are looking particularly lovely this morning. That shade of muslin does suit you so."

Considering the gown was cream-colored, Prue wasn't sure that compliment was worth giving.

Miss Fairbanks offered a wan smile. "Thank you, Mrs. Westfall. Miss Westfall looks very crisp today. Calico does lend itself to much wear, doesn't it? But one would never know to look at her."

Prue barely avoided scowling at the fair girl, not seeing anything amiss with her calico, considering they were destined to be out of doors on such a beautiful day. Muslin was all well and good for finer wear, but it would fray easily on the smallest bit of brush.

Just because Prue had a fortune did not mean she was going to be walking around in silks all day.

"Oh, I know," her mother was saying to Miss Fairbanks now, and Prue took it upon herself to skirt around them and take up some of the breakfast spread for herself. "I have been telling Prudence for ages now that she needs to be on the front end of the new fashions instead of clinging to outdated and rustic trends."

Prue closed her eyes as the spoon in her hand began to tremble.

"Mrs. Westfall, for shame!" the other girl in the room protested with a laugh. "Calico is hardly rustic, and it is quite suitable for the country. And the pattern is lovely on Miss Westfall."

Prue opened her eyes and glanced over at the girl, surprised at the easy defense. She had a miserable time with names and faces, but she tried desperately to remember hers now. She was young, but so was every other young woman here compared to Prue.

Amelia Perry, that was it. Her father was someone important in Society, though Prue could not recall why, and Amelia was more of an heiress than Prue, which gave her some comfort.

She was prettier, wealthier, younger, and spoke perfectly.

She ought to be more pursued than Prue was.

Mrs. Westfall simpered loudly. "What a sweet creature you are, Miss Perry! So good and kind to my poor girl. It will be such a pleasure when her new gowns are finished so she may look just as fine as the pair of you, especially now that she has the fortune to sustain some lovely things. If only she had her cousin Miss Howard's taste."

Prue sat down in the nearest chair and tried her best to block out anything and everything her mother was saying, knowing she wouldn't be able to succeed entirely. Her mother tended to talk incessantly, and she was used to that, but did she have to do so at such a volume? And to boast of Prue's fortune while criticizing her choice in gowns in the same breath? And to further praise Eliza, who did not have the status to secure an invitation, nor the taste of which was boasted?

It was ridiculous. Her mother hadn't found any fault with the dress when they were in their rooms, but once in the view of others, she suddenly spotted so many flaws she was blinded by them.

Miraculously, her mother suddenly grew much quieter, and, fearing she may have perished on the spot, Prue looked up to find her. The briefest bit of relief hit her when she saw her mother now conversing with the other two chaperones, who kept their conversation at a much more appropriate level, leaving the girls to enjoy whatever silence they wished to maintain.

"I really do admire your calico, Miss Westfall," Amelia Perry suddenly said in a low voice, leaning closer to Prue. She smiled warmly, displaying a pair of bright dimples. "It's a good color for you. And I wear calico all the time at home, so I don't know why your mother thinks it inappropriate."

Prue licked her lips quickly, trying to think of a proper response.

Amelia covered her hand gently. "Don't worry, you don't have to respond. I know it can be difficult for you. I just wanted you to know I meant it." She smiled again and went back to her breakfast without a word.

Prue stared at her in wonder.

She had never spoken more than three words to Amelia Perry in all her life, though it may have sounded more like twelve when she did so, and still, this girl was willing to defend her to her mother, and be kind to Prue without any witnesses?

A lump of emotion lodged itself in Prue's throat, and she tried in vain to swallow it down. Her eyes misted over, and she turned her attention to her plate, blinking hard.

Her mother would never forgive her for becoming emotional in the public setting of a breakfast room.

It took her the entirety of her small meal before she was free of the temptation to cry, and somehow, her mother had managed not to scold her once during the eating.

Thank goodness for appropriate table manners.

"Good morning, ladies!" boomed a too-jovial voice from the entrance to the breakfast room.

Prue jerked slightly and looked towards him with the others. He was one of the flattering fools the night before, and he beamed at the entire room.

"It is a fine morning, and if you fair maidens have finished your breakfast, we gentlemen would love your company to walk the grounds and take in this fresh air."

A walk? In a small group and with two men already showing a penchant for paying her too much attention? Her refusal could not have flown to her tongue more swiftly.

But she hesitated and looked past him to see the other two men, one of whom was another of her admirers from the night before, and the other...

Her stomach settled considerably when she saw Camden's face poking out from behind the shoulder of the other.

He gave her the slightest of smiles but showed no other signs of familiarity, which she appreciated.

Her mother would have sniffed that out in three seconds in this small company.

As it was, Prue suddenly found herself pinned with a death stare from her, so she knew what she would be doing regardless of the answers from the other two ladies.

Amelia looked over to Miss Fairbanks, then at Prue, who met her gaze with the smallest smile known to man and then turned back. "We accept, Mr. Applegate. Will you permit Miss Fairbanks and me time for a change of clothes? Only Miss Westfall had the foresight to dress appropriately for a walk in the countryside."

Mr. Applegate, whose named Prue would never have remembered, bowed with considerable flourish. "Of course, Miss Perry." He looked at Prue directly. "Miss Westfall is as wise as she is fair."

Huh. Not particularly wise, then.

All right.

Camden's expression was difficult to see, given that Mr. Applegate was rather squarely in the way, but the compliment fell flat in the room.

The short but awkward silence lent itself to Prue's habit of blushing, and Amelia rose quickly, Miss Fairbanks only moments behind.

"We'll return momentarily," Miss Fairbanks announced airily, sliding from the room. "Mrs. Gates, will you be our chaperone on the walk?"

Her chaperone smiled indulgently, though Miss Fairbanks was gone. "Of course!" She gave Prue a warm look. "Come, Miss Westfall, let us fetch a wrap and bonnet for you."

Prue pushed back her chair and nodded, following without a word.

Her mother grabbed her wrist when she passed. "Be polite and agreeable," she hissed.

"Yes, M-mother," she whispered.

"Don't stammer!"

Prue nodded once and trailed behind Mrs. Gates back up to her room. Mrs. Gates rambled on rather kindly, but Prue was not paying any attention. It was clear Mrs. Gates knew about her difficulty with speech and treated her as though she could not speak at all. But she was kind about it, if overdoing things, so Prue indulged her.

Wrap and bonnets set, they returned down to the gentlemen, and Camden smiled when she approached, gesturing towards the door.

"Shall we wait for the others outside, Miss Westfall?"

His gentlemanly tone was so perfect, so pristine, that Prue had a hard time reconciling his supposed reputation with the man before her.

Mrs. Gates tutted in fond admiration behind her, and Prue barely avoided rolling her eyes. Well, if she didn't want to spend time with Camden before, she certainly did now.

"Y-yes, please," she replied, lifting her chin. "Thank you, M-Mr. Vale."

She proceeded out of the door, and he followed, Mrs. Gates coming behind at a polite distance. They all waited on the gravel drive for the others, and Prue leaned her head back a little to feel the sunshine.

"Good morning, Prue," Camden greeted in a quiet voice.

Prue sighed heavily, making him chuckle. "Good m-morning."

"Did you take a dislike to Applegate's flattery just then?" he inquired, looking up into the sky at the few clouds. "It was difficult to see your face, but I know I nearly clocked him from where I stood."

"It was r-ridiculous," she said without shame. "As if I could be as w-wise as I am fair. O-one has to be f-fair at all to be as w-wise as they are fair."

Camden made a noise of disapproval and Prue opened her eyes to look at him. He stared at her with a furrowed brow.

"What?" she demanded.

He shook his head. "That's not the point I was going to argue, but we don't need to get into all that. Suffice it to say, I do not agree." He smirked at her and raised a brow. "And what did your mother say when you walked by her? Did she tell you which gentleman to walk with?"

Prue snorted softly. "N-not at all. She told me to b-be polite and agreeable, and not to st-stammer."

"Pity," Camden replied, his voice suddenly filled with disappointment. "Thirty seconds in, and you've already failed in all three. So much for obedient daughters."

She scowled over at him. "Am I not p-polite and agreeable, Camden?"

"Not to me." He shrugged easily, his broad shoulders somehow more pronounced now than they had been in the dark eveningwear the night before. "I've only ever known abuse at your hands, and it's really a miracle I agreed to walk with you at all today. It will take me the rest of the day to recover, I am quite sure of it."

Prue stared at him, torn between amusement and confusion. He was an intriguing puzzle of a man, that much was clear. He teased her so easily, just as he had the night before, despite knowing almost nothing about her. It was natural, relaxed, and set her at ease faster than anything else she would have expected.

And this from a sort of man who should have been paying her no mind at all. He was starkly handsome in a classical way, but something about him seemed wrong. Well, perhaps not wrong so much as dangerous. His hair was dark, his eyes a shade darker, and he had a commanding presence that drew others in, including her. He was utterly impressive in his attire, though it was not nearly as fine as the evening before, yet at the same time did not seem at all overdone.

It was all perfection there, and Prue envied him his flawlessness.

"That was a joke, Prue," Camden told her softly, his voice breaking through her reverie.

She flushed quickly, though without her usual fervor and panic. "I know," she assured him. "Just lost in thought."

Thoughts of *him*, but he didn't need to know that.

He gave her a fond smile. "Can I get lost in your thoughts, too?"

Prue frowned a little, unsure if he was trying to be amusing or flirtatious. She needed him to be the comfortable man from the night before, not another one of the suitors making her uncomfortable.

"It seems a better place to be lost than this," he went on, oblivious to her confusion and gesturing at the house. "At least your thoughts would make sense."

Relief had never tasted so sweet, and Prue smiled at the sensation. "I thought you said I wasn't a creature of s-sense."

He looked back at her quickly. "No, I said you *were* a creature of sense, you goose. Don't make me more of a villain than I already am."

"You don't even know how much of a villain you are," she reminded him.

"True, but I imagine it sometimes, and that gives me entertainment enough."

Prue laughed a little as the others finally came out of the house, Miss Fairbanks and Amelia looking far more attractive than Prue ever could. Mr. Applegate and the other gentlemen came out with them and gestured towards the gravel path leading away from the house.

"That way, if you please, Mr. Vale," Mr. Applegate called.

Camden looked at it, then turned back politely. "I think you had better lead, Applegate. You know the grounds better than me, I may prove a terrible leader."

Applegate chuckled and tipped his hat at Miss Fairbanks. "Miss Fairbanks, if you will lead with me…?"

Pleased, Miss Fairbanks curtseyed and moved to the front with him, Amelia and the other gentleman following.

Camden waved at Mrs. Gates then. "Come along, Mrs. Gates,

I'll follow with Miss Westfall. We wouldn't want you tripping over a stone and having no one to help you."

Mrs. Gates colored in delight and did as she was bid, smiling at Prue with the pitying smile one might give a simpleton in the streets as she passed.

Prue watched her as she retreated in front of them, scowling a little.

"Gracious, Prue Westfall," Camden muttered as they finally walked together. "What's that for?"

How to explain the torment of being in her situation to a man who could not hope to understand? She exhaled audibly, choosing her words with care.

"It's c-complicated."

"So am I, but that doesn't change anything," he returned, clasping his hands behind his back. "Tell me anyway."

She gave that some thought. "I understand that c-conversing with me is difficult," she began.

"Not so difficult," he broke in. "I'm doing it without any effort at all, and I hate difficult things."

Prue gave him a hard look. "D-don't brush it off. It is harder than speaking to anybody else." She returned her gaze to Mrs. Gates's back several paces ahead of them. "I don't expect anybody to go out of their way to engage me in conversation. But I don't want to be pitied for it, either. Do you have any idea how many people talk at me instead of to me, thinking I cannot respond at all?"

"I have some, yes," he admitted, surprising her.

She looked up at him again. "Have you? How?"

He glanced down at her, then at the horizon. "I have some experience with girls who cannot always speak clearly. A cousin of mine, Molly, stammered nearly constantly. Worse than you, I think."

"Did she?" Prue asked in a hushed voice.

Camden nodded once. "From what I gathered, your stammer is a symptom of your anxieties. It comes out when you are nervous or embarrassed, gets better when you are angry, and eases once you are comfortable. Stammering isn't your true challenge, your emotions are."

She'd never really thought about it, but she supposed that was true. "Debatable," she allowed, smiling a touch, "but we'll go with that."

He grinned quickly. "See? No stammer there."

She shrugged a shoulder. "Safe."

Camden shook his head. "Still not a good answer from my point of view, but far be it from me to contradict a lady." He sobered, and his throat worked on a swallow. "Molly's problem was, in fact, the stammering. It got worse with her anger and irritation, and she was rarely embarrassed about it. She was angry with it. Hated it. And the more anger she felt, the more she stammered, until she was fairly choking on every syllable."

Prue winced and shook her head sympathetically. That poor girl. Being trapped without a voice was the most paralyzing feeling in the world, and to have no way out of it seemed a torment worse than death.

"I grew up very close to Molly," Camden went on. "I was used to her way of speaking, and knew how to calm her enough to help her be clearer." He laughed a short laugh. "She had so much wit, and so short a temper, she could eviscerate me without any effort at all, and her having to stammer so badly to even get it out. It only made the insult so much better to hear her say it."

The fondness in his tone was evident, and his smile was filled with such warmth and love, Prue suddenly envied Molly a great deal. Not for having Camden particularly, but for having someone in her family to understand her and encourage her in such a way. To be loved as she was and not wish her changed to be better than she was…

Her father had been that way, but he'd been gone so long now, she had nearly forgotten what his influence had been like.

"Perhaps that's why I've taken to you, Prue," Camden suggested, looking down at her once more. "Last night, you reminded me of Molly in so many ways, it was second nature to treat you the same as I always did her. Ergo, I have no difficulty with you."

She smiled at him then. "That's very good of you. Not many people have the patience to bear with our difficulties. Where is Molly now? Is she well?"

He swallowed with some difficulty. "Molly died many years ago.

The doctors think her stammer was a symptom of some medical complaint, and when we were about fifteen, she took a fever and never recovered."

Prue's heart stopped in her chest, and she stared at Camden's profile in stunned silence.

Curse her curiosity to know more about him and his cousin, to understand how he could make her so comfortable so quickly, to help her…

"Not quite the sort of thing one ought to discuss on a country walk, eh?" He sighed and looked over at her. "I'm sorry, Prue. I didn't think of it."

"You're sorry?" she repeated incredulously. "Camden, I'm the one who should be sorry!"

He shook his head quickly. "Not at all. Don't set to crying or anything. I only meant to explain myself further, and Molly is the best reason of all for me."

Prue exhaled, looking away and finding her eyes blurring, despite his insistence on not crying.

"No, don't do that," he said at once as she blinked repeatedly. "I don't do well with tears, I'll bungle something up, and our newfound friendship will be at its end."

She chuckled at that. "Quick, tell me something else!"

"Hmm…" he began, making a show of thinking, "I prefer dark hair to fair. I have never managed to make a good tea. I cannot whistle anything except bawdy tavern songs. My sister used to call me Camelot."

Prue choked on a laugh, and any semblance of tears was suddenly gone. "Are any of those actually true?" she asked, still giggling.

Camden nodded almost proudly. "All of them, in fact. Although I can whistle 'God Save The King', too."

"I'm sure that is very useful."

"It is." He tilted his chin to give her an expectant look. "Your turn."

She returned his look with one of her own. "For what?"

He scoffed loudly. "Come, come, my dear, you didn't think this was going to be a one-sided friendship, did you? I share something with you, you share something with me. I have shared five things now, and I am not receiving anything for my efforts."

Prue rolled her eyes dramatically. "I shared last night."

"What, that you're a Spinster with a capital S?" He shook his head with determination. "That counts as one thing. Four to go."

What could she share with him? She frowned in thought. There wasn't much about her to share that wasn't perfectly obvious. She was quite, in a word, dull.

"Is it really so challenging a task?" he chuckled when she did not answer. "It shouldn't be. Tell me anything at all, Prue."

"I h-have a hard time saying anything about myself," she told him, her reluctance rather evident.

He nodded patiently, smiling a little. "That's one."

Prue huffed, laughing in spite of herself. "I didn't mean for that to be one of them! I just wanted to explain!"

"Then feel free to share more than four things," Camden replied. "Over-sharing is encouraged."

Now she laughed outright, putting a hand to her face. "This is ridiculous. I'm not fascinating at all!"

"That's two, though I disagree most heartily." He tsked loudly. "We really must work on this, Miss Westfall."

She clamped down on her lips to keep from giggling again. "Fine! I like the color blue most of all."

"Bravo! That's three." He nodded and looked her up and down. "And I like blue for you, it's quite fetching. Excellent choice."

Really, her cheeks were going to crack from smiling and laughing too much, she was so out of practice. He'd just complimented her, but without any sort of airs and flattery, and in such a comfortable way that she hadn't even blushed at it.

An attractive man was complimenting her and paying her attention, making her talk about herself, and she wasn't even blushing and hardly stammering at all?

What in the world was this?

Prue looked up at Camden with a newfound appreciation for whatever it was he possessed that eased her so. "I think this house party might not be the terrible thing I imagined it to be after all."

His pace slowed just a hint, and he gave her a searching look. Then his mouth curved up on one side and he nodded once. "That's four, Miss Westfall. Very good." He nodded again, then looked ahead. "And I quite agree."

Chapter Four

A man's motivation is a curious thing. This writer doubts if even they understand it most of the time.

-The Spinster Chronicles, 15 June 1816

"Riding."

"No."

"Shooting."

"No."

"Lawn bowls."

"No."

"Charades."

"Lord, no."

Camden groaned in mock agony and looked at Prue with no small amount of irritation. "Good heavens, woman, have you actually done anything in your spare time?"

She threw a glare at him that she was really quite proud of. "Yes."

"She knows the word yes!" he crowed, raising his hands as if surprised. "Progress!"

Prue was not amused.

He dropped his hands and scratched at his brow. "Do tell me, then, what you do in your spare time."

"Read."

His head hit the table without much effort at all. "Read, she says." He shook his head against the hard surface. "Of course, she reads."

"I'm *shy*," she insisted impatiently, sitting back in her chair roughly.

Camden raised his head to look at her dubiously. "You keep saying that, Prue, but I haven't seen much proof."

She scoffed loudly. "Then you are blind."

"You're timid, yes," he allowed as he straightened. "But you are also completely terrified. Of everything, and everyone."

Prue gestured with her hand as if to say "of course," and he frowned at that. "Look, you're a young woman of…?"

"Twenty-five," she offered without a hint of remorse.

He would have said younger, but he'd accept twenty-five. "Twenty-five, then, and you've never ridden?"

She shook her head. "That's not what I said. You asked if I go riding. And I don't. But I have ridden."

Camden dropped his head to the table again. "Prue…"

"I don't live in the country!" she exclaimed.

"Shh!" He lifted his head to glance around.

They were outside with all the rest of the guests, and they were currently sitting at a small table with some light luncheon, but the chaperones were not too far away, and the other guests were either fetching more food or starting some lawn games. The table next to them bore a dozing Applegate, whom nobody was particularly keen to awaken, and if Prue got any louder, her mother would look over.

He hadn't interacted with Mrs. Westfall at all yet, and he was not particularly inclined to start. All he could determine at this time was that she valued her own station as much as Prue's, so she spent her time cavorting with the other chaperones and mothers to increase her circles.

He had no desire to be included in any of her circles.

"You live in London, I know," he told Prue, "but you can still go riding in London."

She shook her head firmly. "Not with my mother controlling the household. She'll never go with me, or do anything active at all, and she can never spare a servant. Besides all of that, we no longer have horses."

Camden stared at Prue and blinked for a few moments. "Did you like riding before?" he asked, his tone rather mild now. The more he learned about Prue's life, the less he liked it.

He did not know much, and she was not particularly inclined to share, but he suspected it was far worse than he imagined.

Prue's brow furrowed a little. "I think so. It has been several years."

He nodded once. "Very well. Tomorrow we will go riding."

Her face paled swiftly, her eyes widening. "C-Camden, n-no…"

"Don't argue," he told her softly. "We won't go with anybody, if you'd rather not. We're not riding for show. But if you liked riding, Prue, you ought to ride again. You have money now, so buy yourself a horse."

She swallowed repeatedly, and her cheeks started to color once more with the telltale flush. "But… b-but…"

He shook his head slowly. "It's just a ride, Prue. Not a race, not a demonstration. A ride. I'll be with you the entire time, and I'll have you know I am a terrible rider, so I will be quite sensitive to your ridicule."

That made her laugh, albeit weakly. "Fine. All right, then."

It was all he could do to not exhale roughly in victory.

They'd had a long walk this morning, and she'd looked perfectly refreshed afterwards, lively and almost sparkling. Then they'd returned to the house, and every ounce of that energy seemed to dissipate in a matter of seconds. She'd been made to return to her room for an hour, as did the other ladies, and Camden had spent the time mulling over the mystifying Prudence Westfall.

Among the things he had mulled had been his motivations for helping her. He couldn't possibly chalk everything up to memories of Molly, though it certainly had been a factor. He wasn't a protective man by nature, as far as he knew.

Granted, he would be a gentleman if a situation arose that required that of him, and he wasn't exactly a villain, but nothing had ever tested his more honorable instincts. If his sister were in danger, he would have moved heaven and earth and burned in the fires of hell to resolve it, but that was family.

He'd have felt no end of guilt if this was all curiosity on his part. That wouldn't be fair to Prue and did not say much about him at all.

He *was* curious about Prue, but that wasn't it.

He didn't like that she was terrified of the attention she was receiving, and he was finding out that it was only one thing on the list of things that frightened her. He could certainly understand being overwhelmed by all the attention, considering she had never received much before. He could help her wade through this change until it was more natural for her, and that would not cause either of them any pains.

What exactly he would get out of this was still unclear.

But he liked Prue Westfall well enough, and that seemed to satisfy him.

Taking her riding tomorrow was a small victory, and, he hoped, a catalyst to opening her up further. There was a great deal he wanted to know, and that curiosity did not give him guilt at all.

She fascinated him with her timidity, considering she could take his teasing well enough and had started to volley a few herself. There was life beneath the shy façade, and he wanted to see it for himself.

Alas for shy creatures. She threw a wall up the moment she realized what was happening. But Camden could be conniving and sly when it came down to it, and he would be undeterred. In helping her grow more comfortable, perhaps even confident, he would find a bit of entertainment for himself.

Entertainment.

What a sad motivation that was. But he'd never claimed to be a man of gentlemanly impulses, and no one who had heard his name would have said otherwise.

The house party would not last long, and when they returned to London, Prue would hear all about him, and that would be the end of it. Odd, but less than a full day of knowing her, and the thought left him discomfited. He'd lose his little friend when this was over.

He stared at her now with a sense of wonder. He was terrible at having friends, couldn't name a single one at the moment but for her. Plenty of former friends, but…

"Come on," he urged, pushing up out of his seat and waving at her. "We're going to play bowls."

Frantically, eyes wide, she shook her head. "N-no. No, a-absolutely n-not."

He stopped and put his hands on his hips. "Prue, do you play games with the Spinsters?"

"S-sometimes," she squeaked, her hands tangling.

"Then come and play with me." He gestured towards the green. "The others are playing croquet."

She chewed her lip and looked over at the chaperones.

He followed her gaze. Mrs. Westfall was looking squarely at Prue, and the look was not a pleasant one. "Good lord," Camden muttered under his breath. "What does that look mean?"

"It means I have to do whatever it is I am not doing," she whispered, her lips barely moving, no stammer in sight.

Camden grunted, taking care not to frown, lest her mother find further fault. "Then we are not playing bowls at all."

Prue looked at him in confusion. "No?"

He shook his head quickly, smiling more for her benefit than his own. "I have a new plan for us, Prue. We are never going to give your mother cause to find fault with you."

She coughed in disbelief. "I will b-believe that when I see it. She loves to find fault, particularly with me."

He'd have glowered if they weren't being watched. "I wondered if that might be the case." He thought quickly, mind whirling. "Can you draw?"

She looked startled, then shrugged. "A little. Not enough to display anything."

"It'll do." He gestured for her to come with him, and this time she did so, taking his arm when it was offered.

"W-what are we doing?" she asked, and he could hear an amused note under the stammering question.

Camden smiled a somewhat superior smile. "Just play along."

"I'm not very good at that," she admitted with a wrinkle of her nose.

"Then don't ruin it."

"No promises."

He bit back a sigh and proceeded over to Mrs. Davies, thankfully not sitting near Mrs. Westfall. "Mrs. Davies, do you, by chance, have any drawing pencils? Or perhaps watercolors and easels? Miss Westfall wishes to draw or paint, but she is too kind-hearted to think of asking. I've only just convinced her that you, as hostess, would be only too happy to oblige, if able."

Mrs. Davies beamed at Prue as though she had suddenly sung a perfect aria. "My dear girl, you only need to ask! I'll have some things brought out for you at once! What are you going to draw?"

"I'm af-fraid I haven't d-decided yet," Prue managed, looking adorably shy, even to Camden. "I'm n-not very g-good."

Mrs. Davies clasped her hands and made a high-pitched noise that Camden did not understand. "Neither am I, dear, but sometimes it feels just lovely to express yourself through art. Never you mind, I'll fetch Charles to show you some lovely places."

Prue's hand suddenly clutched at his arm painfully.

"Poor Davies," Camden said at once, almost yelping. "He is being so attentive to Miss Perry, I should hate to ruin his chances there." He leaned closer to Mrs. Davies. "You know how particular her father is about potential suitors, ma'am. It'd be better for him if he kept at it and made a favorable impression with her."

Mrs. Davies' eyes widened, and she looked down at the green, where indeed her son was playing croquet in the same party as Miss Perry. "Right you are, Mr. Vale," she whispered conspiratorially. "You are very good. He can show Miss Westfall another time, perhaps tomorrow. But we shall fetch the supplies, and Miss Westfall can make do with the orangery, yes?"

Prue nodded with a warm smile he hadn't expected, and Camden gave Mrs. Davies an acknowledging nod. "An excellent thought, Mrs. Davies."

Mrs. Davies glanced down at her son with some speculation, then smiled at the pair of them and left in search of a servant.

"Well done, Miss Westfall," Camden praised as he exhaled slowly. "And you said you could not play along."

"I couldn't promise to do so when I didn't know what you'd be doing," she replied as she smiled up at him. "But once I saw your plan, I could follow."

He raised a brow at that. "And you always follow?"

Her smile dimmed a bit. "Yes, I tend to."

That didn't sit well with him, but there wasn't anything to be done about that. After all, he was a follower himself. In a very meandering sort of way, but still.

"And why drawing instead of bowls?" Prue asked him. "I really am not very good."

"It's an excuse," he explained as he led her around the green a little. "Once you are drawing, word will spread to the others, and in an effort to display their talents, if any, the other girls will also want to draw. As drawing is more of a solitary activity and not a truly competitive one, it will be well within your comfort level."

Prue grunted a soft sound. "Until the other men come to praise my work, and I know they are lying through their teeth."

"We always lie through our teeth about the accomplishments of women," Camden assured her. "Not just you. Don't take it personally."

She nodded, seeming to steel herself. "I will try to keep that in mind. Perhaps tomorrow when you are all out shooting, the other ladies and I will draw, and no one will pay any attention."

Camden looked down at her in surprise. "So, it isn't just the men's flattering that upsets you?"

An odd shiver seemed to ripple through Prue, and she shook her head almost sadly. "Ever since I inherited, everyone is flattering me and paying me compliments. Men and women."

"And this is a problem?"

"For me, it is." She cleared her throat softly, and her ears and cheeks began to slowly flush. "I am more uncomfortable with this than being neglected and ignored."

He had never heard anything of this sort come out of a woman's mouth in his entire life, and he had thought his cousin so similar to Prue in so many ways. But even Molly had loved attention if it was favorable.

She *wanted* to be neglected? It made no sense at all.

"How is that possible?" he asked.

Prue lifted one shoulder. "Neglect is what I am used to. It's comfortable."

Camden shook his head slowly. "I'm hardly going to neglect you, Prue, so you may as well forget that. And I refuse to blame anyone for liking you."

She looked up at him, her lips curving. "No?"

"No. As it happens, you are a very likable person." He made a face as if it was a most inconvenient thing.

Prue tried for a chuckle that almost convinced him. "Then I shall try to be less likable. For your sake, at least."

Camden smiled, but he didn't look away from her. She had freckles on her cheeks, which he had failed to notice before, and that undoubtedly made her look younger than she was. He liked them. They gave her an almost spirited air, even if she rarely exhibited such things.

He wanted to see that spirited Prue. Racing across a landscape on foot, laughing with the effort of keeping up, or perhaps even winning. No hiding in corners for her, once that side of her was unleashed, and she would never notice the stares or whispers of others. She might never be able to take compliments with ease, but that was one of the more endearing qualities, and it could stay right where it was.

"That is very good of you," Camden murmured, smiling at the images swirling in his mind, and the plan that was forming. "But I'm afraid it won't work."

"No?" she asked, her tone rather mild, even for her.

He shook his head, though she wouldn't see it. "No. You see, I am determined that I shall like you, despite your best efforts, and once I have made up my mind about something, there is really no turning back."

That earned him a bewildered, if amused, look. "Why in the world would you decide something like that? It seems rather foolish."

"Because I make you comfortable," he shot back. "Is it so odd that my making you comfortable makes me like you?"

She smiled in earnest, and it did wonders for her features. "This house party is going to give you a very skewed sense of my nature, Cam. You think this is bad? You should see me when there are rooms filled with people, when I've got friends on either side of me and still cannot find my voice, when..."

"Don't work yourself up on purpose to prove a point," he interrupted with a look that was only half-teasing. "It won't work. And don't talk me out of it, either. I told you, I very rarely like anybody, so this is a new experience for me. I'll protect you from too much attention, and you give me the rare privilege of liking someone without any real purpose to it, even if it doesn't make sense. Agreed?"

Prue laughed once, and it was clear she thought he was mad.

Which was fair enough, as he probably was.

"Agreed," she replied, shaking her head. "But I hold you to no promises."

Mrs. Davies returned to them then and waved for them to follow her to the orangery, so Camden had no time to ask about a lack of promises.

Why was she always saying that?

He'd have to pay more attention there. If he'd said he was going to like her, he fully intended to, and he saw no reason why that should change unless she was some sort of criminal or madwoman. But as it was growing abundantly clear that she was neither of those things, he felt safe enough to proceed accordingly.

She ought to expect that he would keep to that.

Why wouldn't she?

They had a silent walk to the orangery, aside from Mrs. Davies, who felt the need to tell the pair of them the history of said orangery, but Camden was not listening, and he doubted Prue was, either. But once they were within, Mrs. Davies left them to their own devices, leaving the door pointedly open.

Ah, so she did know who Camden was, did she? Fair enough.

The orangery was made almost entirely of glass windows, and they could see the lawn bowling from where they sat. What exactly did she think was going to happen there?

Apparently, Camden underestimated his own reputation.

Prue dropped her hand from his arm and moved to the easel that had been set up. She eyed it carefully, then looked up at the plant it was in front of, her brow furrowed.

"Not pleased with the subject?" Camden asked, folding his arms.

She shook her head, then looked around the orangery for a moment, smiling when she spotted a small, unobtrusive, almost hidden plant with tiny white flowers sprouting from it.

Why did that seem perfectly fitting?

Prue grabbed the easel and set it near the plant, then brought the supplies over. When she was settled, she looked over at Camden, who had chosen to sit in one of the small chairs nearby. "I'm really not very good at drawing," she said again. "Don't expect anything."

He shrugged and pulled a small notebook from the pocket of his coat. "That's all right. I'm barely passable myself, but it never stops me."

Her eyes narrowed. "You draw?"

He shrugged again. "On occasion."

"And what will you draw?" she pressed.

He gestured faintly to the room. "Oh, something in here, I suppose. There's plenty to choose from. And I won't look if you don't."

Prue fought a little smile, then nodded and turned to her easel and began to sketch.

And Camden pulled out his pencil, opened the notebook, and, after a moment, began to draw what captured his attention the most.

Her.

Chapter Five

A long ride on horseback can do wonders for a soul. Not so much for the body, though.

-The Spinster Chronicles, 14 April 1818

"You know, for someone who says they haven't ridden in years, you're showing a remarkable skill for it."

Prue looked back at Camden with a wry smile. "I rode a lot when I was younger. We lived in the country then. Oxfordshire."

"The fact that you can say Oxfordshire without trouble is absurd," he replied as he brought his horse up alongside her.

She giggled, tossing her head back a little. She couldn't believe that she had been fighting his suggestion that they go for a ride just because of her fear that it would be embarrassing. Or that she would be on display somehow. Or what he might think of her.

She had ridden all over Wetherington before her father's death, with and without a groom, much to her mother's dismay. Her father had laughed at that, thinking it all a very fine thing that his shy daughter was a bold rider in her own right. Granted, she had not been particularly daring where her riding was concerned, but children were limited in that regard.

If they hadn't lost Wetherington, she might have actually become a confident rider.

But lose it they did, and she no longer rode.

She inhaled deeply, then released it slowly, taking in the fresh air around them. She'd forgotten this feeling, this complete and utter freedom that she had never found anywhere else. How often had she escaped her mother's criticisms as a child by riding out? Or practiced her breathing in the midst of the hills behind their home? Or found consolation in the breeze of riding when she'd disappointed someone again? Or hidden from Eliza's torment in a refreshing ride?

She'd forgotten all of this.

She'd never thought her situation particularly tragic before, but now she wondered.

"What was that?"

Prue looked over at Camden in surprise, honestly having forgotten he was there with her. "Pardon?"

He gave her a bemused smile. "Something rather significant just happened in the confines of your mind, and now I am wild with curiosity."

Did she dare share something so private with him? Despite their spending so much time together lately, they really knew nothing about each other. Hardly anything they shared was deep or genuinely personal, and she wasn't sure she wanted to change that.

He had been very good to her, it was true, and had lived up to all that he'd said. He was by her side whenever he could be, whenever it was feasible, and she was so very grateful for the reprieve from having to worry about what might happen. But she also did not have to extend trust particularly far with all of that.

Could she tell him?

"I'd forgotten," she murmured before she could think about it too much.

Camden's brow furrowed. "Forgotten?"

Prue nodded slowly, letting herself smile with all her newfound joy. "I'd forgotten that I love to ride."

He stared at her for a long moment, and then he returned her smile, but only just. "That's a sad thing to forget."

"Isn't it, though?" She tried to be nonchalant about it all, shrugging one shoulder and leaning down to pat her horse gently. "Perhaps I will buy a horse for myself when I see the new estate."

"You should."

His voice was so firm, so sure about the notion, and it made her smile. "Don't you think I should examine the place first? It could be a terrible place for riding."

"That's true," he allowed, making a face of consideration. "From whom did you inherit?"

Prue chuckled to herself. "Aunt Harriett. My father's sister."

"That's good. I was afraid she'd be related to your mother, and then she wouldn't have led any sort of active life at all." He shuddered rather dramatically, drawing a laugh from Prue.

"I'm not entirely sure she was any more active than my mother," she told him. "I hadn't seen her since I was a child, and she seemed frail then."

Camden shook his head insistently. "If that's the case, all the more reason to believe the estate is just fine. She only just passed, she was undoubtedly a very robust woman. I take that as a very good sign indeed."

She was not about to argue the point with him, as there were entirely too many eccentricities involved with her father's family. And she could not share much about her father, or else she would share entirely too much about herself.

It was too soon for that.

"Perhaps," was all she said in response.

She glanced over her shoulder at the groom, trailing dutifully behind and looking somewhat bored.

Poor man. Despite Prue feeling very free riding now, she was not particularly adventurous. She had no desire to be truly saved by Camden, or by the poor groom. She would never get over such embarrassment, she knew that much, despite being comfortable with Camden.

It was one thing to be saved by him in a social situation when she was uncomfortable. It was quite another to have to be saved for the sake of her own life or at the risk of injury.

Her face began to flame as she thought about it.

"Four things, Prue."

She looked at Camden quickly. "Four things?"

He nodded, smiling almost smugly. "Four. About you."

"Why?" she laughed, twisting in her uncomfortable sidesaddle to see him better.

"Your cheeks are coloring without any provocation that I can see." His look turned almost scolding. "That means you embarrassed yourself in your head, and I mean to distract you. Four things. Don't delay, or it will be five."

Prue barked a laugh and shook her head, looking up at the overcast sky. "I hate talking about myself."

"No," he said sharply, "you said that last time. That does not count."

She groaned and squared her shoulders. She could do this, she could tell him things about herself without feeling vulnerable. Surely there were small enough things that would give little enough away while still satisfying his requirements.

He wanted to distract her. Perhaps it would help.

"I hate the color orange," she said quickly, keeping her gaze straight ahead. "I cannot sing. I don't like birds."

"Slow down!" he protested, almost whining from his horse. "I need to process."

Prue barely flicked her gaze in his direction. "And I used to read upside down."

"Up…" He nudged his horse ahead, so he could see her more clearly. "Upside down? Explain."

She bit back a smile. "Upside down. I would lay on my bed or twist in the chair so that my head was off and read a book that way."

He gaped at her but somehow smiled as he gaped. "How long did this go on for?"

"Until I was eighteen or so."

He laughed in disbelief, a deep, almost booming laugh that filled the surrounding hills. "That is incredible." He turned his laughing eyes back to her. "Tell me you haven't stopped entirely."

Prue hesitated, then slowly shook her head, smiling. "No, I haven't. It is still my preferred reading position."

"Yes!" He made an exultant face, then grinned at her. "That is the best thing you have ever shared."

"It doesn't take much to please you, does it, Cam?" she asked with the utmost patience.

He scowled a little. "I beg your pardon. I am only trying to get to know my new friend beyond the polite niceties of a drawing room or ballroom. Is that so wrong?"

No, it really wasn't, but that didn't make it any more comfortable than being asked questions in either of those places. All she could say for this scenario was that she was relaxed with Camden, for whatever reason, and nothing she was sharing was embarrassing.

Well, perhaps the reading position, but if that got out to the public, her mother would deny it most emphatically. Prue had come close to sudden death when she'd discovered how her daughter read, which was why Prue never read that way anymore.

Unless she was alone.

Which she almost never was these days. Never alone. Never time to feel or to breathe, never time to think for herself, or to simply be. She was surrounded.

All the time.

"Four things, Cam," she said quickly, interrupting her own thoughts with a frantic edge. If he was going to make her share things she did not want to, he had to return the favor.

She desperately needed a distraction, and she needed it now.

"I was afraid you'd say that," he muttered.

Prue only gave him a look and waited.

He stared at her, then reared back a little. "Do you have any idea how intense that look is, Prue?"

She raised one shoulder. "Some."

No, she didn't. She never looked at anybody that way, not even the Spinsters. How could she? There were five others, and each of them had something to say. She loved each of them, individually and collectively, but saying anything to them took a considerable amount of effort just to be heard. They would never know she felt that way, and she would never tell them, but she also could not ignore the fact.

She never took a stand.

On anything.

She had an intense look? What a bewildering thought!

Camden heaved another sigh, which he seemed to do a great deal in her presence. Was he tiring of her already? He couldn't... He wouldn't...

"I have no friends but you at this moment, because I'm an idiot."

Prue's panic faded, and she stared at him in horror.

"I love to fight," he continued, his tone not changing in the slightest. "Not as in arguing, but with fists. And I don't lose."

He… fought? That did not make any sense; he was so patient and comfortable. He was relaxed and easy, and yet he brawled with fists? Intentionally? And enjoyed it?

So many questions filled her mind, overwhelming her as much as excessive conversation did. She would begin stammering in her mind soon, and then she would be lost.

Could her father's pattern find her there?

"I have a sister," Camden went on, completely oblivious to Prue's situation. "No other family. Just Lydia. She's older, so we can blame my major character flaws on her lack of example. But don't tell her I said that."

Prue found herself smiling, catching the change in tone there. He adored Lydia, no matter what he said, but he hadn't really said anything about her. With all that he was sharing, to have so much kept back about her seemed to indicate a significance to the subject.

That may have been the most authentic piece of himself that he could have shared, and he hadn't said anything about her at all. For a woman who could not manage to say much at any given time, she certainly understood the importance of what could be kept hidden. No matter what else she learned about Camden Vale, that would be a point she would hold above all the rest.

"And I don't have any home but London," he finished, looking at Prue with some pride. "London is it, and London is all. There. Four things."

Prue watched him for a long moment, waiting to see if he would explain any of the things he had said.

He watched her as if he expected the same.

And no one said a word.

Slowly, the edges of her panic began creeping back in, reminding her that it had not fully abated, that the distractions could only go so far…

She cleared her throat and patted the horse again. "Do you know, I can't even remember the names of the men who tried to dance with me last night?"

"No?" he answered, ignoring the awkward avoidance of

explanation over the things they shared just as she had done.

She shook her head. "I rarely can. I have so much else going on that names and faces tend to fall by the wayside. Not exactly a fine example of a proper London miss, am I?"

"With as many Seasons as you've endured, I think we can grant you an exception with names and politeness."

Prue winced at that, though she knew he probably did not mean for it to sound as painful as it did. If he heard what he said, he gave no indication.

So many Seasons. So many people.

So many faces.

"Is there anyone of significance that I should note here?" she asked, her voice shaking a little, though she did not stammer once. "On the off chance that it comes up."

"Well," Camden mused, "surely you know Mr. Davies."

She rolled her eyes and nodded at that. "Of course."

"He'd be a good match for you, once he decides if he is going to be his own man or his mother's creation."

Prue clamped down on her lips to avoid laughing out loud. "That's not entirely fair."

Camden gave her a look. "His mother invited the women. He invited the men. None of the men have a fortune to rival his, and he is intentionally supposed to be the most attractive one. What can you derive from that?"

"Well…"

"No really, think about this." He moved his horse closer to her, his eyes suddenly lit. "There are plenty of wealthy women in London, and plenty of men to match them. But this is a specific group of people. None of your other Spinster friends are here. Why?"

"I refuse to speculate on motivations," Prue snapped, no longer finding humor in this. "Parents may go to extraordinary lengths to help their children make a good match, and if he chooses to go along with that, why should we criticize it?"

He raised a disbelieving brow. "This isn't about a good match. This is about financial gain. That's it. You of all people should know that."

"Oh," she said with some venom, her mind clouding with

everything that had been building up within it, "because I am a poor, plain, shy, stammering spinster who has never managed anything resembling courtship? And now I am so very fortunate as to have an inheritance that makes me suddenly a prospect to gentlemen with monetary gain in mind for a marriage? Yes, I understand that is the only reason I am here. Why else would I be? I had nothing to offer before, and now I do. There couldn't be anything else in store for me, so it is quite lovely that I suddenly have so much money as to make me appealing."

Camden stared at her with wide eyes, no hint of the teasing, relaxed man from before.

Slowly, almost so slowly she couldn't feel it, her cheeks heated, and she felt the familiar waves of emotion begin to roll in. She wrenched her gaze away, letting the tide of heat and irritation wash over her.

"There is so much more to being a spinster than sitting in corners and being neglected," she whispered, though she knew he would hear. "I have a fortune now, and while I despise the attention from the men only wanting that fortune, there is a small, rather neglected part of me that hopes, despite everything stacked against me, that a good match can be found in the midst of them all. Not a love match, but a good one. I may have been dragged here by my mother, but just because I cannot handle the increase in attention does not mean that I have given up on everything else."

There was still silence beside her, though she could see him out of the corner of her eye.

"I don't know what you are playing at, Camden Vale," Prue managed, feeling her panic coming on, "b-but I cannot disp-parage anyone for t-trying to settle their f-future in the way they f-find best. So, d-don't expect m-me to join in y-your attempts."

"Steady," he said softly, "steady…"

It was too late, she was too far gone, and her breathing became labored. "I c-can't… I'm n-not…"

"Molly, stop," he ordered. "You're all right. Stop."

Impossibly, despite her anxieties, Prue gasped at that, the firm command that was neither harsh nor given in a raised voice. She found the air and the calm, and could slowly, shakily exhale. No need for the pattern, not when she had been stunned out of her impending attack.

Molly?

She looked at Camden feeling suddenly bone-weary and thoroughly drained. He appeared no less surprised.

"Forgive me," he said quietly, his tone somehow vacant. "I don't know why I said her name."

Prue wet her lips, the choking sensation fading from her throat. "I remind you of her. It m-makes sense."

Camden shook his head. "But not enough to forget you." His brow furrowed deeply and he looked away for a moment. "Forgive me."

"All right," she replied.

He swung his head back around. "Not for that. For what I said. Prue, I'm not a fine gentleman like the others, so I often say and do things I probably ought not. I never meant to cause you grief or anxieties. Surely you must know that about me, at the very least. Our friendship and association were begun under those understandings."

That was true, and she could nod in acknowledgement of them.

He nodded in return. "I'm a terrible friend, which is why I have none at present. I've forgotten how to behave with them, so I will require some leniency as I try to do better by you."

"I think you will find me most lenient," she said without a stammer, and rather pleased to have done so.

He smiled at that. "Yes, you are probably a very lenient, understanding creature, are you not? Always see the good."

"Hardly," Prue protested with a rough laugh. "That would be my friend, Izzy. I see the good and the bad, and I am not nearly as nice as one would expect a shy girl to be."

"That's promising." Camden smiled further, seeming much more like himself already. "Right, shall we turn back? I'll tell you all the names of the others here, and by the time we reach Tinley, you'll be ready for them."

She made a face. "I suppose, though ready seems a poor word choice."

He laughed and turned his horse, waving at the groom, who turned as well.

Prue rode back at a faster pace, letting Camden tell her all the names he wished, though she would not remember many of them. She was only partially listening.

Molly. She wished that she knew just what Molly had been like, what she had meant to Camden, how similar they truly were. Their impediments sounded rather closely connected, even if they were not identical. The premise for helping one who stammers could not be very different, so it only made sense that he would find similarities in attempting to calm Prue when it came to it.

It wouldn't work if she were genuinely having an episode, but it could help to ward off the worst of it.

He had said on the first night that they had met that she reminded him of Molly, and she hadn't minded then. She wasn't entirely sure she minded now, except it picked at her thoughts in a rather insistent way.

Was he spending time with her and helping her because he wanted to help Prudence Westfall with her difficulties? Or was he trying to find a way to somehow be reconnected with the cousin he had lost? Were his motivations from a selfless place, or one of a painful selfishness?

Did it matter, if it resulted in the same thing?

She wasn't sure, and she was not sure she wanted to know.

Perhaps she should not be so comfortable with him. The ease of their first meeting had caused her to have more confidence in him, and in this, than she probably should have. She had never seen herself as being particularly naïve, but she supposed that was what this was.

If only Georgie or Grace had been here with her. They could have helped her to see things for what they were and to act in a manner that would benefit everyone without any trouble at all.

But they were not here. And if they were, they would have to be told about her fortune, if they did not know already, and they would want to know why she had not informed them of it before.

Change, she supposed, was the only reason she could offer. She did not like change. She had not wanted things to change. She was the quiet, mousy Spinster, the one without particularly strong convictions, and nothing of significance to offer to any man. But with little to offer, one stood a chance of a good match that could actually mean something rather than one entered for less favorable reasons.

With a fortune, she was suddenly a prospect for far more than before, and her place within the Spinsters would have to alter. She would still be the quiet, mousy one, but now she would need to be more like Charlotte, turning down offers of marriage because they did not suit, refusing courtships when they were thrust upon her, and being forced to consider every man that approached her as a potential marriage candidate.

She did not want any of that.

If she married, she wanted comfort, not wealth. She wanted companionship, not fortune. She never wanted to doubt that her husband had married her for any reason that she could not be proud of.

Not this. Anything but this.

When they arrived at the stables, the groom helped Prue dismount and was very kind about it. She smiled at him gratefully and started back to the house without waiting for Camden.

He hurried behind her, slapping his gloves in one hand. "Prue? Are you all right?"

"Just thinking." She gave him a weak smile. "We're a miserable pair, aren't we?"

He frowned at that. "I'm not miserable, and I don't want you to be. Can we be hopeless instead?"

Prue's smile miraculously became genuine. "Yes, by all means. Let's be hopeless."

He tapped the brim of his hat with his crop and moved around the side of the house to enter another way.

Prue shook her head. Camden Vale might have been the strangest man she had ever met, but he was rather entertaining, in his way, and he really was a good sort.

Confusing, but good.

She returned to her rooms with a quiet sigh and began removing the worn riding habit without the maid, who had seen her come and could be heard trotting down the hall.

"Prudence!" her mother barked from her bedchamber. "How dare you go out riding alone at a place like this!"

"I w-was escorted, Mother," she called back, shrugging the jacket off. "By a g-groom and…"

"That is not what I mean!"

The maid arrived and started helping Prue out of the rest of her things, and Prue decided she was not going to inform her mother of just how she had spent her morning. There was no point to it.

Her mother appeared in the doorway to her bedroom, still in her nightgown. "You are only to go riding out in the company of others, Prudence! That is the whole point of our being here! No more time alone, do you hear me? I am going to make some arrangements for you at breakfast. You will draw with the other ladies, in the same room. You will sew with the other ladies, also in the same room. You may be excused from participating in the musicale this evening only because you are abysmal in that area, but you will attend, and you will be pleasant."

"Yes, Mother," Prue replied as her eyes glazed over.

"Honestly, girl, I don't know why anyone would invite you anywhere if it weren't for your money."

"Neither do I, Mother."

"Hurry up and change. Miss Perry will be going down to breakfast soon, and you must learn what you can from her."

"Yes, Mother."

Chapter Six

One's choice of words is crucial to one's character, and one's choice of actions speaks volumes of the same. One requires words, the other thought. Which just proves that you can only trust evidence of both, as anything else isn't indicative of anything.

-The Spinster Chronicles, 4 February 1817

He'd called her Molly.

Molly, of all things.

He hadn't even been thinking of Molly when he'd called her Molly, so he had absolutely no reason to have done so.

And he'd heard her stammer when he'd apologized for it. That was a significant sort of stammer, and it had echoed in his mind the rest of the day, into his dreams the night before, and throughout breakfast now.

Molly?

Prue was not Molly. Not even close.

They could not have been more different in looks and temperament, as Molly had never been shy a day in her life and Prue was paralyzed with it. But they did share that vibrant streak riding through everything else, however hidden Prue's was. Even their stammering was different, in both sound and reason. Molly had stammered incessantly, and Prue only conditionally.

Molly had been his best friend, and Prue…

Well, he wasn't really sure what Prue was, or how to feel about her. She constantly surprised him, and generally, surprises were not pleasant for him, but in her case, it seemed to be. If nothing else, she'd made this house party almost enjoyable for him, which was miraculous.

Or it would have been enjoyable if he'd been able to spend any more time with her. Since their ride that morning, he hadn't even been able to exchange pleasantries, let alone have a conversation. She was surrounded nearly all the time, and not even by men vying for her attention.

The men had gone out shooting after breakfast, and the ladies had stayed behind, much to the dismay of a few. And the shooting had been dismal. Camden wasn't sure how it was possible, but none of the men gathered at this house party had the ability to carry anything by way of substance in conversation.

He'd had the best shooting day of his entire life, but only because he'd been too agitated to be as haphazard about his aim as he usually was. It hadn't given him any favorable points with the others, who complained he was stealing all the grouse from them, but it did satisfy him.

And he had wanted to share his triumph with Prue, but returning to the house had led to being forced into admiring all the artwork of the ladies. Prue's was no better and no worse, earning equal praises, if not a little more. And as the entire gathering had been present, Camden could not even whisper something moderately entertaining or comforting to her.

He'd heard her faintly stammering from across the room, and her face had been the color of a sunset, her eyes lowered.

It irked him to see her so uncomfortable and not be able to do anything about it. But she did not seem to be in much distress beyond her usual vices, given that the men seemed determined to praise every woman with the same effusiveness. Less overpowering, he supposed, if the cloud of perfumed words was spread about.

After forced admiration, they all had to wash and change for dinner, which had been fairly harmless as far as formal meals went, though he had been seated next to two of the silliest girls he had ever come across in his entire existence. They had learned relatively quickly that he was not the talkative sort, and so their attentions had been diverted to the other men surrounding them, and Camden was only referenced when a dry comment was requested.

Prue did not speak much, he noticed, but Miss Perry seemed to be mindful of her, which comforted him. Miss Perry was a good sort of girl with an easy manner, and she would be a good companion for Prue if they wished to maintain any kind of acquaintance after this.

He hoped she would. He did not know any of the other Spinsters, but surely it could be good for Prue to associate with others that were not so meanly relegated.

Provided, of course, that her mother was not controlling every moment as she seemed to be doing now.

While the other chaperones seemed to be letting their charges have some freedom and leeway, Mrs. Westfall watched her daughter like a hawk, and that was entirely unfair to hawks in general. Prue stayed the exact shade of a strawberry for the entire meal. No one else seemed to pay attention to it, but if they had seen Prue at various events throughout London, which he had not, perhaps they were used to seeing her look like this.

If that were true, he wondered why none of them had done anything about it yet.

Actually, a better question might have been why hadn't *he* done anything about it yet.

Standing here in the back of the room, waiting for the required presentation of musical abilities from those who may or may not have been in possession of the talents necessary for such displays, Camden couldn't have said exactly why he was waiting. Or what he was doing. Or how he felt about any of this.

He had the sneaking suspicion that it was more than curiosity and nothing like entertainment.

But he couldn't be sure.

Prue looked well, flushed cheeks and lowered eyes aside. She was dressed just as finely as any of the other girls this time, nothing at all lacking in her appearance. At least four of the girls were wearing the same off-white color, two with patterns, while Prue and Miss Perry's gowns were without.

She looked like all the rest tonight.

For some reason he refused to identify, that bothered him.

Prue wasn't like Molly, she was not like Miss Perry, and she was not like any of the others. In truth, she wasn't like anybody he had ever met before, and she deserved to be an individual, distinct from all the others.

Unfortunately, that was the one thing that did set her apart. While she deserved to stand out from the rest, doing so would terrify her into a stuttering storm of flushed frenzy from which she would never recover. She wanted to blend in, to hide, to be neglected and ignored.

And yet, she wanted to be seen.

To be found.

It was a paradox of contradictions that he found himself caught up in, wondering which side of her would win out, and how she would find the balance. And, it seemed, he would be invested in her and her concerns for the duration of this house party, come what may.

Standing against this decorative and useless pillar, surveying the room, he could only hope that Prue was not going to be forced into participating this evening, as he was reasonably certain she would have expired on the spot. She seemed more at ease as no one paid attention to her, her flush fading to just the tips of her ears.

But with her mother stuck as a fixture on one side of her, he doubted she would truly be at ease the entire evening.

He should go over to her. Sit beside her. Say relatively inappropriate things to keep her entertained throughout. Ward off unwanted suitors.

He should.

Yet here he stood.

"Vale, what are you doing all the way back here?" Charles Davies asked as he came over to him, looking somehow too resplendent for a musical evening.

Camden raised a brow at him and settled more fully into his leaning. "Surveying, Davies. Taking stock of the room. Waiting for enlightenment."

His answer seemed to amuse Davies, and he sipped on the beverage he held. "Well, come on. Don't seclude yourself back here all evening. There are several young ladies who would undoubtedly enjoy spending a quantity of time with a man of your humor and caliber."

"I find myself quite comfortable here, thank you."

Davies looked back at him, puzzled and uncertain if he should be amused or not. "But Vale… You will not have any conversation or entertainment back here."

"On the contrary," Camden protested with an easy smile, "I shall have the best company and the best entertainment."

Davies frowned at that. "How so?"

Camden shrugged a shoulder. "My own thoughts, and my own insights. I shall not shock anybody, nor shall I find anybody particularly tiresome. Truly the best of both worlds."

"But… you will be alone."

"Ideally, yes."

Davies chuckled uneasily and shook his head. "You are such a puzzle, Vale. I've not seen you speak more than five words to any young woman aside from Miss Westfall, and yet you clearly have no interest in her."

Camden shrugged again, unwilling to rise to the contradiction he probably should have offered there. Why should anybody suspect anything? He did not need ties binding him to Prue, and she most certainly would find no benefit in having ties to him. He had somehow managed to save her without bringing any sort of rumors to either of them.

What a marvelous, miraculous wonder that was.

What a dense group of fools they were surrounded by here.

"Your point being?" Camden pressed, not bothering to hide his boredom.

Davies huffed a little, still smiling good-naturedly. "What in the world are you even doing here, Vale, if you have no interest in any of the women? Why waste your Season on such efforts?"

His Season? It was a five-day outing in the countryside in close proximity to London, not a five-month endeavor in the wilds of Africa. He had sacrificed nothing more than nights at his club and random engagements that would have bored him.

"Why did I come?" he repeated, eyeing his companion blandly. "Because you invited me, Davies."

That didn't seem to settle with him. "That cannot be true. Surely you are invited to many places, and you choose not to attend. So why this one? Why here?"

"Why so inquisitive?" Camden asked. He offered a wry, derisive smile. "It is really not overly complicated. I had nothing better to do, and I felt sure some entertainment would be at hand. Boredom, Davies. Sheer and utter boredom brought me here."

Davies looked a trifle bothered by that idea, but he managed a smile all the same. "Well, I am grateful we could appease whatever tedium is currently filling your life, Vale. And for the sake of my mother's reputation as a hostess, try to look a little more enthusiastic about your presence here and the entertainment at hand."

On cue, Camden forced his countenance to brighten and smiled so forcibly that his cheeks ached with the strain.

"Oh, heavens," Davies murmured, eyes wide. "Don't do that. Never mind. As you were, Vale." He nodded to himself and moved on, glancing over his shoulder as though Camden were some sort of perplexing spectre.

Camden bit back a chuckle as he let his features relax into their usual state. Davies wasn't a bad sort, nor even one of the more ridiculous gentlemen of Camden's acquaintance, he simply lacked in the areas of sense and stamina. And possibly substance, but that remained to be seen.

This whole venture of a house party with heiresses seemed a bit of a stretch for Davies, and for his mother. As far as Camden knew, they were decently set up, and quite respectable as far as fortune and station went. The house was well-designed and not in apparent want of repairs or upkeep. Unless the family was better at hiding their needs than Camden suspected, there was no hint of anything to suggest a fortune was needed.

He suspected the ambitious Mrs. Davies was to blame for this, no doubt trying to get her not-so-dainty toes into the realm of the upper crust.

His eyes moved across the room to the seated guests, all settling in for the forthcoming music, and he found Prue again. Head up, eyes forward, ears red, mouth set. She might have been a statue for all the life in her, and the only thing that moved was her chest when she breathed and her eyes when she blinked.

No sign of enjoyment, anticipation, anxiety, or sorrow.

Nothing.

He wanted to make her smile. He wanted to see her vibrant. He wanted…

Her mother leaned over to her suddenly, and Prue somehow straightened further, her mouth curved just a touch at the edge, and her cheeks pinkened at an alarming pace.

What in the world…?

The music started, and Miss Fairbanks commenced with her aria, but Camden didn't care about that, nor did he listen.

He watched as Prue's slender throat worked on a swallow, a slight tremor coursing through her. Despite her hint of a smile, she looked more miserable now than she had before. Whatever drama was attempting to be portrayed in the song, it only gave voice to the turmoil that young woman endured at this very moment.

Someone needed to save her.

She deserved saving.

"Walk with me."

Prue rose without having to think about it, clasped her hands before her, and followed her mother along the row of emptying seats.

The second interval of the evening could not have come at a worse time, but there was nothing for it. Prue had sat as still as a statue, properly poised, perfectly attired, and, after correction, wearing a vaguely attentive expression. A pleasant one, at least.

If a grimace could be considered pleasant.

She had only just become comfortable again after her last reprimand and could have enjoyed several more minutes of music without the embarrassment of new flaws. She desperately needed something to intervene now before she had to endure another attempt at polite conversation.

The day had become unbearable after her ride with Camden that morning. She'd endured flattering for her artwork, which had been perfectly average even for her. The compliments hadn't been too incessant, as the other girls had received the same, but it had been uncomfortable. Her mother, on the other hand, had thought it all very agreeable and found fault with Prue's lack of gratitude for them. Had she been sitting closer, she would have jabbed Prue in the ribs for each and every apparent slight. Blessedly, she had not been that close, and Prue's ribs thanked her immensely at the moment.

But she greatly feared that gratitude would be short-lived. During the first interval, her mother had taken her around the room, parading her like a prized stallion before buyers on display. Then she'd dragged her over to a group of four men, all standing about and conversing together with no other ladies in their midst.

"Good evening, gentlemen," she'd greeted with a lofty tone. "You all know my daughter, Prudence?"

And then, to the horror of all, she had backed away and quite literally shoved Prue forward.

If they hadn't been taking notice of her before, they did at that moment.

Haltingly, she'd done her best to speak with them, though their questions tended to require only the shortest of answers from her. It had been a mercy for her nerves but had wreaked havoc upon her later when her mother protested at the lack of real conversation.

Prue had tried to explain that she could hardly be blamed for lack of conversation when their questions had not allowed for elaboration, but she'd been shushed at the first stammering syllable. There were no excuses, it seemed, and all evidence of her speech difficulties had to be concealed.

At least Amelia was sitting beside her this evening, which had spared her some difficulty. Her mother would take great care not to announce her flaws and failings in a way that might give Miss Perry any cause to think badly of either of them. Not when Prue's gown was nearly identical to hers, her hair of a similar style, and her comportment only a shade behind.

Prue had never been so properly behaved in her entire life.

It was mortifying.

The idea of having to endure her mother's torment yet again was more than she could bear, and she was fairly shaking with every step.

"I beg your pardon, Mrs. Westfall, Miss Westfall," Amelia said suddenly, breaking into Prue's apprehensive thoughts as she hurried over to her.

Mrs. Westfall beamed at her. "Miss Perry, you move with such grace and such poise!"

Amelia dimpled a lovely smile. "Thank you, Mrs. Westfall. I wondered if I might borrow Miss Westfall for a time. Several of the ladies are quite fond of her gown and how it flatters, and they begged me to fetch her, so they might inquire about it and make her better acquaintance."

She indicated the group in the corner, mixed with ladies and gentlemen, none of whom were looking in their direction.

"And some of the gentlemen," Amelia continued, lowering her tone conspiratorially, "have expressed interest in knowing Miss Westfall better, as well. I thought I might come and smooth the way."

She could not have said anything more perfect to convince Prue's mother, who gestured for Prue to take Amelia's arm eagerly.

"Yes, yes," Mrs. Westfall urged, widening her eyes meaningfully at Prue. "Of course, Miss Perry, you are too kind to my poor, shy girl."

Amelia inclined her head with the sort of regal air that Prue could never achieve. "Thank you. I shall return her at the end of the interval."

Without waiting for a response, she steered Prue away, their pace perhaps a trifle hasty for finely-dressed ladies.

"I had to get you away," Amelia hissed as she rubbed Prue's arm gently. "I promise, this is a gentler group than what you had before, and no one will press you."

"Th-thank you," Prue murmured, feeling a trifle lost amidst her overwhelming relief.

Amelia smiled at her, the dimple in her right cheek appearing. "You are quite welcome, Miss Westfall. Please call me Amelia, and let's be friends."

Friends? With her?

Prue could hardly believe it, and she nodded, managing a smile. "I'd b-be delighted. And you m-may call me Prue."

"That would be delightful." Amelia grinned at her, then cast a teasing eye at the group. "Mind you pay close attention to Mr. Andrews there. He's been known to mutter the most extraordinary things to whoever stands near him. Quite amusing, as I understand it."

Prue nodded, looking at the tall, handsome man they approached. "Is he as s-severe as he l-looks?"

Amelia shook her head rather slowly, her eyes twinkling with mischief. "I have it on excellent authority, my dear Prue, that he is all reserve, no severity, and smiles so rarely that one might wish upon it. Shall we try to get a good wish out of him?"

It was the silliest notion Prue had ever heard, and yet she found herself filling with a rare sense of fun. "Y-yes," she said with as much firmness as a stammer allowed. "Let's."

Chapter Seven

It is often in extremity that one finds one's better nature. And undoubtedly one's worst nature. Which begs the question: what are we at all other times?

-The Spinster Chronicles, 9 September 1816

Irritation was becoming a closer associate than was undoubtedly good for Camden, but he didn't suppose there was any help for it.

Not while he was here, at any rate.

He'd not had a single moment with Prue all day long, and after enduring the same odd affliction yesterday, he'd grown rather irascible about the whole thing. If he had not known better, he'd have thought that she was intentionally avoiding him. Except she had not avoided anything.

She had been there all the time, but somehow out of his reach.

He'd watched her quite steadily all throughout the musicale last evening, and it had to have been some comfort to her to be seated next to Miss Perry. But every time her mother leaned over to say something, Prue's flush increased, and just when it would fade, a new comment brought it back.

Miss Perry was oblivious to that particular aspect, but she did seem to help Prue relax, and he would swear that he saw Prue smile once or twice.

He'd moved in her direction during various intervals intending to get her away, but her mother forced her to walk the room, taking her directly to some of the gentlemen nearby. They'd all turned on Prue at the same time, seemingly fascinated by her and everything she had to say.

Camden could not bring himself to save her from that, not with her mother at her side, and considering what Prue herself had said… She still hoped for a good match and wanted to find it.

What if one of those poor sots were genuinely interested in her?

He doubted it, but there was no certainty in these things.

Miss Perry saved Prue at one point, steering her away during an interval before her mother could do so, and taking her over to some of the other ladies and gentlemen who seemed far more comfortable.

It was not until he'd laid in bed last night that he realized that he had spent the entire night doing nothing more than watching Prue. Oh, he'd listened to the music, certainly, and he'd applauded as he'd felt so inclined, but his attention and focus had been on the small, shy, uncomfortable, blushing girl trapped in a situation with no escape.

The irony struck him with such amusement he'd nearly laughed himself to sleep. He, who had grown so used to not caring about anyone or anything, had forgotten to think of himself and his own concerns in the face of a greater cause. The rescue of Prudence Westfall was suddenly paramount in his mind, and essential to his personal satisfaction with this event they endured together.

He'd chalked it up to their bizarre introduction a few nights ago and how it had thrown them together in such a peculiar way, and her outburst that morning. Surely he would not feel so concerned and protective after he'd had a decent night's sleep.

Now, however, sitting in the dining room with the other men after the ladies retired to the drawing room, he was convinced otherwise.

He was more concerned, more protective, and far more irritable. He'd not even greeted her today, nor she him. There hadn't been an opportunity.

That mother of hers was going to be the death of Prue, and he wouldn't be able to do anything about it. The ladies had begged for carriage rides today, as the weather had been fine enough to do so, and Charles Davies had arranged to satisfy them. Or, more likely, his mother had. Parties of six or seven had piled into each of the two barouches, which Camden happened to know they had rented from the local inn, and around the grounds they had gone.

Once he'd seen that Prue was settled in between two chatty girls and three other men had clambered into their carriage, he'd begged off of the whole excursion. He refused to subject himself to the torture of their company just to save her.

Besides, her mother had gone along in that one as well, and he thought it best that he not make her better acquaintance.

The trouble was that the carriage rides had turned into the teams for lawn games, and Prue was expected to participate.

There was no way to save her from that.

He'd volunteered to participate in any capacity but had been informed that having excluded himself from carriages, he forfeited his right to lawn games.

That was the most idiotic thing he had ever heard, but he could not argue the point.

At least it had been croquet and not bowls, and Prue had been decently capable enough. Not incompetent enough to draw sympathy, not skilled enough to earn overt praise. Not that it stopped some from giving it to her, but there was nothing to cause her to stammer nervously. She had been flushed most of the time, and he noticed she seemed to take her shots when a majority of the others were distracted, which made him smile.

Probably more than it should have.

But even her mother had been pleased with her if her gushing to the other chaperones had been any indication. It was odd, but there did not seem to be any correlation between Prue's being pleased and her mother being pleased. It appeared more the opposite, in fact.

Camden's mother had been gone for some years, but he was fairly sure that it was supposed to run along the same lines.

He'd have to ask Lydia about that one the next time he saw her.

"Vale, did I hear correctly that you exchanged fists with Phillip Turner some months past?" Charles Davies asked from the other end of the table where he smoked a cheroot.

Camden raised a brow at him, trying not to be put off by the puff of smoke that had blown in his direction. He wasn't opposed to men smoking in general, despite having an aversion to the stuff, but that by no means indicated that he wished to take on the scent himself.

"It is true," he allowed, wishing he didn't have to discuss it. Most of the time he did not mind recounting his fights for the ears of others, but he wasn't particularly proud of this one.

Phillip had been a friend of his, but after that fight…

"What was it?" Applegate demanded, leaning forward with a new energy in his eyes. "His wife?"

Camden almost laughed at that. Mariah Turner was a lovely, vibrant woman, and he would undoubtedly have fought over her if she had been free for the taking, but there was a strong bond in the Turner marriage, and Camden was not foolish enough to consider interfering.

Plus, Mariah would have had his head and beaten him senseless.

She was small but mighty, and he happened to know her left hook was perfect.

His jaw gave a faint twinge in reminder.

Camden smiled easily for the benefit of the others, drumming his fingers on the table next to his barely touched glass of port. "Not at all. He accused me of cheating, and I took exception to the accusation."

Mr. Gardiner puffed a particularly billowing cloud of smoke. "And was he right to accuse you? Were you cheating?"

Two of the other gentlemen looked at Gardiner as though he had lost his senses, apparently knowing Camden's proclivity for fighting without much provocation.

Camden stared at him for a long moment, letting the cool confidence of the man ebb back into wary hesitation as he drummed his fingers much more slowly.

Then his lips curved slightly. "Not that game. I never cheat with friends, which he ought to have known. Well," he amended, smiling more smugly, "not when there is money involved. I always cheat with friends when playing for sport and glory."

That earned him a round of chuckles, but Gardiner did not seem particularly satisfied. "Then why the fight? If he knew you cheated normally, and you did not this time…"

Camden shrugged with nonchalance. "I'd cheated the game

before, and he knew that. And I'd had too much to drink, so my good sense was rather absent. It was a rousing fight, you should have seen it."

Gardiner finally accepted that and chuckled. "Remind me not to fight you, Vale."

"If you suggest it, Gardiner," Camden answered, spinning his glass of port a little, "I will happily oblige. Just see that your affairs are in order before doing so."

Again, there was a round of laughter, and then Davies rose from the head of the table while Gardiner looked slightly taken aback.

"Should we join the ladies? And then we will proceed into the ballroom for our final dance of the party."

The words shook Camden a little. He'd forgotten that it was the last evening. Everyone would be leaving tomorrow, and then what? What would become of his little friend when she was surrounded by many others who might not be as polite about their pursuit of her?

He nearly shoved his hands into his hair at the sudden catch of panic in his chest. What was happening to him? He barely knew the girl, and he was not solely responsible for her care. Here he was irritated about not talking to her, worrying about what would happen to her when he was not there, and yet he had done so very little. He was no hero, especially not for someone he had no particular interest in.

But she trusted him, however foolish that was. She felt safe with him. That was a weighty thing, and he felt the burden of it.

And Prue was a lovely girl. Precisely the sort that deserved all the good in the world, despite having little of it. Surely any man would exert himself to assist someone like that.

If they could see her.

"Vale?"

Camden looked up to see the rest had filed out while he had sat in his odd stupor. He shook himself and rose with a smile.

"Apologies, Davies. Just ruminating on the return to London and the Season."

Davies chuckled and clapped him on the back as they left the room. "It will be nice to have more variety, eh?"

Variety? Camden rolled his eyes at that. With the sort of

creatures they'd invited here, they had the silly, the spoiled, the sweet, and the spinster. What more could he want?

He mentally winced. Spinster. That title only went to Prue Westfall.

And he wondered if she was even deserving of that label.

How much evidence did a man need in order to properly save a damsel in distress?

Prue made her way to the ballroom on the arm of Mr. Frist, who talked so much of himself it was a wonder he did not court himself. The small mercy in this was that he did not require her to answer, so she only had to walk and endure listening.

She'd managed that for all twenty-five years of her life, she could surely manage another minute of it.

But once inside the ballroom, there was no telling what could occur.

Camden hadn't said a word to her in over twenty-four hours, and she was beginning to wonder if his words about not being a hero mightn't be too true. There had been ample opportunity, both the night before and today, if he would have only paid attention.

Today had been difficult, and she was already blushing over what the ballroom would bring. Still blushing might be a better turn of phrase, as she had been this same shade most of the day.

All of that should have been painfully obvious to Camden, though he had hung back for the whole of it. It would have been so easy for him to come in and ask for a moment with her, or to turn the conversation away from her, or anything to alleviate her anxiety. Even his presence would have done the trick, but he hadn't even done that. Not a single thing to help her, despite being so kind to her the first few days.

Perhaps he had tired of his efforts. Perhaps the reminder of his cousin was too painful, and he had opted to remove himself from the situation. Perhaps he had heard stories from the others about her or the Spinsters…

Perhaps…

"Dance the first with me, Miss Westfall," Mr. Frist suddenly said, his certainty of her answer clear.

She had to. She had to dance with anyone who asked, or her mother would have a great deal to say on the subject.

She swallowed with some difficulty, her throat choosing that moment to close itself off. Rather than attempt a stammering answer, Prue nodded once.

He smiled at her and praised her ceaselessly, which only made everything worse. He swept her into the formation of the dance, taking up the lead position.

Lead.

She had to lead.

Her face flamed worse than before, and she lowered her eyes, her breathing turning unsteady.

The jaunty music began, and she moved before she knew what she was doing. Her motions were not at all fluid, and she was astounded that she recalled the steps at all. She did not have to think about it, did not engage with a single person near her, and let her body move as its instincts allowed.

It seemed all those years of observation and painful dances with uncomfortable partners had been useful after all. If she could not speak or smile or breathe, at least she could dance.

"Come, Miss Westfall," Mr. Frist called out too loudly, drawing attention to her inattention. "Smile! It is a dance, not a lecture! Smile for us all!"

Out of habit, Prue looked to her mother, who had obviously heard, and the severe widening of her eyes and tightening of her mouth told Prue everything.

Swallowing a weak sob without any accompanying tears, Prue forced her lips to curve into a smile that physically pained her.

It would convince no one that she was happy, but it counted as a smile.

Hopefully, that would be enough.

Her feet still moved with the dance, her arms tingled with anxious sensation, and the only part of her face she could feel was that agonizing smile. Her chest ached with every breath, and her throat seemed to constrict in time with her pulse, which was rapidly accelerating.

Breathe in, breathe out. Fear…

So much fear. So many people. So many eyes on her, so many faces, words, things…

Somehow, she managed to finish the dance, and the music and applause were faint in her ears over the buzzing that had begun.

She needed a chair, a reprieve, and no approaching would-be suitors.

"Please dance the next with me, Miss Westfall," someone asked.

"No, me!"

"Miss Westfall is so light on her feet, she must dance the next two with me."

Her hand was placed in another, and she was pulled into another line, seeing everything and yet seeing nothing at the same time.

The music struck up once more, and again, she was familiar enough to dance without thinking.

At least this time they were squarely in the middle and no one would mind her.

"Miss Westfall, you are lovely as the sunrise and twice as splendid," her partner gushed.

She dipped her chin in response, which only closed off her breathing more.

"What has been your favorite moment of the house party?" he continued. "What has struck your fancy? Do tell me, and I shall ensure you have such entertainment every week this Season."

Prue parted from him in the dance, frantically trying to remember how to formulate words, let alone anything that would be considered a response.

"W-w-w…" she tried, stammering so severely she shook with the effort. Her mother's glowering face rose in her mind with a vengeance.

Stop stammering, Prudence!

"W-w-walk," she coughed as tears formed in the corners of her eyes.

Her partner could not keep the strain of his effort at patience and tolerance from his expression, and it rendered the tightness in

Prue's chest further still.

"Oh, yes, country walks are a most lovely excursion," he prattled on, his voice not as enthusiastic as his words. "Do you walk much in London? Hyde Park, perhaps?"

Lord, he wanted her to speak more? She could barely hear his question over her own panic, her face flaming in indignation, the tingling of her arms spreading into the pit of her stomach and down her legs…

"Y-y-yes," she hissed through clenched teeth.

"And Regent's, too, I'd wager. Tell me, do you approve of the new flowers there? I find them a bit distracting. Which flowers would you have planted there?"

The tears in her eyes were going to leak out, would become obvious, would draw more attention…

Attention. Sympathy. Horror.

Shame.

She tried to form an 'L' for lilies, got so far as her tongue pressing against the roof of her mouth, when she stumbled suddenly, crumbling to the ground.

"Oh! Miss Westfall!"

"Miss Westfall!"

"Dear lady!"

And somehow, over the distressed exclamations… "Well, that figures."

Her breath hitched in her chest loudly, and she moved to cover her mouth.

Only her hand would not obey her.

"Clumsy dolt, Alderton! If you cannot dance with someone as light as Miss Westfall, stand over in the corner and be useful!"

Camden's voice cut through the haze, and a pair of hands gripped Prue's arms and practically hoisted her from the floor. "Come, you will dance the next with me, Miss Westfall. And the rest of this one, if you are not injured, and if the musicians would carry on!"

They did so immediately at his loud suggestion, but Prue could not hope to dance, not when she could no longer feel her feet or take in a single breath or see straight.

"I c-c-can't… I-I-I c-c-can…" She shook her head frantically, her breathing rolling into an equally frantic realm. "C-C-Cam…"

"I know, I know," he assured her gently, rubbing her arms. "Outside we go. We're on our way."

The fresh night air hit her then, and she inhaled sharply, nearly collapsing with the sensation.

"No, no, come on, over here…" Camden urged, half carrying her to the right.

She was seated then and hunched over, covering her face with her gloves, which were damp from the perspiration of her palms. Her sobbing, gasping breaths reached a peak then, a hard edge wracking each against her chest…

Breathe in, breathe out. Fear in, fear out.

Breathe in, breathe out. Fear in, fear out.

"What was that, love? What did you say?"

Prue shook her head, hiccupping on tears and words and breath.

Breathe in, breathe out. Fear in, fear out.

She moved her hands to the sides of her face, seizing upon the image of her father, graying and wrinkled as he had been, his eyes crinkling but steady. Fixed on her. Holding her gaze.

Breathe in, breathe out. Fear in, fear out.

"Yes, exactly," Camden soothed. "Yes, Prue. Breathe…"

Had she said the words aloud? She must have done; how else would he know? Had she stammered? Had she been coherent enough?

Breathe…

"Yes," Camden said again, and it occurred to her that he was rubbing soothing circles on her back. "Very good, again."

She did so instinctively and found her lungs filling with the cool night air and not her panic. Her face burned, but that began to fade, and her eyes cleared. She still tingled all over, but at least she was calming.

"I'm s-sorry," she whispered, her hands sliding down to her throat. "I'm s-so s-sorry."

"For what?" Camden asked, taking one of her hands in his and squeezing. "You didn't do anything wrong. Miss Fairbanks tripped you, and I would have called her out if she had been a man. That wasn't your fault. And anyone could see how overwhelmed you were, and with Alderton egging you on."

"S-stop," Prue hissed painfully. "I d-don't want to rel-live it."

He rubbed her back again. "Shh, it's all right. What was it you said? Breathe in, breathe out…?"

"F-fear in, fear out," she finished, nodding slowly. "My father used to say that to me when I g-got too overcome. He would take my face in his hands, just as I was doing, and make me look at him. Tell me to breathe, and he'd breathe with me. It's the only thing that has ever fully calmed me."

"It sounds as though he was an excellent father," Camden murmured, smoothing his hand over her dampened hair.

Prue nodded and swallowed, then exhaled heavily. "He was." She slowly turned to look into the ballroom. "W-what will they think?"

"Doesn't matter," he quipped. "Not even a little. And don't worry about your mother, I sent Miss Perry to distract her for a time out of the ballroom once I saw your state. The others won't pay any attention, I promise."

"They will," Prue whispered, her ears beginning to burn again. "They will. They always do."

"Not if I took you outside while they all finished the dance and told Davies to dance like a clodpole to distract everybody else."

Prue looked up at him, curious in spite of her sudden exhaustion. "And is he?"

Camden looked over her head, smiling in satisfaction. "Brilliantly so. He looks like a right idiot."

She exhaled roughly and dropped her head into her hands again, shuddering with relief. "Thank you."

"It's my pleasure. Truly."

"Saving me is your pleasure?"

"Truly is."

She shook her head against her hands. "Not possible. Nothing about me is a pleasure, let alone saving me in my distress." Another shudder rolled over her, and Camden's hand followed gently to soothe it.

"I don't know about that."

"No, it's true. I'm a trial to everyone, especially my mother and m-my friends, and I don't know why anyone bothers!" She whimpered a weak sob.

"Prue, don't. There is so much to praise," he insisted, surprising himself with his fervor.

She shook her head insistently. He was too kind, too blind, too ignorant of the way of things. "Didn't you hear how they flattered me? You said yourself, men lie through their teeth."

He hissed, and she looked over at him only to see him shaking his head. "Prue, I didn't mean… Sometimes we are sincere. Sometimes we do mean everything we say. And you should like it and take it as a compliment."

Prue smiled a very tight, thin smile. "They never have before, so I have no taste for it." She exhaled and looked back into the ballroom, clasping her hands before her. "I just wish to be left alone."

"Well," he sighed, "then we have another problem."

She looked up at him wryly. "And that is?"

He shrugged, something new in his dark eyes. "I don't think I can leave you alone." He stared at her for a long moment, his hand stilled on her back, and added, "I know I can't."

Her head tilted in a question. "Why not?"

"Because I see you," he admitted with a rawness she did not anticipate. "And I like what I see."

Prue's lips parted in surprise, and a swallow caught in her throat that had nothing to do with panic. She forced herself to swallow and licked her lips quickly. "I… don't know how to respond to that," she breathed, her cheeks coloring faintly.

Camden smiled gently and patted her back. "That's all right. Speaking is a bit of a problem for you when overcome. I have that effect on all women, so you are quite normal in that regard."

His teasing was missing the necessary air, but it made her smile and roll her eyes all the same, and the tension within her faded away completely. "I really must hear that reputation of yours in its fullness. I have no idea what to believe."

"Only the good is true," he assured her, rising from the bench.

The cold night air rushed in on her with his vacancy, and she shivered. "And the bad?"

He shrugged again. "Probably true."

She coughed a laugh and shook her head. "I will keep that in mind."

"Can you dance now, Prudence Westfall?" Camden asked, holding out a hand. "It may be our last night of dancing. London approaches, and our ties will break."

"And your reputation will come to light." She nodded and put her hand in his. "I suppose I must, if I ever will."

He chuckled and squeezed her hand. "I'll save you, Prue," he murmured, his eyes on hers again. "All night, I'll save you."

Her heart clenched within her, and she nodded, unable to speak, to tell him how much that meant.

Or to ask the question, "And after that?"

She was too afraid of that answer.

But tonight, she could dance.

Chapter Eight

Leave-taking is really the most inconvenient thing in the world. Well, it is on the list of most inconvenient things, at any rate. Several other things take precedence. Garters, for example, are much more inconvenient. But leave-taking is unfortunate all the same.

-The Spinster Chronicles, 2 October 1815

Camden had not slept well at all the night before, which would usually indicate that he would be remarkably surly to anyone that crossed his path.

Not this morning, however. Walking the grounds of Tinley, he found himself mostly content. Tired, but content.

Mostly.

Despite the dramatics of it all, he had enjoyed last night possibly more than any other ball he had ever attended. There had been some truly spectacular balls in his time, but at this moment none could surpass it, and that was a perplexing thought. Nothing had happened but saving Prue from the idiots, helping her to calm, and then dancing with her twice.

Twice.

Other than that, he'd stood near her chair, and they'd chatted easily for the rest of the evening. Others would come and join them on occasion, but no one tried to flatter or puff themselves up for Prue's benefit. She had danced with Mr. Andrews, who had shocked everybody with that request, and while Prue had not smiled in the dance, she had not turned any colors either. Davies had asked if he might have an opportunity, and given his willingness to make a fool of himself for her, Prue had allowed that as well.

Camden had only danced with Amelia Perry besides, and his good opinion of her was growing more by the day. It was becoming clearer to him that she was too good for the company present, and while she would never require his assistance or protection, he would consider the idea if it was presented to him.

Whatever that meant.

Truth be told, it was probably the most innocent evening he'd ever had after a social engagement like this. Not that he'd ever been really wicked at any other time, but this may have been the first occasion where he'd had no ulterior motives.

At all.

It was an odd feeling, somewhere between liberating and bewildering.

And today, they were leaving Tinley House to return to the glory and splendor of London. No more limited company, no more structured activities, no more enduring sycophants just for the sake of politeness...

No more saving Prudence Westfall.

That did not sound particularly appealing at this moment, even after what last evening had brought them. In truth, it was not as much a matter of saving as it was soothing. Assisting. Reassuring.

Caring.

He nearly stumbled a step and felt his eyes widen as that realization sunk in.

Good heavens, he cared. He honestly cared about Prue and her situation, her comfort, her feelings... He cared enough to act, not just to sympathize.

He cared. About her.

He exhaled a rough burst of air and shook his head. It was undoubtedly time to return to London and his usual way of life. He needed normalcy and sanity, which one did not tend to get from London Society, but once there, he would find restoration of his usual cares and concerns.

Not that there were many of those, but he enjoyed it that way.

Camden Vale did not care. That was what they all said, that was what he had always believed, and that was what he intended to keep to.

Except this time, he did care, and he did not know why.

She was nothing, a tiny slip of a woman who feared attention and praise the way most women feared the reverse. She was certainly sweet and undeniably witty, and for some reason, he seemed one of very few people who knew that about her. She had seen fit to confide in him, to trust him, to let that more impish side of herself shine through the fortress of her anxieties.

What a surprise it had been to discover just how very far from nothing she truly was.

It would not be necessary to save her in London. She had friends there who were more familiar with her situation and knew how to aid her in her distress. She would be protected and cared for by far better individuals than Camden, and he wouldn't have to do anything at all.

She couldn't possibly need him after this. He hadn't even heard of her before coming to Tinley House, which meant that her difficulties could not possibly be as spread about as she thought. Here, there was little to distract from them, so it was understandable that it should seem so pronounced. Once there were more to gossip about and more people to see, Prudence Westfall and her shyness would be a small matter indeed.

And yet…

He swallowed with a harshness that startled him. Once he had been her protector and her friend, could he cease being so?

He'd lost all his friends before this because of idiocy and willpower, so he knew it was possible, but this wasn't like the others. He hadn't done anything particularly stupid this time, and neither had she. No pride to patch up, no apologies waiting to be delivered.

A friendship such as this, unlikely as it was, did not follow the same form and pattern as his others, and he was entirely unsure what he was supposed to do with it.

Was a friendship of convenience supposed to last beyond the convenience?

Did he want it to?

Despite his warnings to her, he really wasn't as bad as everybody made him out to be. He might be a rapscallion, but he was no villain. He might lack manners, but he was not cruel. There were times he was improper, but he was never wicked.

He wasn't always a gentleman, but he was rarely less.

What exactly did that make him?

She was right; he was confused by his own reputation. He'd never cared enough to really change anything about it, and now he wondered if he should have. Camden Vale could not be friends with Prudence Westfall as things stood. It would take a gross undertaking of the reformation of his character and an establishment of a new one, and probably with some flare and dramatics to emphasize the thing.

And Prue would not do well with flare and dramatics.

So that was it, then. The rogue and the spinster would part ways here, just as the road diverged outside the gates. She would go her way and he his. They might meet at events in London. There might be a shared look or a secret smile, a nod of acknowledgement, perhaps a hint of warmth in their eyes. But that would be all. Once in London, she would hear all about him, and there would be no more saving, no more dancing, and no more terrace escapades unescorted.

Which was as it should be.

Mostly.

He circled around to the front of the house to find carriages lined up, waiting for their occupants to appear. The horses snuffled and blustered a little, making the grooms and drivers chuckle as they soothed them. Camden smiled a little at that, oddly wondering which carriages belonged to which guests and if he would be surprised by them.

A bit of bustling at the doors drew his attention, and he saw Mrs. Westfall proceeding towards the carriages as though she were some sort of royalty. Her head was held almost impossibly high, and her dark traveling clothes, along with those blessed airs of hers, made her seem more like a pompous widow than anybody of importance.

He looked past her, as much as he was able to without straining, to see Prue following at a greater distance than he expected, seeming somehow more fragile and petite than ever before when compared with her mother. She had absolutely none of the same airs, and reminded him again of a very young girl, though she was older than most here.

She wasn't even looking ahead when only in the company of her mother. She was just as timid there as she was when surrounded by a dozen people, though she had never quite managed that attitude with him after the first ten minutes.

There was no life in her like this.

No life. No spirit.

Nothing that made her Prue.

But everything she reduced herself to be.

Glancing back at the carriages, where her mother was now preparing to board the simplest one of all, Camden looked at Prue and cleared his throat.

Prue jumped a little, her eyes widening. He saw her swallow, and then she turned to her mother. "Mother, did you b-bid Mrs. Davies farewell?"

Mrs. Westfall stopped and turned on her heel, not seeing Camden as he stepped further away. "I made my farewells to her last night, Prudence. Did you think I would be so rude as to neglect our hostess in such a way?"

Prue shook her head quickly, her fingers suddenly knitting together. "Of course not, Mother. It's j-just she m-mentioned something to me at breakfast about wanting to c-continue a discussion in London."

Mrs. Westfall looked suspicious. "What discussion?" she demanded.

"She d-didn't say," Prue told her with all the innocence in the world. "But I b-believe she said you discussed it l-last night."

Now Mrs. Westfall seemed almost gleeful, and she marched back towards the house. "Do not go anywhere, Prudence, we will be leaving the moment this conversation is finished," she barked as she passed her.

Prue watched her go, then turned to Camden with a raised brow.

He grinned and strode towards her. "Is there a real conversation that is going to take place inside now? Or did you make that up just to have a private word with me?"

She returned his smile. "As a matter of fact, yes. I wasn't going to tell her before we left, as I have a fair idea of what it will pertain to, but now…"

Camden tilted his head at her, his grin turning crooked. "You sacrificed keeping something from your mother just to speak with me? Good heavens, Prue, I'm rather flattered."

Prue rolled her eyes, still smiling. "I keep a great many things from my mother, Cam. It isn't anything special."

He had to laugh at that and marveled at how changed Prue was now from the creature he had just seen. "What's the conversation about?" he pressed, losing some of his teasing air.

Now she looked uncomfortable and averted her eyes. "Mr. Davies and myself."

"Ah," Camden murmured with a slow nod. "And am I to congratulate you, then?"

Prue glared at him quickly. "You know better than that, don't you?"

He shrugged. "Do I?"

She scowled and sputtered softly. "Mr. Davies has never said anything to me to indicate any particular interest. His mother is eager to have him marry anyone of fortune, and as my mother tends to be fairly boisterous with regards to her interests…"

Camden barked a laugh, interrupting her attempt at an indignant speech.

Now Prue sighed and let herself smile again. "She is very determined."

"So I see," he replied, still chuckling. "You will undoubtedly find yourself engaged before you reach London."

Her cheeks flushed, and his smile softened at the sight. Even the thought of it embarrassed her.

Poor thing.

Prue met his eyes wordlessly, her gaze unexpectedly open, the lack of barriers taking him by surprise. It was the clearest, steadiest gaze he had ever seen, somehow filled with secrets and yet completely without them. He was at once disarmed and fascinated, and more confused than ever.

"Cam," Prue began, hesitation rampant in her tone.

He was shaking his head before she could say anything else.

"Don't," he told her. He couldn't bear having her showering gratitude on him, making this moment more of an ending than it already was.

She gave him a look, something raw and vulnerable that nearly stole the feeling from his knees. "I h-have to."

That stammer…

Camden sighed, glanced at the door, and stepped forward to take her hand. "No, you don't," he told her gently. "I'm only glad I was out on that terrace when you came racing out."

Prue smiled at the reminder and nodded once. "You scared me to death."

"I have that effect on people," he quipped, though he couldn't manage the lightness he'd hoped for.

She said nothing, but her smile remained.

And so did his.

He cleared his throat and turned their hands, so he could shake hers. "Well, goodbye, Prue Westfall. If you ever need saving in London…"

Her smile turned wry, yet somehow sad. "But you aren't the saving type, as I recall."

"True."

They stared at each other again, silent but for the horses and the sounds from within the house.

"Goodbye, Camden Vale," Prue murmured, her hand gripping his with more firmness than he'd expected. "Thank you for saving me."

The thought crossed his mind to take her hand and press it to his lips, not in a romantic sense, but more of a teasing, gallant air. Yet it remained firmly in his hold, and he returned the pressure.

"My pleasure," he told her, with an honesty he hadn't managed in years.

Her slender throat moved on a swallow, and she nodded, releasing his hand and moving to the carriage.

He ought to help her up, see her situated, say something more…

Yet here he stood.

Watching.

Too soon, her mother reappeared, a satisfied smirk on her lips, and she bustled past him without a word. Then they were off, pulling away and rambling down the road of the estate and out of his sight.

He stared after them for a long moment, then turned back towards the grounds.

It would be well to walk them again.

Prue gnawed on the inside of her cheek as they approached London once more, grateful that it was not a longer journey from Tinley House, though her mother had managed to doze off on the trip, her mouth gaping rather comically as her snores escaped.

London, for all its being her home, was one of her least favorite places in the world. Too many people, too bustling, too much expectation and restriction. If she had any strength in her character, she would have told her mother that she wished to spend what remained of the Season at her new estate, but she had not.

And a life in the country would not be the haven she expected it to be if her mother was with her.

At least London would have the Spinsters. She'd only been gone a few days, but she had missed them terribly. They would have been such a comfort at the house party with all that had been going on and would have found a way to make her laugh about it.

She would have gone mad had Camden not taken her on.

She sighed as she leaned her head against the side of the coach, watching the countryside fade into the London streets.

Her farewells to Camden this morning had seemed somehow more poignant and culminating than she had expected. As though they were parting for life and not for the time being. As though the friendship they had struck up was no longer in place, dissolved now that they had no need of it.

It was a forlorn feeling, losing a friend who had been so attentive.

Well, when he remembered to be attentive, that is.

She had yet to decide if his behavior last night made up for the almost two days of neglect previously, but she could be persuaded to forgive him.

Not that it would matter. He would not be asking for

forgiveness, and she would probably never see him again under the same circumstances. Their paths would most certainly cross at various events, but she crossed paths with several people who paid her little attention.

She'd never minded before.

Would she mind now? Would she notice his absence when her usual friends and associates were about her? Would she look for him when she returned to the routine of her life? Would she find herself looking to be saved?

Would he be watching?

Questions rose and swirled and threaten to engulf her completely, none of which she could bear to properly contemplate. She closed her eyes against them, letting the swaying of the carriage soothe her as much as it could. There would be enough to be getting on with without worrying about Camden Vale and his intentions.

Not that he had any intentions. He didn't. He wouldn't.

And she shouldn't care.

London was dangerous ground for a woman in her position, but even more so for a woman in her condition. She knew that the attentions she had endured at Tinley would only be magnified when the rest of London caught wind of her inheritance, if they hadn't already. Those that had been at Tinley and had gossiped about her would spread it around once returned, and then more and more would do the same.

She felt no panic at the moment imagining all of that. Rather, it seemed a far-off dream, a hallucination, something that another girl would have to endure, and she would watch with sympathy. She was too fatigued to contemplate how she would react to such advances and attentions. She had no reserves to draw upon, and London would see to it that she did not have a chance to build any up.

Prudence Westfall was an heiress now, and in London, that was a significant thing to be.

She would have to deal with all of that soon. She would have to manage invitations and calls, attempts at courtship from men who had never paid her attention, requests for friendship and associations from girls who had never seen her as an ally… Everything she had never been, she would now become.

The only thing that had not changed was herself, which had never gotten her anywhere in the first place.

She could not do this alone. She could not endure another event like Tinley. If Camden hadn't been there to assist her, it would have been a complete disaster, and disasters for heiresses were worse than death.

She needed her friends.

Prue looked over at her mother, who was now rousing and scowling out of the window blearily.

"Mother," Prue said quickly, hoping to make the request before her mother was too lucid to plan, "might I call upon Charlotte Wright after we arrive home?"

Her mother looked at her for a long moment, blinking as though she did not understand. Prue couldn't blame her, she'd managed the entire question without stammering, which was a rarity with her mother, and if she had only just woken…

"Charlotte Wright?" her mother repeated, her brow darkening. "She's not much wealthier than you now, and thus is less of a valuable connection."

Oh, Charlotte would be delighted to hear that. Prue nodded and folded her hands in her lap. "Yes, Mother. But she does know how to m-manage Society so well, I thought it might be w-wise to confer with her on the topic."

Again, her mother blinked her large, owl-like eyes. "It's an excellent idea, Prudence," she finally said, a bit confused as she found herself saying anything praiseworthy about her daughter. "Yes, call upon her, by all means. I will not accompany you, I am far too fatigued. Take a servant."

A hot burst of elation hit Prue's stomach, and she forced herself not to smile at all. "Yes, Mother." She looked out of the window and bit the inside of her cheek again.

It was Wednesday, which meant the Spinsters would be gathered to discuss the upcoming articles for the Chronicles. She could remind herself that she was not alone and friendless in this, nor was she unprotected. She could manage this new way of life with their aid.

She could.

They arrived at the house and entered to find flowers, cards, and a somewhat frazzled-looking pair of maids trying to decide what to do with more flowers that had just arrived.

"Harper," her mother chirruped, taking everything in with a calculating eye. "What is this?"

The butler stepped forward, his slender figure seeming somehow frail now. "Cards and gifts for Miss Westfall, ma'am. They've all arrived in the last few days."

A slow, satisfied smirk filled her mother's face, and she turned to Prue with the same look. "Go upstairs and change, Prudence. Call upon Miss Wright, and then return here straightaway. There is much to be done. And mind you don't spend too long with that hussy. Eliza and your aunt and uncle are coming for dinner, and I must beg their advice on this matter."

Prue blanched and hurried up to her room, any hopes for a collected manner vanishing in the face of her new reality.

Flowers, cards, gifts… And to be subjected to Eliza after what she'd just been through?

She couldn't breathe, and despite having just arrived, was wild to be gone again.

Once changed and accompanied by a footman, Prue climbed back into her carriage and rolled on towards the Lambert residence, the unofficial meeting place of the Spinsters. She could feel tears welling behind her eyes, but she forced them to remain there. There was nothing the Spinsters could sniff out so well as distress, and obvious signs would make short work of all of this.

Thankfully, it was a shorter trip to Izzy's than Prue anticipated, and she disembarked from the carriage without any assistance, rushing into the house as though it were the only safety she would know in the world.

Bonnet, gloves, and spencer were handed off to a maid, and she was taken to their usual parlor, holding her breath every step of the way.

The others were already within, chatting with their usual eagerness, and she was pleased to see that Lady Edith Leveson was actively engaged in the conversation. She was a recent addition, and somewhat of a novelty, being a widow as opposed to a spinster, but Prue liked her immensely, finding her far more reserved than the others, but with none of the shyness that held Prue captive.

Edith wasn't shy. She was rather more like Charlotte than Prue if Charlotte would behave a little more like Prue.

Though she had not even been gone a week, she felt as if a lifetime had passed since she had seen any of them. Somehow, it hurt to admit that.

"Prue!" Izzy squealed when she caught sight of her. She jumped up and came over to hug her. "Oh, we missed you! And your last Quirks and Quotes was so popular, you should have *heard* how people have been going on about it!"

Prue smiled and hugged her friend in return. Izzy was a veritable ray of sunshine no matter what was happening, never spoke ill of anyone, and was never anything less than perfect at any given time. Being around her made one comfortable, content, and warmed by her goodness.

It was more soothing than ever now.

The others rose and hugged Prue in turn, and she smiled as Georgie passed on Tony's greeting as well.

"He'd have been here, too," Georgie assured her, rolling her eyes, "but Francis wanted him to go to the club, and since Hugh is being a right troll…"

"Too right," Elinor Asheley muttered darkly from the corner.

She was far too young to be a spinster, with or without a capital S, but they let her participate with them anyway. She had strong opinions, a cynical nature, and purposefully held herself back from anything resembling a courtship.

It was the oddest thing.

Georgie looked at Elinor in exasperation. "Yes, thank you." She looked at Prue, still smiling. "But he will be here later, and says he has a task for your next article."

Prue nodded and situated herself between Edith and Grace on the sofa while Izzy poured her a cup of tea.

"Prudence Westfall," Charlotte said slowly from the other side of the room, looking Prue over as though she had never quite seen her before. "What is this I hear about money and lots of it?"

The room stilled as Prue looked at Charlotte, letting her warm, curious, dark eyes take in everything that Prue's fair ones might show.

Everything rose to the surface, the fear, apprehension, anxiety, and fatigue warring for primary position, and all jumbled together until Prue did the one thing she had sworn not to.

She burst into tears.

Chapter Nine

"I cannot believe that you failed to get a single gown with lace on it. Not a single one! You are *hopeless*, Prudence Westfall."

"It really is quite sad, Aunt. All that money and the lamb doesn't know what to do with it."

"Quite so, Eliza."

"There is still time, Aunt. Do let me take my dear cousin to procure some proper lace items next week. You know I have quite the eye for these sorts of things."

Prue couldn't do anything about the rampant flush from her shoulders up, but she made every conceivable effort to have no other reaction to the conversation happening around her, despite being the subject of it.

It was the only way to survive.

A night at the theater was usually something that Prue enjoyed immensely, but when a box was secured for her family, including her cousin, it was one of the worst things she could have endured.

And if her mother agreed to Eliza's offer…

"That would be so good of you, Eliza," her mother said with a simpering sigh of affection. "It would be just lovely to have you assist Prudence in such a kind way, wouldn't it, Prudence?"

"Yes, Prudence," Eliza hissed, sitting just to Prue's left. "Wouldn't it?"

Prue swallowed in response.

"We'll all go!" her aunt suggested brightly, her voice warbling as it always did. "A delightful outing of women!"

That would be better, Prue was sure, but if she knew Eliza…

"Oh, but Mama!" her cousin protested on cue. "I was so hoping to have some private time with Prudence! We weren't expecting to be up here for the Season, and I want to hear about everything I've missed! You know that nobody has the sort of details a wallflower does, they see and notice everything!"

"Very true, darling, very true."

Really, it was as if Aunt Howard had no idea of anything except what Eliza said. Prue had never given any of them the notion that she saw or heard or noticed anything of significance at any point in time. Of course, what Eliza had said in this case actually *was* true, but she had no reason to suspect that Prue would be such a source for her.

And while she certainly played the wallflower on occasion, she hadn't thought one could actually *be* a wallflower. If she were anything, surely she was more like wallpaper…

Prue sighed a little, wishing that the performance would begin so that her cousin might be a little less invasive of Prue's evening.

"I saw that," Eliza told her, keeping her voice low.

Prue did not look at her.

"You're not going to have it so easy, lamb," her cousin went on, her tone turning almost sinister. "You have a fortune now, and I am going to take full advantage of that. You will be my patron, like it or not."

There was no need to respond to that. No question meant no need to answer. Prue knew very well that the slightest stammer on her part would evoke a vindictive response from Eliza, and she was only barely holding it together at this moment.

"Say something, lamb," Eliza said as she leaned closer. "Say something."

Prue clenched her teeth hard, her cheeks somehow flaming more than before.

"Glow, little lamb. Glow."

Her palms began to sweat and she her jaw began to ache with the pressure of her teeth.

"Baa," Eliza bleated with a laugh. "Let's hear it. Baa."

Prue closed her eyes. She tried to swallow but couldn't seem to manage it.

Eliza chuckled and sat back against her chair. "Simple women never get anywhere, Prudence. Remember that."

Being back in London had not done anything for Prue's comfort, and Eliza was more menacing in her efforts than she had been in years. Thanks to Prue's fortune, now the family connections were even more worth preserving, not that there had ever been a question of it before. At least her uncle seemed to have some idea of the difficulty Prue was facing, as he appeared to be giving her more sympathetic looks than usual.

It didn't lead him to act in any sympathetic way towards her, but she hadn't expected that.

Dinners with the Howards. Outings with the Howards. Now, the theater with the Howards, and, if Eliza had her way, shopping with the Howards.

It seemed that the suitors would not be Prue's greatest problem in London, but rather her own family.

That shouldn't have surprised her.

Changes were happening faster than Prue would have liked, and her mother was on a rampage to turn Prue into the proper heiress she imagined she should be. The new gowns had arrived, and only half of them were the ones Prue had liked. The rest had been additions from her mother.

Every Wednesday was now for callers, and soon they would add Fridays, as well. Tuesdays and Thursdays were for making calls herself, and Mondays were for shopping. Saturday and Sunday, she had a reprieve from set tasks, aside from church services, and even those had been turned into an opportunity to look lovely while being pious.

Given the fervency of Prue's prayers of late, she rather expected she was more pious than any of the clergymen.

A new maid had been hired specifically to be Prue's lady's maid, and while Prue had balked at the change at first, she found herself rather enjoying having Bessie around. She was not at all chatty and had a tasteful eye, which was the most comforting thing that she could have possessed. There would be no more catastrophes like the orange dress a few weeks ago, now that Bessie was entrusted with all things appearance for Prue.

That had surprised her, as her mother tended to have a vested interest in such things, but no more. Bessie had once been lady's maid to Mrs. Miranda Sterling, she'd been told, and that was quite good enough for Mrs. Westfall. Prue thought that seemed a bit farfetched.

Having met Miranda herself, she could not imagine anyone being anything for her only once. She was the sort of woman who engendered lifelong devotion wherever she went.

But she had yet to work up the courage to ask Bessie about that rumor, and she did not think she would any time soon.

At least this evening she knew she looked well enough. Bessie had chosen to adorn her hair with the sort of simple elegance that Prue had always wished for but had never been able to manage herself or describe adequately enough. It flattered the shape of her face and the texture of her hair so well that she wondered at having ever worn it any other way. Soft ringlets danced near her ears and were matched by thicker, longer curls in the back, pinned amidst plaits and white ribbons to match the white details on her blue silk gown.

Silk. Of all the silly things for a wallflower and spinster to wear, silk seemed chief among them. It hardly suited her, no matter how flattering the shade and cut. According to her mother, that was because there was no lace anywhere to be seen.

The musicians near the stage started into their first piece, and Prue exhaled very slowly, taking great care not to do so audibly. She was now to be corrected on the tone and frequency of her sighs, as well. Because heiresses do not sigh.

Apparently.

She would have to tell Charlotte that one. How distraught she would be.

The opera commenced, and while Prue couldn't recall which opera they were seeing, she did not particularly care. Any of them would have been a welcome reprieve, and she was only grateful to have time to listen and reflect. The drama on the stage just might distract her from the drama in her own life, or else enhance it.

They would commence to an evening of dancing and music at Lord and Lady Mortimer's after the opera, which meant that Prue would be getting home rather late, which meant that she would have quite a headache tomorrow, which was unfortunate, as she would be forced into accepting callers shortly after breakfast.

At least there was a limit to the number that came, or that her mother allowed, and Prue had never been so grateful for small public rooms in her life. It was saving her the trouble of more chaos than she already faced, and while it had not been much of an issue thus far, if things continued the way they were going, they would need the size restriction.

The Spinsters had been stunned by Prue's admission of her inheritance and fortune, and only Charlotte had scolded her for the secret, and then just for a few minutes. Prue's tears to them the other day had startled them all, as she generally avoided crying before them at all costs, and their love and support had relieved much of her anxieties at the time. There had been no significant events as yet where Prue had been forced into her usual difficulties, but the smaller gatherings were proving just as challenging, though in different ways.

Card parties were less about the cards and more about her. Taking tea had nothing to do with the beverage and everything to do with negotiating relationships and events. Rides in the park were anything but refreshing and turned into interrogations.

No panicking, no need for saving, but she had certainly flushed and stammered, as she did, and that seemed quite enough. Some of her initial suitors had already cried off, and she wished them far, far away. Others were utterly devoted to the idea of making her like them, though nobody seemed to actually try to understand just what it would take for them to do that. With the ridiculous characters she had seen thus far, she began to wonder if any of their methods actually worked on the sentient females of Society.

They must have done, or there would not have been half so many marriages as existed.

Two weeks since Tinley House, and she was more at sea than ever.

Smaller parties meant that not all her friends would be in attendance, and in some cases, none of them were. She had yet to attend an event where Izzy, Georgie, or Grace did as well and had not even seen Amelia Perry yet. She had seen Charlotte numerous times, but given the congested nature of Charlotte's circles, they did not do much by way of association. She knew very well that if she had trouble, Charlotte would have bowled the entire group over to get to her, but no occasion had driven them to that yet.

Come to think of it, Prue wasn't entirely sure that such extremes would have made her feel any better. It spoke to Charlotte's loyalty, most assuredly, but the scene such antics would have created might have done more harm to Prue's delicate frame of mind than anything else. Provided she noticed, at any rate.

Low, rumbling sounds drew Prue's gaze across the seats to her mother, aunt, and uncle, only to find two of the three dozing without shame. Her uncle stared straight ahead at the stage, though it was quite clear that he was neither seeing nor enjoying anything before him. It was entirely possible that he was, in fact, asleep with his eyes wide open.

Such talents would have explained his lack of accomplishment in Parliament and his subsequent replacement, but that was neither here nor there.

Prue smiled a little and looked back at the stage, biting back the need to sigh again, this time with resignation. The tenor currently performing with all of his might was only fair in his talents, and it was quite a shame, as the music was extraordinary. But without the vocal ability to match what the musicians provided, there was not much to see there, so Prue took the opportunity to glance about the theater.

There were a great many people in attendance, and some of the patrons she could see were those who tended to plague her with questions about anything they thought might be of interest to her. If they had seen her enter tonight, as some certainly would have done, she would need to remember to have answers and opinions at hand.

Not that anyone wanted to hear her opinions, given the difficulty she had with basic answers when provoked, but she would have to be prepared for every eventuality.

A late arrival in an upper box across the theater caught her attention, and she watched as a dark-haired man in eveningwear situated himself in a chair, no companions near him.

He looked up at the stage then, and Prue's eyes widened as she recognized him.

Camden Vale.

He watched the stage for a moment, then raised a brow as if to say, "This is the best he has?" which she echoed in her own mind, smiling at the thought.

At that precise moment, his gaze met hers, and he stilled.

Prue's breath caught in her throat, and she prayed she did not look as stunned and bewildered as she felt.

His dark gaze held her, kept her staring back at him rather frankly, and he did the same. She did not find herself becoming embarrassed or even flushed, oddly enough. On the contrary, it was as easy as staring at a wall, for that is all the expression he maintained.

No flash of interest, no smile of encouragement or amusement, nothing to indicate she interested him in the least. There was, however, also no flash of sympathy or derision.

What did he think? What was he feeling?

What did she think and feel?

She couldn't even decide that at the moment.

She didn't think, she didn't feel; she only stared at him. And he stared at her, and neither of them seemed in any way inclined to change that.

As the tenor finished his poor attempts, neither of them applauded. Then he absently did, just three times, and Prue found herself slowly raising a brow at him, which made his mouth twitch, and he very slightly shrugged one shoulder.

Smiling to herself, Prue returned her attention to the stage but found herself glancing back over on occasion, and he always seemed to be watching her.

What did that mean? Why would he do that? What did he see, what made him look, why…?

It couldn't mean anything. It couldn't. It was only the surprise, surely, and she was looking at him as well, and without much reason to.

She just wanted to. Whatever that meant.

So, he was in London. She wasn't sure that she had expected him to be anywhere else, but without seeing him out and about, she'd gotten used to the idea that he was gone. From London, from Society, from her life…

But there he was. Not gone from London, not gone from Society, and…

Well, there was no need to jump to any conclusions, no matter how her knees suddenly shook with the urge to leap.

She was bound to see him eventually, and now she had done so. And he had not seemed in any way ashamed of her, which was something significant, in her estimation. He, who had seen her at a very low moment, knew how bad she could get when overcome, had not made any move to pretend he did not know her.

He was here, and he was alone, which made her sad. She'd settled on the idea that he'd been kind when he'd said he had no friends but her, something to make her feel at ease and give her reason to trust him, but there he sat in a box by himself. He seemed quite contented there alone, which Prue could certainly understand, being quite comfortable on her own herself.

But with how entertaining Camden had been with her, she could not see why he would not be surrounded by friends at any given point in time. He might be somewhat unconventional for a gentleman, but that was becoming more and more of a popular trend and ought not to put many off from associating with him.

It hadn't stopped her.

The Spinsters had no idea that she had ever associated with him. Despite confessing her fears and anxieties to them, as well as the full situation of her inheritance, her mother, and her experiences at Tinley House, she had neglected any and all mention of Camden Vale.

He was her secret.

Why, she hadn't dared to contemplate, but with all that he had said and led her to believe about his reputation, she had no doubt that some, if not all, would have some powerful objections to being in any way tied to him through friendship, convenience, or anything else.

She was terrified of what Elinor's research on him would reveal, and the opinions of those who did not know him could unfairly sway her against a good impression.

You don't know him either, she reminded herself. Not really.

No, that was true, but when a man treats a woman kindly and with gentleness and patience when there is absolutely nothing to be gained by it, it ought to say something about the true nature of the man. There was no possible benefit to aiding Prudence Westfall in the midst of her anxieties at a house party for wealthy young women to be flattered by potential suitors. There was nothing advantageous in paying any attention to a spinster so shy she could not bear compliments from others or being noticed.

Yet he had done all those things.

How wicked could a man like that be?

It didn't even matter if he were wicked or not, they were hardly going to move in the same circles and continue the odd friendship they had formed. He was only in the same theater as her this evening, but so were dozens of other eligible men, and some of them were wicked, some of them were good. There was no reason to dwell on it.

She looked over at him again, and this time he smiled as she did so. Not in a teasing or arrogant way, but the same sort of soft smile he had given her any number of times at Tinley. Nothing that had ever made her flutter, blush, or fidget there.

Now, however, it had all those effects on her. She felt a fluttering in the pit of her stomach, she felt her cheeks grow hot, and suddenly she was feeling restless. Her throat began to burn, and she started to rub her fingers together as anxiety twisted at them, despite not feeling any sort of panic anywhere else.

Eliza was sitting beside her, smug in every respect, having every intention of taking complete advantage of Prue's fortune and shyness, and of making her life as difficult as possible.

Her mother was pressing her into more and more uncomfortable situations and encouraging every attention Prue had ever wished miles away.

She would be flattered and fussed at for the rest of the evening, probably embarrass herself, stammer needlessly, and come close to fainting, despite having friends at hand.

At this moment, none of those things mattered.

Camden's smile seemed to somehow force all those things to the back of her mind. They were still there, looming in the distance, but nothing about them irked her now.

Slowly, Prue inhaled and exhaled, keeping her eyes trained on his, letting the corner of her mouth curve into what she could only hope was an adequately responsive smile.

They might never have a moment like this again in their lives, particularly not after their farewells at Tinley, which had played over and over in her mind and in her dreams until the pain and awkwardness ate away at her. They might never again dance together or speak a single word to each other.

But in this theater, in this first act of this mediocre opera, they could smile at each other.

Camden dipped his chin in a nod, a hint of his mischievous nature showing forth, and then he returned his attention to the stage just in time for the final strains of the aria.

The theater applauded the end of the first act, and Prue felt that something had broken with the sound. A bit belatedly, she joined the applause and waited for further torment at the hands of her family.

"Miss Westfall!"

Prue turned in her chair to see Amelia Perry standing in the entrance of their box, grinning unabashedly at her, and looking a shade of lovely that Prue could only ever hope to achieve.

"Amelia!" Prue greeted, relief washing over her. She rose and went to her, taking the girl's outstretched hands and letting her kiss her cheeks.

"I couldn't believe it when I saw you!" Amelia squealed, squeezing her hands. "I was fidgeting the entire first act, I was so excited to see you." She suddenly seemed to recollect there were others in the box and she curtseyed perfectly. "Mrs. Westfall, it is so good to see you. I do love that color on you, it does you such credit."

It did no such thing, but her mother beamed anyway and curtseyed in response. "Miss Perry, you are so good. May I introduce my sister, Mrs. Howard, her husband, and their dear girl, Eliza?"

Everybody greeted her accordingly, though Eliza had a

speculative light in her eyes that Prue was very wary of.

"I wonder, Mrs. Westfall, if you would permit me to steal Miss Westfall for the interval," Amelia begged with the sort of charm that could not be refused. "I have missed her so."

Eliza raised a brow that Prue could only pray that Amelia hadn't seen.

"And Miss Howard is more than welcome to join us," Amelia continued, smiling at Eliza in a way that only ignorant people would.

Prue could have kicked the silly girl in her perfect shins for the suggestion.

"My brother is on his way to escort us," Amelia went on, still smiling, "and we shall be quite looked after."

Mrs. Howard clucked excitedly. "Oh, what a dear creature! Yes, you may take my Eliza along, if my dear sister agrees to part with Prudence."

"Naturally, if Miss Perry wishes it," her mother allowed indulgently, "and Mr. Perry will not find it too taxing to mind you all?"

Amelia shook her head, her rich brown curls dancing against her translucent skin. "Not a bit of it. He is quite used to minding me, and that cannot be an easy thing."

"No, it is not," a distinctly male voice replied drolly from behind her. A man with coloring equaled to Amelia's, though his skin was a bit tanned, appeared, his mouth curved into a pleasant smile.

"Mrs. Westfall, Mr. Howard, Mrs. Howard, Miss Howard, Miss Westfall," Amelia said with a suddenly formal tone, though she smiled informally, "my brother, Frederick Perry."

He bowed with absolute precision, still smiling. "Charmed, ladies. Sir."

Now Eliza looked positively delighted and glided over to them. "So, you are to escort us, then, sir?"

He apprised her politely. "I am, Miss Howard, if you do not find it burdensome to be escorted."

She smiled slowly. "Not in the slightest. I pray you will allow me your arm, sir, as I have somewhat of a weakness to my ankles. Walking does do me good, but I am not quite steady, you see…"

He offered his arm at once, all cordiality. "But of course. Amelia, if you and Miss Westfall will follow, and stay close?"

"Naturally," Amelia replied easily, linking arms with Prue. "Lead the way, Fred."

They all nodded at the parents, then proceeded out of the box.

Mr. Perry kept a steady pace for them, and an even steadier stream of conversation with Eliza, which was surely some trick of madness.

He needed to be warned.

"Amelia," Prue murmured, feeling a stammer rising as they followed, keeping her voice low. "My c-cousin…"

Amelia patted Prue's hand easily, her dimple flashing with a smile. "Not to worry, Prue. Fred can handle her."

No, he couldn't. No one could.

"You d-don't understand," Prue insisted, whispering as best as she could. "She is…"

"Oh, I know all about her, Prue," Amelia overrode with a knowing look. "Trust me, I know. And I saw the pair of you before the start of the opera, and I saw how she made you look, to say nothing of the lace monstrosity she chose to wear. I might have doubted what I'd heard about her before, but now I see it is worse."

"Then your b-brother," Prue stammered, eyes wide. "He…"

"…has a remarkable talent for enduring unlikable people," Amelia finished with a sly smile. "And is quite devoted to me. This way, I get you all to myself for a few minutes, and you don't have to contend with *that.*"

Prue found herself laughing and pulled Amelia closer to her side. "I missed you, Amelia."

"And I you," Amelia replied with a wink. "Now, let me tell you what I've heard about Mr. Andrews…"

Chapter Ten

There are some people who add nothing of value to Society and ought not to participate in its activities and entertainments. Whether for reasons of morality or moronic tendencies, these individuals would be better served being trampled. If we all someday burn because of the general degradation of Society, feel free to blame these pox-carriers for your singed status.

-The Spinster Chronicles, 23 January 1816

"Oh, Mr. Applegate, you are such a wit! Such a surprising thing in a man of your intellect and station, and rather a pleasant one. If you asked me to dance the next, I would accept."

"Erm, Miss Howard, I…"

"Never mind my dear cousin. She is terrified of all creatures of the male persuasion, and I am to aid her in finding those truly worthy of a woman of her position as it now stands. It is really the least I can do for her, such a dear, shy thing."

"In that case, it would be an honor to stand up with you next, Miss Howard."

Prue watched as Eliza placed her hand in Mr. Applegate's outstretched one with a flourish, letting him lead her away.

"Have you ever heard the sound a lamb makes when it cries, Mr. Applegate?" she heard Eliza ask before the music began again.

Prue closed her eyes and craned her neck as an irritated shiver raced down it.

"You really need to stand up to that tart, Prudence."

She glanced over at Lady Hetty, sitting beside her, and smiled sadly. "How, my l-lady?"

Lady Hetty returned her smile, creating even more lines on her withered face. She patted Prue's hand with an equally lined hand, covered by crocheted half-gloves.

By telling her she's an impudent tart and isn't charged with anything where you are concerned."

Prue made a soft noise of amusement, feeling bone-weary after enduring first the theater and now this ball. "I never wanted Mr. Applegate to pay me compliments, Lady Hetty."

The older woman chortled. "No, I should say not. But it is the principle of the thing, my dear. And for her to speak such horrible things about you while she is trading on your name to further herself…" She shook her head, tsking loudly. "Not at all respectable."

Prue shrugged a shoulder. "I'm used to it."

That earned her a look. "And that is a tragic thing."

It was, wasn't it? Prue had grown so accustomed to being insulted and degraded by her family, let alone embarrassed by them, that the shift to a grander scale had almost no additional effect on her. It was just as embarrassing to have Eliza telling potential suitors in ballrooms of her ties to Prue as it was for her to gossip about her in tea rooms. Being scolded by her mother in the park was just as embarrassing as being scolded by her at the theater.

She was accustomed to their treatment of her. It did not make it easier to bear, just the way of things.

"Surely your cousin doesn't want Applegate for herself," Lady Hetty scoffed as she watched the pair of them dance.

"I doubt it," Prue sighed, wringing her fingers together. "She just doesn't want m-me to have him. Or any of them. She is very jealous of m-my attentions."

"She should be jealous of your nature, not your admirers," chimed in Izzy as she approached them and took up position on Prue's other side, smiling warmly. "She's only two years younger than you, and no closer to marrying than you were even before your inheritance, but if she were not so mean…"

There was another laugh, and Prue looked up to see Georgie approaching with Tony. "Don't even finish that sentence, Izzy. Eliza

Howard is a viper and a menace, and nothing good can or should be said about her."

Prue hiccupped a startled laugh as Tony snickered, giving his wife a proud look.

"Who are we speaking badly of and can I join in?" Charlotte asked as she joined them, pulling at her gloves a little. She glanced around, looked where Prue was looking, and then snorted loudly. "Oh, good. Toad face. I don't give three figs for Applegate, but he doesn't deserve that."

Lady Hetty cackled and thumped her walking stick on the ground in apparent approval.

"Where's your contingent, Charlotte?" Tony asked as he looked around as if attempting to find them. "I would swear they followed you in here."

"Very funny, Anthony," Charlotte replied with a sniff. "I predict they will be here in no less than five minutes."

"Ugh," Georgie groaned. "Take them over there, Charlotte. Away from Prue."

Charlotte grinned at that and looked down at Prue. "Not interested in sharing, sweet lamb?"

Prue gave her a sardonic look that drew chuckles from her friend. "No."

"Ah," Charlotte sighed, adjusting a perfect ringlet, "I do love when you are firm."

"Take them a-all," Prue insisted.

"I'll take some," Izzy offered wryly. "Anyone have a fortune I could borrow?"

"If only," Prue muttered with a sour look at the gentlemen nearest her, all of whom were glancing in her direction. "They're g-going to start coming over s-soon."

Izzy took her hand and squeezed it gently. "I'll be right here the entire time. You're not alone."

Prue nodded and swallowed.

"I'll just be over there being myself," Charlotte assured her, indicating the corner just opposite. "Unless I am dancing. But you give me any sort of signal, and I'll come."

"Tony will dance with you if you need a reprieve," Georgie

reminded her with a smile. "And we can even get Lieutenant Henshaw to come dance with you if you'd feel comfortable. Maybe even Mr. Morton."

The mention of Tony's friends set Prue's cheeks to flaming, but she nodded again. "I m-might be."

Charlotte sighed, giving Prue a half-exasperated, half-sympathetic look. "So convincing, lamb. Who is distracting your mother?"

Prue shook her head, feeling more nervous now than she had only moments ago. Her friends were loving and kind, but their assurances were overwhelming her, reminding her of all the things that could happen tonight, everything that could go wrong. It felt as though she were their new project, something requiring strategy and observation, with everyone taking up a position with Prue in their line of sight. Rather like the watch everyone in London presumed the Spinsters took up with the younger ladies in London.

They didn't, but it probably would have happened like this, if they did any such thing.

Charlotte said something in her lighthearted way and then left them, Tony took Georgie out onto the dance floor, and Grace and Elinor appeared, jabbering and gossiping about several members of Society.

Prue didn't listen to any of them. She fixed her gaze on the dance, watching the couples go through the motions, noticing the expressions of each. Did any of them feel the same way she did about these things? Did they fear observation and attention? Did they wish to dance, but in a private setting and without any expectation rather than on display and with the risk of rumors starting?

"Miss Westfall," an intrepid young man greeted, bowing before her. "You are looking particularly lovely this evening, and that is a paltry expression indeed. Might I have this dance?"

Prue stared at him without speaking, fairly certain she had never met him in her entire life.

"You don't even know her, Thomas Baldwin, so you can just slink off and find someone else to prey upon," Elinor sputtered, waving him off.

He glared at Elinor and curled his hand into a fist before striding away.

Prue looked up at Elinor in surprise, but the girl was shaking her head at the retreating figure.

"He's a friend of Hugh Sterling," Elinor spat. "I've heard him call you a duck, and a goat, and recently, 'mine for the pillaging'. He's not dancing with anyone I have ever said a kind word about, let alone you."

Izzy stared at Elinor, her eyes wide, her brow furrowed. "You're turning into a termagant, you know that?"

Elinor shrugged without concern. "All the better for me."

Prue exchanged a slightly worried expression with Izzy, then watched the dancing again.

"Miss Westfall," began another man.

"No," Elinor said abruptly. "Move on."

"Elinor," Izzy hissed as he, too, left with a glower.

"What?" she replied, utterly ignorant as to the problem. "We are protecting Prue from the vultures, are we not?"

Grace met Prue's eyes, and Prue did everything short of actually pleading with her to do something as her cheeks flamed. Grace nodded once, smiling for effect. "Elinor, did you say Thomas Baldwin was an associate of Hugh Sterling?"

Elinor's gaze sharpened at the name. "Yes. Why?"

"I would swear I saw him paying a call to the Wiltons just yesterday." Grace widened her eyes as if in dismay. "You don't think…"

Elinor grabbed Grace's hand and pulled her away. "No, no, no. Come with me, we are going to speak to the Wiltons. That must stop right now."

Grace winked at the others as she let herself be pulled away, and Prue breathed a sigh of relief that had Izzy and Lady Hetty snickering.

"I applaud her enthusiasm with your defense," Lady Hetty commented dryly, "but the delivery leaves something to be desired."

"That is one way to put it," Izzy agreed. "That girl…"

Prue shook her head, exhaling slowly again, wishing her mortification would fade. Sitting beside Lady Hetty would keep some of the men away, as she terrified nearly everyone, but those who considered themselves to be important enough would not be put off by it.

She had to make a show of participation in the activities of the evening, or her mother would never let her hear the end of it. But the list of men with whom she felt comfortable enough to dance with was short indeed. Additionally, Eliza's penchant for spreading whatever stories she wished to provided a different set of problems entirely.

"Is Eliza dancing with Mr. Frist now?" Izzy asked in an almost hushed voice. "That's the worst pairing I've ever heard of."

"Almost as bad as Mr. Frist and m-me," Prue muttered to herself.

Izzy heard, though, and giggled at it. "I suppose that must be true. But it's not favorable."

"No one is favorable when paired with Eliza," Prue told her.

"Prudence Westfall!" Izzy laughed, covering her mouth. "That is the most delightfully spiteful thing you have ever said! Where in the world did that come from?"

Where? Oh, the bitterness of twenty-something years of enduring the patronizing, sniping, coldly cutting remarks of someone to whom she would be forever bound through the bonds of blood and family. From being tormented again and again by people who should have loved her and treated her with gentle consideration and kindness. From a dark corner of her mind that said and thought all sorts of things that she would never say aloud for fear of mortification and punishment.

Prue smiled tightly at her friend. "I'm in a f-foul temper."

Her hand was gently squeezed. "It's all right, lamb. You can be whatever you need to be tonight."

The trouble with Isabella Lambert was that she was endearing, enduring, and patient to a fault. The kindest, gentlest heart Prue had ever known, including her own, but so well liked by absolutely everyone that her being a spinster at all was astonishing.

Not that there weren't reasons for it. Izzy was plain and had no fortune to speak of, though there was a little money, and she was so accommodating that nobody thought about her in that regard. It was a tale almost as tragic as Prue's, though for different reasons.

Izzy wasn't shy, though she wasn't particularly outspoken, and she had no visible display of her insecurities as Prue did.

She should have been the heiress.

Not Prue.

She didn't even know if she could adequately understand the legalities of her inheritance, let alone the ins and outs of the details. She hadn't met with the solicitor managing the affair yet, aside from the initial revelation of the inheritance itself. What if she couldn't oversee her own finances the way she would need to? What if she bungled everything and lost it all?

What if the man she married, if she married, squandered her fortune and left her with less than nothing? What if she chose the wrong husband and would have been better off a spinster heiress? What if her fortune was all she had to offer, and without it she was worthless?

"Prue?"

She shook her head at Izzy's gentle, unspoken question.

She couldn't explain the torment inside her at the moment.

"What if" were the two most terrifying words in the world to her.

They tended to thrust themselves into her mind with startling frequency.

"Miss Lambert," a kind-faced gentleman greeted as he bowed before them, "might I have the next dance?"

Izzy smiled politely, ready to decline, but Prue squeezed her hand. Izzy glanced at her and Prue nodded quickly.

"Of course, Mr. King," Izzy replied, smiling in earnest. "I'd be delighted."

She rose and left with her partner, and Prue looked down at the gloves in her lap. It was fine that she was by herself with Lady Hetty. It was. She needed her friends to live their lives as they would have done, not stop everything just because Prue needed some assistance. She would never forgive herself if one of them had a chance worth taking and they were prevented from it due to tending to her at this time.

She could sit here vulnerably.

She could.

The jaunty tune began, and Prue glanced at the dancing to find

Eliza now dancing with Mr. Gardiner, of all people.

It occurred to her then what was happening. Somehow, Eliza knew who had been at Tinley, and she was taking great care that those men who had tried for Prue there were not permitted the slightest chance to pay her any particular attentions. Which meant that, among others, Mr. Davies, Mr. Andrews, and…

…Camden.

They would all be targets for Eliza's manipulation and intervention, and Prue knew only too well how skilled and devious Eliza could be when she had the proper motivation.

She could *not* let Eliza get within ten feet of Camden Vale. Anyone else was a minor detail, although she would have hated to see Mr. Andrews fall victim to her, as he really was a fine enough man and had treated Prue with great respect. He needed to be warned as well, though Prue knew at once that she could not be the one to do it.

Amelia could tell him, assuming she could find Amelia amidst this melee. She was here, undoubtedly, but she could not be restricted to the corner as Prue was. She was too young, too fresh, too fair to be a wallflower, and deserved to dance and enjoy all of the delights of the Season.

But this was imminent danger, and Mr. Andrews had to be warned.

She scanned the room quickly, her heart pounding in her ears. Mr. Andrews was certainly here, but she had seen no evidence that Camden was. He could be safe tonight, but any other night in any other public place, he would be at risk. And he didn't know Eliza, had no experience in dealing with her, and Prue's need for privacy had kept her from sharing any of those crucial details with him at the house party.

Please don't let him be here, she thought furiously.

Her breathing began to quicken, and she tried to find something, anything, to resemble calm. Not finding him would be a good thing, right? Seeing him would make her panic more… It would mean Eliza could have a chance to meet him, talk with him, influence him…

Would he listen to her? Would she infuse her conversation with enough truth to gain his trust? Would he like her vivacity and wit because it was more on display than Prue's had ever been?

Images of Cam and Eliza waltzing together, laughing uproariously as they glided smoothly about the room, flittered through Prue's mind rapidly. The pair of them speaking together apart from anyone else. Cam's sly smirk of a smile being exchanged with Eliza's superior smugness as they both looked at Prue while she was inundated with fools.

Baa for me, lamb. Go on.

Prue bit back a whimper as her imagination took hold, Eliza's favorite taunt filling her ears.

"Miss Westfall? If you are not engaged for this dance, might I persuade you?"

A dance… Yes! She could see much better from the center of the room than from her chair here. If Cam were here, she would be far more likely to see him there.

Without thinking, she put her hand into the gloved one before her and let herself be led, looking around with as much thoroughness as she could.

Her mother saw her and smiled indulgently, which was an unsettling sight and feeling, but Prue pushed all that away. There wasn't time to worry about what her mother would think of her dancing with whoever this was.

She caught sight of Izzy, standing just outside of the dancers, watching her in stunned bewilderment, and she let her gaze move quickly past. The Spinsters were not used to Prue dancing with men she did not know extremely well, but things were different now. Georgie and Tony were in line with her, albeit further down, and they, too, took notice of her. Eliza was now partnered with Alderton, which was no great loss to Prue, though Eliza seemed pleased enough with herself.

"Miss Westfall."

She looked straight ahead at her partner and blanched to see Simon Delaney standing there. He was not the sort of man she would have danced with under any circumstances.

Ever.

And that had been decided before he had tried to seduce young Lucy Wilton a few months ago. That catastrophe had only been prevented by quick thinking and action from Tony and Georgie.

No one else knew that, of course. They only knew that Simon Delaney was a younger son of a wealthy family and a bit of a rogue, but in all other respects perfectly acceptable.

But not for Prue.

Never for Prue.

And a quick glance to either side of her told Prue he had put them in the lead position.

Her throat constricted painfully, and she did her best to hide a distressed gasp.

Delaney noticed her conflicting emotions and smirked at it, evidently knowing precisely what she was thinking and feeling.

"Smile, Miss Westfall. And if you cannot manage that…" He broke off and bowed with the rest of the men while the women curtseyed, and then he proceeded around her in the pattern. "… then perhaps you might baa…"

Prue inhaled sharply, her lip trembling at the derogatory bleating.

Eliza.

Her eyes burned as she moved as was required, desperate to keep whatever composure she could while her cheeks turned scarlet with her humiliation. The other men she had to interact with as part of the dance seemed concerned with what they were seeing in her face, but their stares and grimaces only made things infinitely worse.

Tony was not in her circle, but she could see his expression, and she knew he knew her well enough to know what was transpiring. He couldn't save her without causing a bigger scene, and he would know well enough to avoid that.

Mr. Alderton seemed amused by it, though he, too, was not directly in contact with her.

Prue tried to search for Cam amidst those watching the dance. Delaney bleated whenever he came near her, and each one chipped away at Prue's resolve and calm. He had never been cruel to her before, had hardly interacted with her in the years she had been out, and yet now he was tormenting her for sport.

It was unbearable, and she had half a mind to feign a swoon on this dance floor just to end it all. But even that image made her lightheaded with anxiety, and she continued through the dance as she had been.

Laughter reached her ears, and she could see it in Delaney's face, in his eyes, in his manner. Suddenly, it was as if she heard it from everyone. All around her. Somehow swirling about her and filling her, dark, menacing laughter…

Mercifully, the song ended, and with the briefest curtsey known to mankind, Prue moved directly from her position back to her chair beside Lady Hetty, who immediately clasped her trembling hand.

Izzy sank down beside her with an arm about her shoulder, and through the haze in her mind, still echoing with laughter, she heard Amelia's voice.

"Prue? Oh, Prue, are you all right?"

"Miss Westfall, you dance like an angel."

"Miss Westfall, the waltz?"

"Miss Westfall…"

"Miss Westfall?"

Prue squeezed her eyes shut, clenching Lady Hetty's hand as if it could somehow make all of this disappear.

"No, lads, this dance has already been claimed. By me."

The clenching tension in Prue's chest suddenly released with a mighty whoosh of air.

That voice…

Prue looked up with her burning eyes to see the face of Camden Vale before her, perfectly groomed, perfectly attired, perfectly present. His white-gloved hand was extended just out of her reach, but his eyes were filled with the steadiness she craved.

"You do remember, don't you?" he asked in the most polite, perfect tone she'd ever heard from him. "You haven't forgotten."

"N-no," she heard herself whisper. "No, I h-haven't."

Izzy gasped beside her as Prue reached out her hand and laid it in Camden's, letting his warm fingers curve around hers, the pressure anchoring her to him.

She released Lady Hetty and rose from her chair, keeping her eyes squarely on his, finding her torrential emotions settling markedly.

"Why is it that you always need saving in the dance?" Camden asked her in a low voice, smiling slightly. "I happen to know you are a most graceful and light dancer."

"Y-you…" she managed, choking on the stammering words.

Camden shook his head slowly. "Alas for lack of privacy. Why don't I talk, and you simply enjoy the dulcet tones I'm about to pour out upon you? I promise not to flatter or flirt and will only say shocking things that will make you laugh. Everybody will wonder what in the world that disreputable man has done to make her look so very pleased, and I shall assure them all that I had very little to do with any of it. That it was all you, and I simply danced my way about." He raised a brow as he bowed before her. "What say you?"

Prue could not have spoken even if she wanted to, though stammering would not have been her prime concern at that particular moment.

She managed a watery smile at him as she curtseyed, nodding as best she could.

"No tears," he whispered as he came to her and took her hands, turning her in the dance. "No tears."

"N-no promises," she whispered back, inhaling shakily.

He smiled at that and winked surreptitiously. "There she is. Welcome to the dance, Prue Westfall. It's a pleasure to see you again."

Prue shook her head in disbelief, too overcome to properly contemplate this miraculous turn of events. "The pleasure is all mine," she assured him, without any stammer at all.

Chapter Eleven

There is a fine line between insufferable and irresistible with regards to the nature of friendships. And quite a lot of dancing occurs along that line.

-The Spinster Chronicles, 1 December 1815

Camden Vale was apparently the saving sort of man.

He hadn't ever lumped himself in with men of that sort, but the proof was there before him. When faced with an unpleasant situation wherein someone other than himself had been in dire straits, he had acted for their benefit, taking no thought for himself.

What a selfless and noble endeavor that had been!

He snorted in derision at himself. Noble and selfless were not words that could be used to describe him in any way, shape, or form. It hadn't been something that he had actively decided upon, he'd only acted on his instincts.

Which had driven him to Prue.

He hadn't known the particular cause of her distress the night before, only that she had been mortified beyond human reason, even for her, and the strain in her features had been clear for all to see. Her partner in that dance, Simon Delaney, was an insolent puppy of a man more adept at cards than in anything else, though he was known as a notorious cheat there. He'd been surprised by her standing up with such a man, but he'd attributed it to her mother's determination to see Prue married off.

Enduring that dance had been almost as painful for Camden as he imagined it had been for Prue. He'd been near to interrupting it several times just for the sake of Prue's pain and embarrassment. But he was satisfied that in dancing with her afterwards, clearing off the others who had come to beg for her hand, he had turned the tide for her, at least temporarily.

But none of that had been selfless. He'd wanted to dance with Prue.

Badly.

Her expression when she saw him made him wish he was a better man than he was, that he could be deserving of such a look. There was not much he could do about that now, but he was trying all the same.

Impossibly, he was changed for having been bound to Prue during the party at Tinley. His manners were much the same as they'd ever been, but he found himself doing fewer and fewer things that would bring another stain to his reputation.

Why, he'd even gone so far as to consider making amends with some of his former friends!

Considered and had started, though he hadn't done very well there, but progress was being made. What had come over him, he couldn't fathom, but something about the shy girl who felt comfortable with him made him wish for former associations he had once known. They had always done him credit, though he had done little enough to deserve it, and reengaging them would undoubtedly do him a world of good.

The list was not a long one, but it seemed to catalogue his faults well enough.

The reminder was not a pleasant one.

But at least he had no amends to make with Prue. He'd done everything right by her, as far as things went, and helping her to overcome her anxieties last night had been yet another brick he could lay at the foundation of their friendship.

He smiled to himself now as he slowly walked through the relatively quiet London streets.

It had been surprisingly natural to be with Prue again. He'd not seen her in weeks, not since their farewells at Tinley, and seeing her across the theater, in far more splendor than he'd ever seen her, had taken his breath away. She had looked regal and elegant, ideally suited to the finery adorning her, and the same spark of life danced in her fair eyes. Her lips curving in a hint of a smile as he applauded the lackluster tenor... The candor in her gaze...

He hadn't realized how much he'd missed her until that moment.

And then to dance with her? After finding her nature so unaltered?

If it were a sin for one to be gleeful at the distress of another, not for mercenary reasons but for the opportunity it provided, then he would be burning in hell for quite some time.

Once Prudence Westfall realized her own strength and overcame her demons and anxieties, she would have no need for saving, or for a man like him in her life. She would slay her own dragons and save herself, if not others around her.

Until then, he rather liked saving her and looked forward to doing so again.

While he could.

"Camden, where are you off to?"

He turned in surprise to see Phillip Turner crossing the street in his direction, and he smiled at the sight, which was a rarity of late. He'd made it a point to avoid Phillip for the last four months or so since their fight, finding it too taxing to his pride to maintain a friendship so tremulous as theirs apparently had been. But after Tinley, he had sought out the Turners, swallowed whatever pride he'd thought himself in possession of, and found that his apprehensions about that moment had been entirely unfounded.

They had renewed the friendship with enthusiasm, and somehow it was as if the past had never happened.

Camden would never tell Phillip how much it meant to him to have that connection once more, as he was hardly the sort to express such sentiments, and Phillip would undoubtedly have been mortified to hear it, but he could not deny that he was grateful.

Phillip gave him a sardonic look, no doubt wondering at the smile Camden wore. "Well?"

Camden shrugged easily, continuing on his way as Phillip fell into step beside him. "I thought I'd call upon Prudence Westfall."

"Really?" Phillip asked, his deep voice laced with interest.

"Yes," Camden clipped with a scowl. He fixed his gaze ahead and maintained as calm a demeanor as he could. "We became acquainted at Tinley House."

"And your sweeping in to dance with her last night after she nearly caught fire was purely to maintain such an acquaintance?"

Camden closed his eyes, biting back a groan. Perhaps not having friends would be a better alternative after all. He'd forgotten about this part of it.

"I don't know much about her," Phillip went on, ignoring Camden, "but after last night, I was curious, and Mariah tells me…"

"Oh, Lord…" Camden rolled his eyes heavenward, unsure if he were praying or not.

"…that she's remarkably shy and stammers incessantly." Phillip looked over at Camden in speculation. "You had a stammering cousin. Can you understand her?"

Camden sighed, wistfully recalling how thoroughly he had thrashed Phillip months ago. "She does not stammer incessantly, and yes, I can understand her, as would anyone who gave it any sort of effort."

Phillip considered that and seemed to be fighting a smile. "So, last night…?"

"Anyone could see that Miss Westfall was distressed." Camden shrugged again. "I simply saw fit to do something about it."

"Yes, because being with you is so much of a comfort."

Camden stopped and turned to his friend, raising a daring brow. "Are you curious about my intentions, or indignant at what your wife thinks I'm doing? Because this feels like a very familiar path we are on, only you were not so amused last time."

Now Phillip grinned outright. "I am perishing with curiosity, and so is Mariah. I don't know if you know this, Cam, but she rather likes you."

That was a hilarious thought, and Camden laughed accordingly.

Mr. Turner did not find the thought nearly so amusing. "She does!"

"I highly doubt that," Camden assured him, shaking his head. "She likes cataloguing my faults, and she likes having you in my presence, so you might somehow become amusing, but that is all."

Phillip chortled beside him. "If you say so, Cam. But she insisted I invite you to dinner tomorrow if I saw you."

"No doubt she has a line of questioning prepared for me," Camden muttered.

"Of course, she does. It's Mariah."

"I have no idea why you married such a demanding woman."

"I fell in love."

"That's your problem."

"So, you'll come?"

"Of course."

They shared a smile, all teasing aside, and then Phillip looked the slightest bit uneasy. "In the interest of full disclosure…"

Camden slowed his step, reluctance suddenly weighing upon him. "Yes?"

Phillip winced. "She's invited Dartmouth, too."

Camden stopped completely and turned around, beginning to walk the other way. "No."

"Cam, come on," Phillip begged. "It's been a year!"

"No," he said again. "Not after… No."

Phillip grabbed his arm and pulled him to a stop. "He's been trying to apologize for months, and you will not allow it."

Camden looked at Phillip's hand and then into his face. "You would think a man with the education of Dartmouth would understand."

Phillip gave him a reprimanding look. "He's at fault, and he knows it. You're the one maintaining distance, though. Why are you pushing everyone away?"

Cam yanked his arm out of his friend's hold. "It's amazing how inconvenient friends are."

"Cam, you didn't even attend his wedding."

He scowled at the reminder. "He wouldn't have wanted me."

"And yet, you were invited."

Camden looked away, eyes narrowing as he peered off into the distance. "Formality."

"You sure?"

Of course, he was sure. Dartmouth had thrown away twenty

years of friendship over a speculation that Camden had refused to join him on, and the fallout from such an apparent betrayal had been great indeed. Rumors had increased, and invitations had decreased, and when the speculation had failed, Camden had been without any of the significant losses of the others, yet he had still been the one labeled at fault.

Dartmouth hadn't been ruined by any stretch, but it ought to have been enough to humble him sufficiently.

Yet their distance remained, and Camden hadn't even considered altering the arrangement.

And yet...

"No," he finally said on a rough exhale. "No, I'm not." He looked over at Phillip, whose expression was all too knowing. "Fine, I'll come. But I cannot guarantee that I won't destroy something if Dartmouth says something wrong."

Phillip nodded once. "I'll tell Mariah to use the second-best china."

Camden rolled his eyes dramatically and turned back towards Prue's house. "Spare me the domestications you have undergone. If I inspected your rooms, no doubt I'd find lace handkerchiefs."

"Only if Mariah left hers in there."

"Good lord, why would she be in your rooms?"

Phillip's rather frank and superior look was enough to make Camden ill, and he did not bother hiding his disgust.

"You'll get there, friend," Phillip assured him. "Perhaps Miss Westfall..."

"Shut your mouth," Camden snarled before he could finish the thought. "If you think that's what this is..."

Phillip was laughing too hard to comment, and Camden pushed him off the sidewalk, but unfortunately, no carriage was rolling by to trample him.

"I'll leave off Miss Westfall," Phillip assured him as he returned to his side. "I've just never seen you actually call on anyone, let alone play the hero. Why exert yourself?"

"I'm no hero," Camden replied in a low tone, "but I'll exert myself for my friends, particularly if it's the right thing to do."

Phillip made a noise of assent beside him, but no other comment came forth.

Camden looked at him in anticipation. "That's it?"

Phillip shrugged. "If it's the right thing to do, why question you?"

"Because it's you. And you're still following me."

"Accompanying you. But only because it's on the way to where I was going anyway."

Camden paused before adding, "And because you want to see where she lives, don't you?"

"Absolutely."

"Are you out of your mind?"

"You cannot possibly be serious!"

"What on earth were you thinking?"

"Do you even *know* how much of a bad idea that is? Because I can tell you just exactly how bad. In detail."

Prue sighed and looked over at Elinor. "N-no, thank you. I don't want to kn-know."

Elinor looked scandalized. "But that's what I do!"

"Camden Vale?" Grace sputtered, looking almost as indignant as Charlotte and Elinor were. "He could not be more inappropriate a candidate for you."

Prue's cheeks colored quickly, but she kept her gaze steady on her friend. "I did not s-say he was a candidate."

Grace reared back a little, then looked around at the rest. "Then what are we saying?"

"As far as I can tell," Edith mused in her natural brogue, sipping slowly on the tea she'd just finished preparing for herself, "we are opposed to the idea of him for anything in general." She shrugged a shoulder. "I have no idea who he is or why this is so terrible, or what even happened. I've only come for the tea." She sipped it again and nodded in appreciation. "Much better than at my house."

"Your house doesn't have two sticks to rub together," Charlotte snapped as she flicked a dark look to her.

"It does so," Edith shot back. "What do you think the tea is made from?"

Prue coughed a laugh and put a hand to her heated face.

The Spinsters had descended upon her unexpectedly this morning, and launched into a campaign against Camden, though they had yet to actually tell her what they were protesting or why. She had only danced with him last night, and only once. He had saved her from what could have been a disastrous evening, stormed back into her life in the most wonderful way, and her friends protested it.

It hardly seemed fair.

It was not as though he had become a permanent fixture at her side after their dance. He had returned her to her seat, and actually maintained a safe distance from her. Nobody would have known he was intentionally standing near her, nor could Prue have described the relief at having him there. He would have saved her again if need be, but his presence had ensured that it was unnecessary.

No one had questioned her last night, and even her mother hadn't said anything on the subject. She was too upset that Prue had looked so ill when dancing to make any sort of comment on her choice of partner.

Eliza would have something to say about it, but she had yet to call.

That would probably come later.

"… and she's not even listening!"

Prue looked up into Charlotte's distraught expression and sighed again. "What, Charlotte?" she asked patiently. "What have I done?"

Charlotte's eyes widened. "You danced with him!"

"I did. And not for the first time."

Charlotte made a peculiar squawking sound and flopped into a chair while Elinor screeched as though Prue had developed an odd rash.

Izzy, who had joined in the protests, albeit to a lesser degree, watched Prue with wide eyes. "I think you had better explain yourself a little, dear. When have you danced with him before?"

Prue shook her head slowly and related to them the rest of the stories from Tinley House, this time including Camden in the details. She told them about the terrace, the dancing, the riding, the drawing… She revealed everything.

Except for the theater.

There was no explaining that.

"You were alone with him," Charlotte replied faintly when Prue had finished. She put a hand over her eyes and sunk further into the chair. "You could have been ruined."

"Shh!" Izzy hissed, looking unsettled herself. "Don't say that!"

Edith looked Prue over in assessment. "She doesn't look ruined to me…"

Prue smiled at her with all the warmth she possessed.

"It's only because he didn't do anything he usually does!" Elinor insisted hotly. "If you knew what I know…"

"No!" Prue interrupted loudly.

Elinor clamped down on her bottom lip, positively livid.

"Prue," Grace prodded gently, her dark eyes round. "Last night… when he asked you to dance…"

"He was saving me from the rest," Prue told her wearily. "He could see that I was growing overwhelmed and agitated, and he knew that dancing with him would put me at ease."

"Nothing about him should put you at ease!" Charlotte protested as she flung a hand out.

Prue shrugged a shoulder and reached for her tea. "It does. I don't even stammer with him."

Charlotte gaped at that, her mouth working soundlessly.

It was enough to make Prue wish she felt like smiling.

"So, is he… courting you?" Izzy asked gently, looking distressed by the thought.

Prue shook her head firmly. "No. He has never said or done anything to make me think his intentions are anything but platonic."

Charlotte mouthed the word 'platonic' as if it were foreign.

Prue ignored her. "We are only friends, Izzy. Nothing more."

"Friends!" Elinor blurted out. "Friends, she says!"

"Elinor," Grace spoke firmly, "shut up."

Elinor covered her face with her hands, her voice audible through the obstruction of her palms, though not coherent.

Prue speared Charlotte with a cold look. "I was not aware that one had to have potential friends outside of the Spinsters approved by the Spinsters in order to keep them."

Charlotte stared at her in outright horror and straightened up very slowly. "Prudence Westfall, if you think I object to your having friends outside of our group, even of the male sort, you are almost as simple as your mother."

Grace snorted a laugh and covered her mouth quickly, as everyone else smiled, even Prue.

"This has nothing to do with friendship," Charlotte went on, still looking as severe as Prue had ever seen her. "It has everything to do with you. I find Camden Vale to be an inappropriate association for you purely because his reputation is that disreputable, and you know my standards in that regard to be very low indeed."

Torn between offended and warmed by Charlotte's concern, Prue only stared back at her, waiting for the next blow to fall.

Charlotte softened a little, smiling at last. "I care about you very much, lamb. I don't want to see you hurt."

Prue returned her smile. "I know."

"Don't see him again, please. At least until we can weed out truth from gossip where he is concerned."

"That seems fair," Izzy agreed, brightening. "We can send Elinor out to be especially discerning there."

Elinor voiced some response from behind her hands that sounded very much like an offended complaint, but no one listened.

Prue looked at them all for a long moment, weighing the options.

"Miss Westfall, you have a visitor," Harper intoned from the door.

"Who is it?" Charlotte asked a bit sharply, earning herself a scolding look from Izzy.

Prue gave the butler a patient look. "W-who, Harper?"

"Mr. Camden Vale, Miss Westfall."

Prue nearly laughed out loud.

"Noooooooo!" Charlotte howled, scrambling to her feet. "No, no, no…"

"I've shown him into the Green Room, Miss," Harper continued, barely raising his tone over Charlotte's.

Prue nodded once. "Very good. I'll s-see him now."

Three distressed sounds came from her friends, but she only turned to Edith with a smile. "Will you ch-chaperone, Edith?"

Edith smiled and placed her teacup on the table. "Lovely. Of course." They rose at the same time and glided for the door, ignoring the protests of everyone else.

Out in the hall, Prue exhaled slowly, and Edith linked her arm with hers. "Well done, my dear. They'll get over it."

"I d-doubt it," Prue muttered, shaking her head. "I've never done anything to upset them in my life."

"Oh, what's a little upset amongst friends?" Edith scoffed as they moved towards the Green Room. "Mr. Vale is calling upon you, not them, and if he puts you at ease, who are they to question it?"

Prue looked at the Scottish beauty with real fondness. "You don't question it?"

Edith gave her a candid look. "I am in no position to question anyone on anything. I'll keep you safe in this interview, but it is up to you to keep yourself safe in the matters where a chaperone has no control."

Prue swallowed at that and shifted her gaze to the room ahead of them. She would not pretend to not understand Edith's meaning, but neither would she dwell on it.

Camden was her friend. More than that was pure fancy, and she had never been fanciful.

Not before this, at any rate.

Edith dropped her arm as they entered the room, and Camden turned at their entrance, smiling politely and bowing to them. He looked somehow more himself in the more natural clothing of a gentleman, and more handsome for it.

Not that he hadn't been handsome in eveningwear, because he had, and no man had ever looked better in them, but this was Camden.

And his smile warmed her to her toes.

"Who is in agony down the hall?" he asked without any sort of preamble.

Prue smiled at his frankness. "Charlotte. She's opposed to your presence."

"Pity," Camden replied, though he showed no inclination to change the situation.

Edith bit down on her full bottom lip as her eyes danced with merriment.

"Lady Edith Leveson, may I present Mr. Camden Vale?" Prue said, gesturing to him. "Camden, this is my friend Edith."

Camden bowed again as Edith curtseyed. "Charmed, my lady." His brow furrowed in thought. "Leveson? As in Sir Archibald?"

Edith's smile turned very flat indeed. "That would be the one, yes."

"Husband?" Camden asked, tilting his head and taking in her mourning colors.

"He was, yes," Edith replied in an emotionless tone.

"My condolences."

"On my choice in a husband?" Edith asked innocently. "Thank you very much, you are too kind."

Camden coughed in surprise but smiled. "I had heard it was a short marriage. Five minutes, was it?"

Edith shrugged, returning the smile. "Thereabouts. But we don't need to dampen this interlude with subjects no longer applicable. I am here to ensure you don't ravish her senseless, so I'll just sit in that corner and keep a weather eye open." She inclined her head and swept to the chair in the corner indicated, sitting gracefully.

Camden stared at her, then looked back at Prue. "I like her."

"So do I," Prue admitted, blushing slightly at Edith's intentions. She gestured to the chairs. "Please, sit."

They both did so, and Camden rested his hat in his lap, smiling at her. "I just wanted to make sure you were all right after last night. I wasn't sure what had happened, but…"

"It isn't i-important," Prue hastily told him, cursing herself for the stammer.

He gave her a look at hearing it, knowing better. "Are you well?"

She nodded quickly. "Very. Thank you."

Camden stared at her, then sighed heavily. "This is tedious," he mumbled. "I don't know how to make polite conversation, Prue. I came to ask if we could be friends again."

Prue tilted her head at him curiously. "I wasn't aware the connection had been severed."

He grinned at that. "I tend to sever things whenever I leave them. Old habits."

She smiled a little. "We are still friends, Cam. I promise."

"Good," he replied, still smiling.

"WHAT IN THE WORLD IS SHE THINKING?" a feminine voice bellowed, making Prue wince.

Camden looked mildly surprised. "Who's that?"

"Georgie," Prue and Edith said together.

"OVER MY DEAD BODY!" a male voice exploded.

"And that?" Camden asked, now seeming to enjoy himself.

"Tony," Prue and Edith told him, again in unison.

Camden sobered a little. "Do you need to go?"

Prue looked at Edith, who smiled and shrugged. "No," Prue responded as she looked back at Camden. "It'll keep. Would you care for some tea?"

Chapter Twelve

"They *all* object to me?"

"No, just most of them. Edith doesn't object."

"But does Edith approve?"

"She says it's not up to her to approve, she's not going to tell me what to do."

"Well, hurrah for the wisdom of Lady Edith Leveson, witty widow and all-around noncommittal bystander."

Prue rolled her eyes and laid a card down. "Just be grateful that Izzy wasn't prejudiced enough to withhold your invitation to this card party. She's not fond of you either, but she doesn't think poorly of many people, and is so desperate to please that when I asked, she agreed."

Camden grunted and looked through his cards. "So, your wishes overrule her good sense, is that it?"

"Miss Lambert has the unfortunate tendency to do whatever anyone asks of her, whether in her own interests or not," Lady Hetty informed him from his other side, her focus on her own cards. "Prudence was wise to influence her."

Camden looked at the aged woman, who had insisted on partnering with Prue for whist. "Wise? For persuading her to invite someone like me?"

Lady Hetty didn't even spare him a look as she discarded. "No one here said anything against your nature, Mr. Vale, which means you should not discuss it, either."

"Personally, I think it's overdone," Miss Perry said across from him. "I've met you a number of times, Mr. Vale, and you've always been a perfect gentleman with me."

He allowed himself to smile at the girl. "That's because you are always finding me at a rather good moment, Miss Perry. My true nature is not so gentlemanly."

She shrugged and laid down a card, her dimple flashing with her smile. "Far be it from me to contradict one who knows you so well as yourself, but a wicked nature would not care so much about the approval of a group of spinsters."

Lady Hetty cackled at that, and Camden gave her a withering look.

"That is quite enough out of you, madam," Camden told her, liking the old lady despite her impudence with him. Or perhaps because of it.

She smirked in response to that and looked across the table to Prue. "Your set, Prudence."

Prue nodded and swept the cards up. "They're only concerned for me, Mr. Vale," she told him in a much softer voice. "Don't take offense where none is intended."

"I'm not used to offense not being intended," he whispered back. "Most people offend me on purpose, and with quite a lot of flair. And you forget, I heard their protests the other day. They would absolutely offend me if given the chance."

He glanced across the room at the Sterling couple, blatantly staring at him. They apparently saw him as the greatest evil on the earth. Captain Sterling was tall, dark, and intimidating, while his wife was fair, fine, and composed, and what he'd heard of them had convinced him that he'd rather enjoy knowing them.

Provided they did not kill him, as they seemed somewhat inclined to do at this moment.

His entrance to this card party at the Lambert residence had been awkward at best. Mr. and Mrs. Lambert had no qualms about it, but they did not seem to be paying much attention to any of their guests, let alone him. Miss Lambert, however, had been more fidgety than Prue and could not manage to meet his eyes. She was hovering not far from them, while a young girl with dark hair and hazel eyes glared furiously at him from beside her.

Was this what Prue felt all the time? It was the single most unnerving experience he'd ever encountered, and he wasn't particularly put off by anything.

Yet, as he looked around, he could see several gentlemen whose eyes were repeatedly drawn to Prue, and the glint in their eyes was not something he found any satisfaction in.

It was the same look a predatory bird had when fixed upon its prey.

And Prue could not possibly be unaware of it, not with the way her cheeks flushed.

"Miss Perry," Lady Hetty said suddenly, rapping her stick on the ground, "would you take me over to the refreshments? I have need of some lemonade, provided Faith Lambert has made it palatable."

Miss Perry snickered and did as she was bid, leaving the pair of them alone at the table.

"Please tell me they're coming back," Camden muttered as he watched them go. "Otherwise, we'll get two young bucks over here, and you'll clam up."

Her blush increased. "They'll come back," she whispered in an almost harsh tone. "And Lady Hetty would take the h-head off of anyone who took her seat."

Camden nodded and sat back against his chair. "That was an excellent edition of the Spinster Chronicles this morning," he told her, folding his arms. "Which one did you write?"

Prue shook her head, a small smile playing at her lips rather fetchingly. "Not telling. Guess."

"Fashion Forum," he said at once, looking for any reaction from her.

Her lips twitched again. "No."

"Dabbler."

She dipped her chin once. "Correct."

He grinned at her admission. "You called Mr. Dartmouth a fine addition to any Societal event, and his wife made him what he was."

Prue's nose wrinkled up as she restrained a grin. "I did. I met them the other day and found them to be perfectly pleasant. Not put off by my stammer at all."

"That's because they are friends of mine, and I told them about you."

Her eyes shot up to his and her smile faded. "You did?"

He nodded once, thrilled that Dart and Julia had met her and made a good impression. Dinner with the Turners had been a marvelous evening, despite his reservations, and he found that Prue's assessment of the couple was remarkably accurate. Julia Dartmouth was the better half of their relationship and had enough energy and vigor to keep Dart on his toes for the rest of their lives. She was beautiful, far too good for him, and had taken Camden down three notches before the main course had been completed.

It was a perfect match.

Dart had been quick with his apologies for the past, and Camden found himself eager to accept them. Whatever financial difficulties Dart had endured a year ago all seemed to be resolved, in part thanks to Julia's fortune, but also due to some wiser investitures, some of which he had a desire to discuss with Camden in the future.

Camden wasn't ready for that, but when he was, Dart would be the one he approached.

"I didn't know they w-were friends of yours," Prue breathed, her eyes still wide. "I would never have… I'd n-never…"

"I loved what you said," Camden interrupted, wishing he could reach out for her hand. "And so would they, if they knew who had written it. They have a genuine understanding of their relationship, and a remarkable sense of humor between them."

Prue still looked red and agitated, and he half expected her to begin shaking at any moment.

"Prue," he murmured. "Breathe."

She did so rather roughly, making him smile.

"So, what exactly are the objections of the Spinsters about me, eh?" he asked, training his eye on Mr. Carpenter in the corner, who seemed to be trying to analyze Prue from his position.

Prue's gaze lowered to her cards, and she was suddenly very intent on her poor shuffling, her cheeks flaming.

"Prue…" Camden nudged her chair with his foot. "Come on. It's my reputation, right?"

She nodded, her eyes still on her cards.

"And you don't know what to believe."

Again, she nodded.

Camden sighed, sensing rather than seeing the struggle within her to be loyal to him while maintaining loyalty to her friends. It wasn't fair for them all to do this to her, especially when she was the one who needed their efforts and support.

"I promise to answer any point of contention with honesty and plainness," he informed her, surprising himself with the energy behind his words. "And I've never said that to anyone."

Prue's shuffling stopped, and he saw her breathe for a long moment, her chest rising and falling steadily. Then she raised her chin and met his eyes, her almost violet eyes surprisingly steady. "They said you were in a duel a few years ago over a mistress you shared with another man."

It was all Camden could do to avoid visibly wincing, and he bristled at the implications, but he had promised to answer everything. He shook his head twice. "Not true. There was a duel, I admit, but she was not my mistress."

Prue tilted her head at that but said nothing.

Camden exhaled and uncrossed his arms, sliding his palms along his thighs. "She was a childhood sweetheart who had been taken advantage of. Her family could not avenge her, so I did. Not to the death, but I did win the duel, for what it's worth."

He watched Prue's eyes as she processed that and saw her bottom lip tug a little as though she bit the inside.

"What else?" he prodded gently.

"Did you lose your inheritance gambling?" she asked him, her tone as steady as her eyes, and they were unnerving enough.

"No. But I did lose a fair amount. Too reckless." He shook his head with a snort. "That was idiotic. But I have never been so reckless again, and now I am fairly respectable financially."

Prue tapped the deck of cards on the table in a halfhearted shuffle. "Did you sell your family estate to salvage your debts?"

Now Camden did wince and had the desire to tug at his cravat.

"Yes, but to be fair, it wasn't worth much and was in poor condition. You'd have hated it."

The quip made her smile a little, and his heart leapt against his ribs. She wasn't upset with his answers yet, and it made him hope.

She straightened a little. "They said you had a warrant out for your arrest."

That was part of his reputation? He didn't bother hiding his surprise and whistled softly. "Goodness, we are going far back. No, I was not wanted for arrest. The warrant was for questioning on a situation that my stupid cousin was involved in. They had to issue a warrant because I was out of the area and needed to be summoned back. Caused a bit of noise, but I was free to go the moment questions were completed, and I never saw a jail cell."

Prue laid the cards down on the table and drummed her perfect nails on them. "If your reputation is so filled with half-truths," she wondered aloud, "why haven't you corrected any of the aspersions?"

Camden shrugged a shoulder, feeling somewhat vulnerable, and yet not at all exposed before her. "What good would it do? People will say what they will say, and I've never particularly cared enough. Those who needed to know the truth knew it, and there is enough truth to the rumors to cause doubt in those that don't know." He smiled a little. "I told you it was confusing."

Now Prue smiled outright, drumming her fingers again. "You did. I was fairly warned."

"It doesn't help that I fight," Camden admitted with an exhale. "I'll fight anyone for the slightest provocation, and that tends to get caught in the rumor mill as well. And I cheat at cards on occasion, which seems to bother some people. But you can believe me, Prue, I have never jilted a woman, been in a compromising situation, or had unpleasant run-ins with magistrates or Bow Street."

"Have you had pleasant ones, then?" she asked with a teasing tilt to her lips.

He let his mouth slide into a crooked grin. "Let's just say Bow Street doesn't like to lose at cards, and magistrates have trouble landing good punches, in my experience, but they do always pay up."

Prue shook her head, rolling her eyes a little. "It's a wonder you're a gentleman, Cam."

"I've always thought so, but no one has officially removed my status." He shrugged with nonchalance, taking the cards from under Prue's hand, his fingers grazing hers in a way that made them both still for the space of a few heartbeats.

He cleared his throat quickly. "So. Any more questions?"

She swallowed, her cheeks coloring, and shook her head. "I don't think so. Elinor probably has more points, but she hates all men these days, so that doesn't say much."

Camden eyed the furious girl for a moment. "She'll give herself apoplexy if she's not careful."

"I know." Prue stiffened as two gentlemen approached, their eyes on her.

"Miss Westfall," they began in eerie unison.

Camden growled at them. "The lady is occupied at present with a card game, which shall recommence when our partners return from refreshments. She has no time for puppies like you. Off with the pair of you."

They looked affronted and were clearly on the point of protesting when Camden started to rise from the table. That sent them skittering off, and they perused more appropriate targets, such as the younger Wilton girls, who clearly appreciated the attention.

Prue looked at Camden in awe as he sat back down in his chair. "Was that r-reaction from your glower or your reputation?"

He sniffed uneasily and shuffled the cards. "Probably both."

"That was most convenient."

Camden drummed the cards on the table once, then looked at Prue speculatively as an idea began to form in his head. "I'm having a thought…"

"So, that's that, and we shouldn't have any more issues on that score."

There was a long silence that stretched on and on, and Prue finally looked up into the faces of her friends.

They all wore the same expression of disbelief mixed with

horror.

"What?" she asked, wringing her fingers together. "He explained everything."

"That's just the first page of my notes on him," Elinor told her in a hushed tone, her eyes wide.

Prue swallowed at that and looked away.

"What else did he say, Prue?" Tony asked from his position, sitting on the arm of the sofa.

His tone was not accusatory, but neither was it particularly warm. Georgie sat beside him, her hand rubbing along his back. She hadn't said anything yet, but her eyes had been fixed on Prue with an unnerving intensity.

"He s-said that h-he…" she began, breaking off to clear her throat and gather her focus. "He said that he had never had unpleasant encounters with magistrates, had never jilted a woman, and had never been in a compromising situation."

Charlotte chortled from the divan she'd pulled over. "He's never been *caught*, more like." She looked around, frowning. "Where's Edith?"

"She didn't come," Izzy reminded her, "because of the number of guests. She's not comfortable yet."

"None of us are comfortable, now that Mr. Vale is in the picture," Charlotte muttered shaking her head.

Prue threw her a wounded look, and Charlotte gestured helplessly.

"Did you have to choose him for a friend?" Izzy murmured, looking as though she would take Prue's hand. "Why not Miss Perry? She is lovely, I am so pleased you have found her."

"Amelia *is* my friend," Prue insisted, desperate for them all to understand. "She saw the situation at Tinley, and she didn't find any fault in Camden's character, nor did she dissuade me from…"

"Camden?" Grace interrupted, her eyes widening. "That's rather forward, isn't it?"

Prue felt her cheeks heat. "Under the c-circumstances, informality was b-best. More c-comfortable."

"All right, all right," Izzy soothed as Prue's discomfort grew. "We'll ignore the propriety of given names."

Prue nodded once. "We called Tony b-by his given name before it w-would have been appropriate, too."

Tony looked stunned at that and looked at the others for help.

"That's different," Charlotte said with a wave of her hand. "Tony is Tony."

"Very descriptive, Charlotte," Tony remarked with a smile in her direction. "Perfectly summed up."

She sneered at him, then returned her attention to Prue. "It's different. We trusted Tony."

Prue lifted her chin. "I t-trust Camden."

Charlotte gave her a pitying smile. "If only you said that without a stammer, I might believe you."

Anger, that rarest of Prue's emotions, flared in the pit of her stomach, and she ground her teeth together. "I trusted Tony before you did, even if I couldn't call him by his Christian name first. What does that signify, Charlotte?"

The room went silent again as they all looked at Charlotte warily.

Prue stared at her friend, whom she loved dearly, she reminded herself, and waited for a response.

Charlotte seemed to be chewing on her words, then looked at Georgie for a long moment.

Georgie only shrugged, which made Charlotte frown.

"I concede that you have some taste and judgment," Charlotte finally relented almost sourly, "but that was never in question here. The case before us is that of Mr. Vale, not you."

"What case?" Prue shook her head in bewilderment. "He wants to associate with me, to be my friend, to help me when I am in distress. Those motives are no different than what Tony feels for me."

"But he *isn't* Tony," Georgie pointed out, speaking for the first time.

Prue looked at her, feeling an emotional desperation for her to understand. "He could be."

Georgie's eyes narrowed a little and her head tilted with interest, but she said nothing further.

It crossed Prue's mind that perhaps she ought to be concerned about what might be happening in Georgie's mind at this moment, but there were too many other concerns at present.

"He said I could believe him," Prue murmured helplessly to no one in particular.

"Oh, Prue…" Izzy sighed, shaking her head sadly.

"Of course, he says you can believe him!" Charlotte insisted loudly, earning a fervent nod from Elinor. "He wants you to!"

Prue frowned at her. "Why would he care what I think?"

Charlotte gave the entire room an incredulous look before gesturing wildly. "He wants your fortune! You may not know this, Prue, but those of us with extensive fortunes are always going to be a target for vile creatures like Mr. Vale. They will manipulate and twist you until you don't know your own mind. All to get their hands on the inheritance."

"If that is true," Prue mused slowly, feeling a rather cynical edge coming on, "then he certainly has a strange way of showing it."

Charlotte's brows snapped down as she sat up. "Prudence Westfall, did you just use sarcasm with me?"

Prue raised a taunting brow at her. "Did I do it wrong?"

Now Charlotte positively gaped, her eyes wide, and she pointed at her. "There it is again!"

"I may take back my argument," Grace announced with a beaming grin. "I vote she keep Mr. Vale on."

"What?" Charlotte and Elinor cried together.

Grace nodded, still smiling at Prue. "He is obviously a good influence on her."

"Good?" Tony echoed, not as surprised as Charlotte, but still disgruntled.

"Entertaining, at least," Grace allowed. She looked at the others. "Mr. Vale was with Prue and Lady Hetty almost the entire time. We can ask Lady Hetty what she thinks of him."

"Knowing her, she'd probably love that roguish lout," Elinor muttered under her breath.

Georgie turned her attention to Elinor. "You needn't be petulant just because Lady Hetty doesn't like you. And perhaps you, too, should be friends with Miss Perry. I daresay she would be a good influence for *you*."

Elinor was instantly indignant. "I am not the issue here. Prue is."

"No, Mr. Vale is the issue," Tony corrected, matching Georgie's severe look and tone. "Prue is as Prue ever was and we love her for it."

Prue's throat constricted at his words, and her heart swelled a little. They might be having a spot of trouble at this moment, it was true, but these were her dearest friends in the world, Tony included, and those relationships were never in question.

All she wanted was to not have to choose between her friends. This was a trying time in her life, and she wanted all of them with her. Around her. Supporting her.

Saving her.

"I don't see why we can't give Mr. Vale a chance," Izzy finally said in the most unconvincing tone ever. "If Prue likes him well enough, that ought to be indicative of something."

"Probably that Prue is as naïve as she is sweet," Charlotte grumbled as she rubbed at her brow. "Or that we are terrible friends for not protecting her better. If not both."

Georgie chuckled reluctantly. "Prue may be a lot of things, but naïve was never one of them."

"There's a first time for everything." Charlotte sighed heavily and looked at Prue with a disgusted expression. "Fine. We give Vile Vale a chance to be less villainous than we have heard. Will that satisfy you?"

Prue smiled in the face of her friend's abhorrence. "It will suffice. Thank you."

That made Charlotte smile back, and she shook her head. "I can never stay mad at you, can I, little lamb?"

Well, she probably could, probably even would, once Prue confessed the rest of it.

"Actually," Prue began, straightening up in her chair, "Camden had a marvelous idea for managing this whole suitor affair."

"Did he?" Tony inquired, mildly intrigued. "I'd love to hear it."

Prue nodded once. "He has offered to pretend to court me. For all intents and purposes, it would appear to be a real courtship, and his character would become transformed into something more gentlemanly. He would see to it that a proper reputation about myself would spread, more aligned to my true nature than what everybody else thinks, and after a reasonable amount of time, once the fervor surrounding my fortune has passed, we will dissolve the relationship, thus allowing more worthy and truly interested men to pursue me."

She exhaled slowly after her recitation, almost verbatim what Camden had told her, and waited again.

For a moment, no one said anything.

And then…

"That is the most ridiculous idea I've ever heard," Charlotte scoffed with a loud snort.

Prue met her eyes steadily, smiling the sort of wry smile Camden usually did. "Well, you'd better get used to it. I've already accepted."

Chapter Thirteen

Acting is a delicate art. One must be believable and sincere, and yet convey all that ought to be conveyed. But great care must be taken that the sentiments in one's acting do not seep into reality. Everything would grow far more muddled then.

-The Spinster Chronicles, 2 September 1815

The pretend courtship of one Prudence Westfall by one Camden Vale was well under way, and quite the talk of London.

Well, of those who didn't have anything better to talk about, anyway.

In truth, there wasn't much going on with it. There ought to have been, but two very significant obstacles stood in the way of any progression there.

Mrs. Westfall and Miss Eliza Howard.

Somehow, the pair of them had decided that they had to be present whenever Camden was to call, despite having been approved by Mrs. Westfall for the courtship. She surveyed every meeting between them as though he was a criminal, which led him to believe that she was not ignorant as to his reputation. And yet, she had given permission for him to call and court Prue, so she could not be as disapproving as all that.

Although, when he made his formal suit and request of courtship known to Mrs. Westfall the week before, she had been astonished by the suggestion. She'd sat in her chair, blinking at him rather owlishly, and could only repeatedly ask, "Why?" as if the very idea was a foreign concept. Camden had not been pleased by that at all, and he'd left the house in quite a foul mood, despite having secured permission.

Her recent participation in this particular courtship had not done anything to improve her position in his mind.

The involvement of Eliza might have been the more bewildering part. She did not live with Prue and her mother, and as far as he could tell, had no fondness for Prue at all, but she appeared to be taking an interest in every detail of Prue's social life. She was everywhere he wished to be with Prue, and while she made no effort to influence Camden one way or another, despite what he'd heard of her, she seemed to commandeer every conversation he wished to have.

He missed having Edith for a chaperone so fiercely he could taste it.

He hadn't spoken more than three words to Prue in over a week, and it was starting to grate on him. She was a complete mouse with her mother and Eliza around, and the strain in her features was painfully evident. To him, at least. The other women seemed completely ignorant, or perhaps ambivalent.

He wasn't sure which was worse.

Today, however, there was a pleasant change in the situation. Eliza Howard had not come for his usual appointment, and it was a fine day, which prompted them to go out and walk the garden.

Mrs. Westfall was no walker and would not accompany them under any circumstances.

Camden had done his best not to appear too jubilant at this development, though he did not particularly care if it was obvious.

He wanted to spend time with Prue, and he would not apologize for it. And if Mrs. Westfall were any sort of mother, she would approve of that.

Apparently, there was some debate as to how much of a maternal nature she was in possession of.

Nevertheless, now he was walking the garden with only Prue for a companion, and Mrs. Westfall kept a steady eye on them from her perch in a shaded corner of the house, fanning herself, although the day was not overly warm.

The exertion of moving from the interior of the house to the exterior must have worn on her.

As yet, Prue had said nothing, her posture and expression perfectly poised, and were it not for the way her eyes flicked over to her mother on occasion, Camden would have thought her sleepwalking.

"Good heavens," Camden muttered once out of earshot as he slowly escorted Prue along the path, "are you under lock and key?"

"Yes," she replied, keeping her face demure for her mother's benefit. "More than you know."

He sighed and made a show of taking her arm as if the stone beneath their feet required it. "I never thought I'd ever have to say this, but it is good to hear your voice. Why is it that I have spent more time talking to your cousin in my courtship of you than I actually have with you?"

Prue glanced back at her mother, still trying to look perfect, then turned to him, smile fixed. "Because my family finds me lacking in most regards, and they are not very t-tolerant of my..." She started to motion a little, then stopped herself. "My..."

"Your speech," he finished, frowning a little.

"Don't do that," she scolded, losing her calm façade for a moment.

He looked at her in surprise. "Do what?"

"F-finish my sentences." She shook her head, glowering at him. "Everyone does that as if it is somehow helpful to say what I struggle to, but it's not helpful at all. It's embarrassing. I can sp-speak, it just t-takes a while sometimes."

"All right," he soothed. "I didn't mean to. My apologies."

"Prudence!" her mother suddenly boomed, scolding her from her seat.

She looked back and nodded obediently at her warning look. When she turned back to Camden, he stared at her, jaw taut.

"What in the world was that about?" he asked her in a very quiet, very dangerous tone.

She swallowed with some difficulty, but managed, "I was not looking pleasant. I must refrain from making faces. It's not proper, and she's already warned me once."

Somehow, his face remained blank as he looked over her head

at her mother, then back to Prue. "Does she think you're a child, Prue? Someone who needs to be chided regularly?"

"Worse," she whispered, shaking her head, trying to make herself smile. "She thinks I'm s-sim… sim…" She couldn't bear to say it and looked at him helplessly.

His step slowed. "Simple-minded," he said slowly, his face wrinkling in disgust. He shook his head and took her down a different path, keeping Prue's face away from her mother. "Stop smiling. Take a moment. Just listen to me for a minute, all right?"

She nodded, letting her face relax, and losing much of the strain from her features.

"If there is anyone simple in this house, despite my limited knowledge of it, it would be your mother," he hissed, somehow managing to smile despite the venom in his voice. "I may not know you as well as your friends in the Spinsters, but I know full well that you have more wit in your smallest toe than she could cultivate in her entire lifetime. You do not deserve to submit to such a person, no matter what ties bind you. You are a full-grown woman, not five years old, and her time would be better spent minding her own infernal business than you."

Prue stared at him, eyes wide, apparently beyond words.

"Do you understand me?" he asked, again with the dark tone, not willing to soften it for her benefit when the matter before them was so crucial.

Prue nodded once, still looking too much like the startled, shy girl from the first night he'd met her.

He swore a bit colorfully, and she glared at him. Oddly enough, that seemed to satisfy him a little. "There," he said, his voice suddenly kinder. "That is the first sign of life I have seen from you since our arrangement was struck."

Impossibly, she smiled, and he felt her sigh as much as he heard it. "I'm s-sorry," she murmured as they walked again. Her brow furrowed for a moment. "And I'm sorry for the stammer."

"Never apologize for the stammer," Camden told her at once, covering her hand where it rested on his arm. "I really don't mind it."

She gave him a grateful look, then returned her gaze to the path. "I am sorry for Eliza, though. She's determined to ruin any chance I have at a real relationship with any man. She thinks that by interfering with you, she'll influence you enough to change your mind."

Camden snorted once. "Not bloody likely."

Prue smiled a little. "It seems to be working with several others, though. She deliberately interferes with anyone that shows interest, and now none of the men from Tinley House speak to me anymore, aside from Mr. Andrews and Mr. Davies. I don't know what she tells them, but it is enough."

That was the most outrageous thing that Camden had ever heard, and he shook his head in disgust. "Andrews is too smart to be taken in by a creature like that."

"And he never showed me any particular interest as it is," Prue added, nodding in agreement. "He should be quite safe."

"Davies, on the other hand…" Camden winced at the thought. "He could be a perfect pawn for her games."

Prue shrugged once. "It would certainly disappoint his mother. Eliza has almost no fortune to speak of, which is why she's being so vindictive."

Camden looked down at Prue with interest. "She's jealous?"

"Terribly." Prue widened her eyes meaningfully, her mouth curving further. "I have the life she deserves, it seems, and if she cannot have it, neither can I."

"Sounds like my cousins would get along quite well with her," Camden retorted derisively. "I only have two, and they took it upon themselves to see that our family never quite reached full respectability. It was astounding that Lydia was able to marry anyone worthy of respect at all after their efforts, but Chadwick is a rather exceptional man, and I don't say that lightly."

Prue's hold on his arm tightened, and she looked up at him with interest. "Is he?"

He nodded, smiling in thought. He didn't speak of it much, but he had great respect and affection for his brother-in-law, though they could not have been more different in personality. "He's a scholar from Oxford. Getting to be quite an important figure, as I understand it, and will undoubtedly uncover the next great truth in this world. And he loves my sister with a single-mindedness that baffles the mind."

"As it should," Prue murmured fondly.

He glanced down at her curiously. "Don't tell me you're a romantic, Prue."

She shrugged with a helpless air that was quite charming. "What woman isn't in some way? I am a realistic woman, and I have no romantic notions for myself, but I have always thought it would be lovely to have that." Her expression darkened momentarily. "My parents never did, and it was miserable to witness."

"What happened there?" Camden asked with as gentle a tone as he could manage. "Marriage for fortune?"

Prue shook her head. "Convenience and connection. Papa was older and needed a wife for respectability and to manage the household and the like. Mother had no fortune to speak of, but it was not a bad match, and she has a decent enough pedigree, so it was favorable." She sighed slowly, the tone one of the saddest sounds he had ever heard. "They could not have been more wrong for each other. Papa was kind and gentle, patient with everyone and everything, laughed in the sort of way you feel as much as you hear…" Her eyes misted over, and she smiled tenderly. "He never thought I was simple. Whenever I had one of my attacks, after helping me breathe through it until I was calm, he would pull me onto his lap and hold me until I was better. He knew there was a difference."

Camden squeezed Prue's hand gently, finding his chest aching uncomfortably at the image she had painted. The indignity of it all was not lost on him. She had lost the one parent that had understood her and cared for her, the one who knew how to set her to rights, and instead had to endure the daily intolerance of the other parent who could not be bothered to see her own daughter clearly.

Prue deserved to have her father be tasked with managing this time in her life, not her poor excuse for a mother. She deserved that warmth and gentleness, not criticism and temper.

Camden wanted to meet Prue's father and shake the man's hand rather warmly, and the intensity of that wish surprised him immensely.

And he wanted to shower Prue with all of the warmth that she ought to have had and once knew.

Which may have surprised him more.

Suddenly, he was concocting a plan, and a strategy to implement it.

"Brace yourself, sweetheart," Camden told Prue with a teasing smile, "we are about to come back into your mother's view. Look pleasant, but not too delighted. No reason to make her think this is all going splendidly."

Prue giggled and adopted a pleasantly dour expression and did her best to avoid laughing while Camden told her stories of his misspent youth, and all the while, his idea swirled and formed in his mind. He would make this courtship something for both of them to enjoy, though it was only for show.

Acting a scene did not mean there was not some truth in it.

How much truth was another matter entirely.

Prue groaned as she looked down at the note in her hand for the forty-seventh time in two days.

The instructions had not changed, and neither had her panic.

Change in plans. Politeness is tedious. Tomorrow, we go to the opera again, L'inganno felice *this time. I have secured a box, and my sister has already agreed to chaperone. Wear your most elaborate gown.*

She screeched and covered her face for the forty-eighth time.

His sister? She wasn't ready to meet his sister, let alone spend an entire opera in her company!

She hadn't seen *L'inganno felice* yet, but she'd heard it was quite lovely, and any chance to attend the opera was welcome, to be sure.

But *this*?

She looked at the note again. Elaborate gown. She didn't *have* elaborate gowns! She had fine gowns, expensive gowns, over-trimmed gowns, unflattering gowns, and old gowns, and that was all. Nothing was truly elaborate in a way that she would feel comfortable displaying.

Bessie had said she would see to it, and she had chosen a pale red, silk gown with a high waistline, low neckline, and short, gathered sleeves that she claimed would show off Prue's slender arms to delightful effect. Matching red ribbons and small rosebud garlands were embroidered along the bodice and at the hem of the skirt, and thin, gold trim accented absolutely everything that could possibly be accented.

It was a piece of art, not a gown, and Prue balked at seeming so on display in such a thing.

Bessie had assured her that this was not exorbitant, nor was it overly elaborate, but it conformed nicely with the style of gowns other ladies of Prue's status would wear to such an occasion.

That wasn't much of a comfort.

Yet here she was, standing atop the stairs in said gown, hair perfectly adorned with plaits, pearls, ribbons, and curls, long, white gloves in place, clutching the note and her reticule with trembling fingers.

"I hate you, Cam," she hissed to herself as she shoved the note into the matching beaded reticule, then exhaled slowly.

She could do this. She could accompany him and his sister to the theater and wear an elaborate gown and not have one of her attacks.

Her mother was staying behind. Eliza would not be with them. The Spinsters might even be there in some number.

She would be fine.

Slowly, carefully, she descended the stairs where her mother and Cam, and undoubtedly his sister, waited. There was a moment of stunned silence from everyone when she appeared, and Prue held her breath, unable to meet the gaze of any of them.

"Prudence," her mother scolded in a huff, "go and change at once, that is entirely..."

She broke off as Camden approached the stairs, his eyes scanning Prue's form with too much intensity.

"Miss Westfall, you are perfection," he informed her, his voice smoother than the silk she wore. "I have no words, only praise and overwhelming feelings." He shook his head and stepped forward, extending his hand. "It would be my honor to have you on my arm."

"Th-thank you," she murmured, blushing as he took her hand and squeezed it.

"Don't stammer!" her mother scolded.

Camden glowered at her. "Do not scold her. Do not correct her. I find no fault in her, and that is enough for you, madam." He pulled Prue along, pausing only long enough to have her cloak secured, and then they left the house.

"W-where is your sister?" Prue asked him, her voice much smaller than it should be.

"In the coach," he told her brusquely, his brow still furrowed. He shook his head and looked at Prue incredulously. "You must have the patience of a saint. How do you stand her?" he asked, indicating back towards the house.

"I don't," she said with a shrug, "but I have no choice."

He paused outside the carriage and gave her a look, again taking in her figure. "I told you to wear something elaborate."

Realizing his earlier behavior to be an act for her mother, Prue frowned, trying to ignore the rising hurt within her. "I don't own anything elaborate," she snapped. "This is the best, or worst, I could do. And it was more than enough for my mother."

He snorted as if that were answer enough.

"Cam! For heaven's sake, don't keep the poor girl standing outside! Get in here!"

He scowled at the feminine voice from within the carriage. "Chadwick, shut her up!"

"No!"

Camden groaned and put a hand to his brow, muttering under his breath.

Prue folded her arms, looked down at her toes, and muttered, "I thought I looked quite well, but trust you to find fault."

He looked up sharply. "I didn't find fault."

She gave him a hard look.

"I didn't," he said again. "I said it wasn't elaborate. And it isn't. But that doesn't mean there is anything wrong with it. I only wanted to draw attention to you tonight, but not because you're with me. I wanted people to look at you, but differently, and I only know how to do that by standing out." He shrugged, smiling a little. "You are different from any other woman I've ever associated with, and I am a bit at ends about it. But I don't find fault in it."

"Cam!" called his sister again.

"All right!" he retorted, yanking on the carriage door and helping Prue in. "For the love of…"

"Better say it in German," the dark-haired woman inside the carriage quipped as she moved over for Prue. "It's less offensive in a foreign tongue." She grinned at Prue and held out a hand. "How do you do? Lydia Chadwick."

Prue stared at her in wonder. "Prudence Westfall."

Lydia dipped her chin quickly then gestured to the almost gangly fellow across from her, who watched his wife in bemused adoration. "That's Mr. Chadwick, he's mine."

"Too right," he replied with a wink. He touched the brim of his hat and nodded at Prue. "Miss Westfall, a pleasure."

She nodded in return, her eyes flicking to Cam in apprehension. He still seemed perturbed, and she was still unsettled by his words. He claimed he didn't find fault, but there was no mistaking the critical eye. She ought to have known she would ruin everything.

Camden tapped on the roof of the coach, and they took off for the theater, his focus now on adjusting his gloves.

"Did I hear you finding fault with Miss Westfall's gown?" Lydia demanded as she stared at her brother in disbelief. "That's preposterous, she looks better than I do."

"Not possible," Chadwick interjected matter-of-factly. "No offense to Miss Westfall."

"None taken," Prue murmured, amused in spite of herself.

"Not helping, Chadwick," Camden grunted.

"I adore you," Lydia sighed with a look at her husband.

"I am going to be ill," Camden announced, not looking at any of them.

"Out the window, if you please," Lydia told him without sympathy. "Miss Westfall and I do not deserve the indignity of sick on our gowns, in which there is *no fault*."

Prue clamped down on her lips hard, watching the exchange with interest.

"I did not find fault!" Camden protested, spearing his sister with a dark look. He turned to look at Prue, his gaze softening. "I didn't find fault."

Prue sighed to herself, then nodded in acceptance.

"I couldn't find fault with you if I tried," he muttered under his breath.

Prue heard him, and snorted, shaking her head as she turned her gaze out the window.

All was silent in the carriage for a moment. "Prue," he said in the gentlest tone she'd ever heard.

She slowly turned back to look at him and found him watching her closely. "What?" she managed, uncomfortable with such direct attention and the effect it was having on her.

He smiled a little; and really, it was a lovely smile. "You are beautiful. In the rarest of ways."

She stared at him in shock. No one ever said things like that, not to her, and especially not people who knew her. She had received flattery and ridiculous compliments with flowery fluff from fools who soon flee, but nothing like this. He was not teasing or flattering, and she had never known any man to say something so sincere, so simple, and so touching. That he was saying such to her was discomfiting, and she was confused by it.

Her face flushed and she looked down. "Th-thank y-you."

"Does that make you nervous?" he asked with concern, again sounding sincere.

She nodded, clearing her throat. "S-say something else, please."

He shifted and drew one knee up. "Did you see your mother's face when you appeared?"

Prue grinned, and he responded in kind.

"Tell me! Tell me, I must know!" Lydia demanded, chiming in excitedly.

Camden looked at her. "If you promise that you and Chadwick heard nothing that I just said to Prue, since it was not for your ears, I will tell you exactly what the bird's face looked like."

Prue covered her mouth as a soft snort escaped.

"I have no idea what you're talking about," Lydia said obediently, her dark eyes flashing. "I've forgotten everything until this very moment."

Camden grinned. "Good girl," he praised before launching into an excellent description of the events.

They all laughed the rest of the way to the theater.

Prue studied Lydia carefully as they arrived at the theater and proceeded to their box, and even into the first few songs. She was very similar in coloring to her brother, but her temperament was very different. The same sort of wit, but she was all good humor and politeness. Her husband was more reserved, but he had no qualms about speaking up with her or with Camden as he saw fit.

And Lydia put Camden quite in his place without a second thought. It was amusing to hear her scold him, always calling him Cam, and always with a mix of exasperation and admiration. It was evident that he adored his sister just as much as she'd suspected he did.

What would it have been like to be part of a loving family such as theirs? It was hardly the time for sad thoughts, but they were there all the same.

The opera itself was a decent enough affair, though not quite to Prue's taste. But there seemed to be much conversation around them, and she thought it quite possible that their box just might be the subject of the discussion. If the number of eyes on them were any indication, they certainly were.

Camden was affectionate and very protective, charming and almost perfectly behaved. Almost, because the wicked gleam in his eyes never faded, and he enjoyed letting people think they ought to be shocked. Once or twice, he leaned over to whisper in Prue's ear, only to tell her to linger, smile, and push him away playfully.

And that somehow took away Prue's fears of the attention, as she enjoyed every moment of it.

A woman enjoying herself must be a topic of discussion.

During the interval, Camden and the Chadwicks took her to walk a little, and Prue felt the stares and attention more than ever.

Camden must have felt her nerves, given the increase in people milling about, for he kept her close to his side and covered her hand, stroking it in soothing circles. He did not make much conversation that required a response from her, which was appreciated, but he tried to put her at ease by amusing her with a sort of commentary on the public.

They paused a step when Tony Sterling suddenly approached

them, his eyes flicking between Camden and Prue repeatedly.

"T-tony," Prue whispered, pleading with him not to make a scene.

He smiled a little at her. "It's all right, lamb. This won't take long." He looked at Camden with a far more severe look.

Camden didn't like that at all. "Yes, Sterling?"

"I have some concerns, Vale, about the attention you are paying Miss Westfall," Tony told him without any sort of preamble.

Camden raised a brow. "Why should that give you cause for concern?"

"Because I care for Miss Westfall," Tony snapped, "and I do not want to see her hurt."

"And you think I am going to hurt her?" Camden replied, sounding offended. "Ridiculous."

"Right," Tony muttered. "I know your reputation, sir. You can have no honorable motives."

"And what are yours, may I ask?" Camden asked, starting to hide Prue behind him a little. "She hasn't asked you to step in, has she?"

Tony looked at Prue, at how she clung to Camden's arm, but no doubt saw her concern, and he relaxed a little. "No, and she appears not to need me to. I mean no offense, Prue." He returned his gaze to Camden, no longer seeming severe, only somber. "I think the world of Prue. I feel very protective of her, rather as though she were a sister." He looked past the pair of them to the obviously curious Chadwicks and smiled a little. "A sentiment I believe you may comprehend, Vale."

"I'll not harm her," Camden told him in a much softer voice, nodding in agreement. "I have her best interests at heart, and I see you do as well. We are on the same side, Sterling, despite what you may have heard."

The two stared at each other for a long moment, and then Tony looked back at Prue. "Do you trust him?"

Prue looked up at Camden, and it seemed he was holding his breath. "Yes," she said simply, with no stutter at all.

The smile she received from Camden could have set the whole room aflame, and she was quite sure she would have stammered incessantly had anyone tried to converse with her.

Tony chuckled and put a hand on her arm. "Very well, I'll stand aside." He winked at Prue, smiling. "And you look very pretty, Prue. No doubt Vale has already informed you of that."

"I have, and she did not like it." Camden rolled his eyes and groaned in exasperation. Then something drew his attention, and he grunted to himself. "Oh good, your toad of a cousin is here, Prue. What a surprise. Time to go back to the box."

Tony looked where he had and muttered to himself incoherently.

Camden chuckled. "Yes, I have that exact sentiment with her, as well."

"As you should. I detest her." Tony gave him a tight smile and started off in the opposite direction. "Pleasant evening, friends."

Friends? Truly? Could it be, then, that there would be no further objections from him or the Spinsters?

It hardly seemed possible, but she would hope with all her might.

"Well," Camden sighed as they turned back for the box, "I can't say that I'm finding this opera to be a favorite, but it may be the best night at the opera I've ever had." He tilted his head a little as he looked at Prue. "And I think I would endure it again… if you were with me."

Prue's breath caught, and she wished her flush would recede, so she could smile properly.

Camden seemed to shake himself and released her hand, his raffish grin returning. "Now, I will call on you tomorrow, and every day after, and I promise to get you away from your mother as often as I can."

"And so will I!" Lydia crowed from in front of them.

"You're not courting her, I am."

"I wasn't asking you."

"You didn't ask anyone."

Prue felt her lips curve into a smile as her heart pounded a joyful cadence against her chest. It was the best night at the opera she'd ever had as well, and there wasn't an easy way to express that. So, she would just smile and enjoy it, hoping that this would be a turning point for her and whatever future lay before her.

Chapter Fourteen

What could be better than a small, intimate gathering of friends? That, dear readers, would depend entirely on the friends invited, the weather of the day, and the gossip of the time. There are no certainties with friends.

-The Spinster Chronicles, 28 March 1817

"Mr. Vale, would you escort me in, please?"

"As you can see, Miss Howard, I already have Mrs. Westfall and Miss Westfall on my arms. I do not have a third arm, alas."

"Oh, Prudence doesn't mind walking in on her own, do you, dear?"

Camden looked at the infernal blonde with all the patience he could muster, which was not much at all. "I already have her arm, Miss Howard, and it would be ungentlemanly of me to release it."

Miss Howard threw her head back and laughed merrily, though it sounded more like an evil cackle to his ears. "But you are no gentleman, Mr. Vale. Surely you don't adhere to such archaic statutes."

He ground his teeth together and tried for a smile, grateful the door was before them now. "I do try, Miss Howard, and it does me good."

Prue's hold on his arm tightened, but she said nothing.

Miss Howard laughed again, and she swept through the door before he or the ladies on his arm did, and he scowled after her.

"Such a lovely, high-strung girl," Mrs. Westfall said with a fond sigh. She rapped Camden's arm with her fan. "She'd make you a good wife, Mr. Vale."

Camden stared at her retreating figure as she entered the house and looked down at Prue in revulsion. "Is she trying to pair me with your cousin while I'm courting you?"

Prue shrugged a shoulder, not looking particularly surprised. "Mother is set on Mr. Davies for me. She said as much before you arrived. You are currently an obstacle."

"How unfortunate for you," he muttered, gesturing for her to enter ahead of him.

"Isn't it just?" she replied, shaking out her pale blue pelisse a little. "Georgie is never going to forgive me for…"

"WHY ARE THEY HERE?" came the indignant screech of their hostess.

Prue winced and looked up as the fair-haired Georgie Sterling approached them, eyes wild.

"Prue!" Georgie exclaimed, waving a hand in the direction Prue's family had just gone. "My first event? Really?"

Prue shook her head morosely. "I tried, Georgie. I really tried. They just… don't listen to me."

Camden grunted and removed his hat as he bowed to Georgie. "I can vouch for that, Mrs. Sterling. They just tried to match me up with Eliza despite the fact that I'm already courting Prue." He shuddered and tried not to gag.

Georgie gave him a sympathetic look. "Poor man. I'll have Tony get you something stronger to drink." She turned to Prue and shook her head, sighing, then reached for her hands. "Well, I forgive you, especially since my dunce of a husband invited Hugh, as well." She rolled her eyes, took Prue's arm, and pulled her along. "Come on, it's not a garden party unless you're in the garden, I'm told."

Camden chuckled and followed them through the house, marveling that Georgie could look at him without twitching already. After that encounter with her husband the other night, it seemed an uneasy truce had been established, and a tremulous alliance was now in place. He might not be on warm terms with the Spinsters, but they were not excluding or cutting him either.

Small mercies.

For all the slow progress he was making here, Prue was taking Camden's life by storm. Lydia absolutely adored her and was fully set on adopting her as soon as she could find a way to accomplish it. She spoke of nothing else when Camden saw her, and no longer seemed interested in anything he had to say unless the subject was Prue.

It was endearing, he would admit, but he could have done without her gabbing about her to his friends, with whom she was unfortunately also friends, and now they would not stop talking about Prue, either. He wanted her to know them better, to be sure, but with this increasing fervor about her, they would overwhelm her with enthusiasm, and she would be far too embarrassed to make any coherent response.

She wouldn't care for that at all, and he had to defer to her wishes and comfort in all of this.

Whatever this was.

He'd loved taking her to the opera, loved spending time with her out in public, loved that she admitted to Tony Sterling that she trusted him… It had meant more to him than anything in recent memory had, and his delight had been unending. He didn't know what he'd done to deserve such a woman in his life, but he wasn't about to give that up.

And she'd looked beautiful beyond description.

He'd complimented her without thinking, belatedly recalling how compliments affected her, but feeling strongly that he had to say something. Some small part of what he felt, what she did to him, how he… Well, there simply were not words. She was the description, picture, and ideal of loveliness, and that was all there was to it.

The fact that her shy smiles were beginning to make his knees unsteady, and her soft eyes set his heart aflame, and the sound of her laugh gave him wings, was just an extension of that truth.

He cleared his throat now as they moved out to the garden where the other guests were milling about. He grunted to himself at the suddenly interested expressions at least half a dozen men cast in Prue's direction, and, after taking in their identities, felt no qualms about striding forward to offer Prue his arm as they descended the few stairs. A bit of a protective glare wouldn't hurt either, he considered, as he did so.

"Oh, good, the goat's here."

Camden slowly turned to look at the whelp nearby with too-coifed hair. "I beg your pardon, sir?" Camden growled.

Prue's hand tightened on him. "C-cam…"

That stammer of apprehension made his fingers curl.

"How many more sad spinsters are you inviting, Georgie?" the man asked as he stared at Prue steadily, oblivious to Cam's fury or Prue's distress. "Going to pair them all off?"

Georgie snarled audibly, which Camden nearly applauded at. "If you have a problem with my guests, Hugh Sterling, no matter their marital status, you can show yourself out. Lord knows *I* would never have invited you."

Prue tugged at Camden's arm, her face flaming.

"I demand an apology, sir," Camden told him, not moving from his position.

Sterling looked at him with mild surprise. "Why?"

"Two counts," Camden growled. "Insulting Miss Westfall and being rude to Mrs. Sterling."

"I'm Mrs. Sterling's cousin," the idiot replied smugly, taking another glass of wine from the table.

"A point I am sure she weighed very seriously against accepting her husband's offer," Camden replied. "He must be an incomparable catch to ensure a lifetime of being tied to you. She must have spent ages in despair over the prospect. Alas for love matches, no one would have accepted you as a relation for convenience alone."

At least two people nearby snickered, but Prue was not one of them. She pulled on his arm again. "C-cam."

"Still waiting on the apology, Sterling," Camden told him, smiling blandly.

Sterling's eyes narrowed. "Or what?"

Camden's smile turned devious. "That is my very favorite question to answer."

Prue pulled on him harder. "Cam!"

He listened this time and went where she pulled, leaving a wide-eyed Hugh Sterling standing in his place, staring after them.

"Sorry," he mumbled to Prue, rubbing her hand. "I didn't mean to embarrass you."

She shook her head quickly. "Not you. Just… the s-situation."

He nodded and took her over to Lady Hetty, who had watched the exchange with interest. "I couldn't hear what all that was about," she croaked, reaching out a hand for Prue but looking at Camden. "I insist on knowing."

"I'll tell it!" declared another voice behind him, decidedly feminine and decidedly amused.

He turned to see a tall woman in elegant clothing, too attractive for her years, and in possession of very bright blue eyes. She grinned at him easily, as though they were old friends. He turned to face her, unwittingly amused himself.

"Miranda Sterling," Prue intoned softly, a hint of a smile on her lips, "may I present Mr. Camden Vale? Cam, this is Mrs. Sterling. She's Tony's stepmother."

Camden bowed but sighed aloud. "How many dashed Sterlings are there?"

Mrs. Sterling chuckled and patted his arm. "I'm the only one really worth knowing, Mr. Vale, aside from my stepsons. They're fair enough, but that one over there drags us all down. Lord knows why. His brother is charming."

"There's more?" Camden protested, shaking his head. "Unbelievable."

"Rather a fertile lot, the Sterlings," she replied. "Present company excluded." She reached a lace-gloved hand out to Prue, who took it at once. "Darling Prue, how are you, dear? You're flushed, but you mustn't let Hugh's bleating trouble you. No matter what he says, he's more goat than you could ever be accused of being. I should know, there are goats on my estate."

Camden liked this woman at once and grinned at Prue's shy smile.

"Thank you, Miranda," Prue replied.

Mrs. Sterling paused, sniffed the air, then turned around, glowering. "Lord above, I thought I smelled a rat. Who invited your cousin, Prue?"

Camden's grin couldn't have grown any further, but he wished it were possible. "Mrs. Sterling, you are a woman after my own heart."

She looked at him in surprise. "Charmed, my dear, but Prue

should be that. I'm only impudent. Call me Miranda and let us be friends."

He inclined his head. "Delighted, Miranda. You may call me whatever you like."

Miranda smiled mischievously. "Oh, you are a rascally one. I may have you take my hound for a hunt one of these days just to test the pair of you together."

Camden shrugged easily and took up position against a tree near the group. "If you like. Hounds tend to like me."

"Rufus likes everyone," Tony informed him as he and Georgie approached. "That won't signify anything."

Miranda sniffed haughtily. "He's not that fond of you, dear."

Tony rolled his eyes and gave Camden a grim look. "I heard about your interaction with my cousin just now. I cannot apologize enough. I'd hoped he would behave himself, but…"

"I wasn't the one he offended," Camden said with a shake of his head. "He refused to apologize for his words, either." He glanced down at Prue, who was suddenly very interested in her gloves.

"Thank you for defending Georgie, too," Tony murmured, looking at Prue as well. "Especially given that we weren't exactly pleased with this connection of yours."

Camden chuckled drily. "I'd have reservations about me, too. But for my respect for you both, I'd have called Sterling out for what he'd said."

"Ah, yes," Tony replied with interest. "I'd heard that you are something of a fighter. That would have been a fine sight."

"Not that fine," Georgie snorted, giving the other ladies an incredulous look. "It's a garden party."

Tony groaned as if in agony. "You ladies have no idea what we men endure for your finery."

"Yes, we feel quite ashamed of ourselves," his wife replied, obviously anything but.

"You wouldn't really have fought Hugh, would you?" Prue asked as she looked up at Camden, eyes wide.

He returned her look firmly. "I most certainly would. He deserves a good thrashing. I still might do so."

Prue's eyes widened further, and she looked at Tony and

Georgie. "He wouldn't."

"He would," Tony and Camden said together.

She fidgeted in her seat. "But it's Tony's house and Tony's cousin."

Camden looked at Tony, his expression hopeful. "Do you mind, Captain Sterling?"

Tony shook his head. "Not at all, I welcome it. Please, feel free."

Georgie cleared her throat meaningfully.

"Ah, but perhaps after the guests have left," Tony clarified, looked at Georgie again, then added, "and don't cause any damage."

They nodded at the group and moved on to other guests.

"Not much fondness between cousins, I take it," Camden commented as he watched them go.

Prue shook her head. "Tony hasn't forgiven Hugh for what he almost did to the relationship between him and Georgie."

Camden made a soft noise of understanding. "Has Hugh asked for forgiveness?"

"No."

He smiled at Prue rather easily. "Then I see no need for Sterling to oblige him there."

Her brow furrowed in exasperation, but whatever retort she would have offered was lost as the rest of the Spinsters arrived and greeted them all, Camden with wariness.

He didn't mind. He fixed his attention on Hugh Sterling on the far side of the garden and prayed for any additional excuse.

She was alone for the moment, and oddly glad for the reprieve.

Sometimes all one needs is peace and time to oneself.

She'd had so little of that lately. Not that she wasn't grateful for Camden's devoted attention and the Spinsters keeping her company, but she'd always had moments of reflection and calm before all of this, and she yearned for it. She missed not having to be on display constantly, and not having her mother and cousin interrupt everything private and personal in her life. She missed her independence, which she ought to have gained with her fortune but had lost instead.

Prue sighed and closed her eyes, tilting her head back a little into the sun, letting it warm her.

"Miss Westfall, would you mind very much if I sat beside you?"

She bit back a sigh and opened her eyes, surprised to see Mr. Davies there, a hesitant smile on his face.

"Not at all," Prue answered, surprising herself. She indicated the seat, and he sat with a smile, putting his hat into his lap.

"Thank you," he replied, still smiling. "I've hardly seen you since our time together at Tinley. You're always so surrounded."

Prue grimaced slightly, "Rather too surrounded for my taste."

"I can imagine so." His expression turned sympathetic. "And I remember Tinley not being a particularly enjoyable experience for you."

"Not through any fault of yours," Prue assured him at once. "Nor your mother. You were both very kind and should not feel any guilt for my discomfort."

He nodded gratefully. "You are very good to say so."

Prue smiled at him a little. "I understand you were of great importance to the smoothing over of my embarrassment that final night. Mr. Vale said you made a spectacle of yourself as a distraction."

Mr. Davies chuckled sheepishly and nodded. "I did, and it was prodigious fun. I'm not one for acting for attention normally, but it seemed as good a reason as any to do so."

"Well, I am exceedingly grateful," Prue told him as she laced her fingers together in her lap. "You can't imagine how much."

He seemed to color a little and glanced over to where Camden stood in discussion with Tony's friend, Lieutenant Henshaw. "Vale's a good sort of chap. A bit coarse, but nothing too outlandish. It's a wonder his reputation does him so little credit. I didn't mind doing as he asked, considering it was for you." He looked back at Prue curiously. "He is rather protective of you, Miss Westfall. Like a brother to watch over you, eh?"

Something like that. Unease clenched at her stomach, but Prue only smiled again. "He has been very kind as well."

There was no need to go into all that.

Mr. Davies' eyes suddenly narrowed, and his smile turned curious. "Pardon me saying so, Miss Westfall, but your… your speech seems much improved on closer acquaintance. Not so much trouble, if you'll forgive me."

She smiled further at his observation and the innocent wonder at it. "It tends to do that, Mr. Davies. Only crowds and attention heighten my anxieties, and with that comes the difficulty. I usually do quite well in private."

His smile spread, and he opened his mouth to speak again when a laugh nearby distracted them.

"Oh, Mr. Davies," Eliza exclaimed, trotting over to him. "You aren't disturbing my cousin's solitary reverie, are you? You know she must collect herself in order to converse at all. Soaks up the solitude like a plant in the sun."

Eliza's dark eyes glinted at Prue as she laughed, and Prue's cheeks colored.

"I didn't mean to disturb," Mr. Davies said, looking worried.

"You d-didn't," Prue tried to tell him, wincing as she stammered.

"Oh dear, she's overcome now," Eliza sighed, shaking her head dramatically. "Poor, simple girl, now she'll be babbling for hours. And poor Mr. Davies trying to be so polite. Truly, sir, it is not worth the effort."

Mr. Davies frowned and fidgeted with his hat. "Oh, but I…"

"Dear Prudence needs to collect herself, sir," Eliza insisted, gesturing for him to come. "She's already turning a frightful shade. Just look at it. Have you ever seen such a shade? Poor thing, she is so embarrassed about it, and it only gets worse and worse."

As if determined to make the situation worse, Prue's face flamed further still, and her hands began to shake.

"Miss Westfall?" Mr. Davies prodded as he rose, looking concerned.

"You are so kind, sir," Eliza preened, crooking her fingers again. "So sweet to my poor, miserable cousin. But she cannot tolerate conversation for long. She'll stammer up a storm and grow insensible. I don't know what will become of her, but such a simple creature cannot hope to be worthy of an inheritance. She cannot make her own decisions; how will the estate survive?"

Mr. Davies wandered away with Eliza, looking back at Prue with some hesitation, but she could see the glimmer of doubt that Eliza had planted, and her simpering tone would convince anyone who did not know her true motives.

"Tell me about Tinley House, Mr. Davies," Eliza was saying as she linked arms with him. "Prudence couldn't tell me anything, she stammered so much, so I must hear it from you."

Prue closed her eyes, ignoring the dampness there, and exhaled slowly.

"Prue? Good lord, what did the vermin say?"

"Little lamb, are you all right?"

Her hand was suddenly grabbed and pried from the arm of the chair she had been gripping, then rubbed soothingly between a pair of warm hands.

"Was it horrible, dear?" Izzy asked from beside her. "I'm so sorry, I didn't see her coming."

Prue shook her head, exhaling once more. "Nothing w-worse than usual."

"And that's what concerns me."

Prue opened her eyes to look up at Camden, who glowered darkly, his arms folded over his chest. She swallowed and gave him a sad smile. "She doesn't want me talking to Mr. Davies. Or anyone. She doesn't want me to be happy or even have a chance at it."

She could see his jaw working ominously and she thrilled at his defensive, protective nature.

Rather like a brother…

Was he? Was this? She didn't have a sibling, she was not sure she could tell the difference, but on her side…

That wasn't it.

Not at all.

"If Mr. Davies can't see what a poisonous reptile Eliza is, I wash my hands of him," Charlotte spat as she dropped beside Prue and put her arm around her. "Good riddance."

Camden nodded in agreement but said nothing.

"She's been doing that with all of them," Grace pointed out with a sigh. "Any man who tries to flatter you, she intercepts."

Prue smiled weakly. "That one I don't mind so much. So many

of them only want my fortune, and I don't want all that attention. She can have it. And them."

Camden cocked his head. "But what if they were sincere in their motivations?"

"Surely one interfering woman isn't enough to prevent such a man from finding a way." She looked at him for confirmation.

He didn't give it. "You wouldn't think so, and yet…"

"Would it stop you?" Prue asked him before she could stop herself.

Camden seemed to stiffen. "Not a fair question," he finally said with a shake of his head.

"Why not?"

He sighed and ran a hand through his hair quickly. "Because I know you."

Her heart began to thump against her ribs. "So?"

He laughed once. "So my answer should be obvious."

Prue did not respond to that, forced her expression to remain blank, and waited.

Hoping.

He exhaled roughly, his lips quirking to one side. "No, Prue. No, it would not stop me. Nothing would."

She couldn't breathe, couldn't think, couldn't react…

"I like him," Charlotte announced to the group. "Can we keep him?"

Grace scoffed softly. "Just last week you called his attentions an outrage."

Charlotte made an unapologetic face. "I have since come to my senses."

"Oh, I wasn't aware you had any," Grace mused with a perfect smile. "What a revelation."

Prue only half listened to them. She was too busy staring at Camden, who was staring at her, and everything else was just accompaniment to their mutual staring.

His soft smile brought out hers, and her heart pounded harder still.

Rather like a brother…

No, she thought to herself, not at all like.

"Well, almost everyone has gone," Georgie announced as she approached, sounding relieved.

That shook Camden, and he turned to her. "Have they?" He looked around quickly, then grunted and handed his drink to Grace. "Hold this, will you, Grace?"

Then they all watched as Camden strode across the garden directly to where Hugh Sterling stood with a drink in hand, and punched him squarely in the jaw, sending Hugh tumbling to the ground.

"Yes, indeed, I like him immensely," Charlotte said again with a dark chuckle. "We are definitely keeping him."

Prue swallowed harshly, her cheeks beginning to flame further.

But she agreed. Quite a lot.

Chapter Fifteen

There is nothing like a ball for grand moments, eager flirtation, and secret heartbreaks.

-The Spinster Chronicles, 9 February 1818

"Don't think for a second that you can sit in the corner all night like you used to do. You're an heiress now, and you've got to start behaving like one."

"Your mother is right, dear. No one will want to court a young lady who is so reserved and antisocial. Not a single beau will come of that."

"I h-have a b-beau," Prue informed her aunt and mother, feeling as though her cloak would strangle her.

Eliza barked a hard laugh from the other side of her father, situated between his wife and daughter, clearly miserable. "Camden Vale? He's not a beau for you, he's entertaining himself with a mouse for a toy. Surely you don't believe for one minute that this laughable courtship of his is anything real."

Prue stared at her cousin, blinking unsteadily.

Well, no, her courtship wasn't real, and she was all too aware of it. It was a ploy to distract the bevy of suitors from overwhelming her, and to ensure she could be more protected and comfortable than she would otherwise be. It was an act to keep her from embarrassing herself with her attacks when all of this became too real for her.

But no one else knew that.

Eliza certainly didn't.

"W-what do you mean?" Prue asked, wishing she had managed a firmer tone.

Eliza made an annoyingly sympathetic sound. "Poor Prudence, you're too simple to even know. Camden Vale is a reprobate. Quite disastrous with women, and rather flagrant in his attentions. His last mistress died of a broken heart when he deserted her, quite perished in the streets for want of him. And he did not care, Prudence. He has no heart, and he's amusing himself with you, pretending to court an heiress to move in better circles than he deserves. He's manipulating you for his own ends."

"It's a wonder I let him proceed in this farce of a courtship at all," her mother grumped, shaking her feathered head. "If it weren't for the attention you receive from it, Prudence, I would not have done. But having him pay you attention is bringing more notice of you, and that is something we must have if you are to secure a good match. Look at Mr. Davies, for example. I saw that he paid you a marked degree of attention at the Sterling's garden party before you went all pink and flustered on him. If Eliza hadn't saved him, you might have embarrassed him and prevented any further interest."

Eliza modestly ducked her chin. "I am only too glad to assist, Aunt. Dear Prudence must be at her best at all times. I shall keep a firm eye out all night to save my dear cousin from herself."

"Oh, such a sweet girl, such a lovely creature…"

Prue swallowed and tried to breathe as silently as possible. She couldn't bear to have Eliza watch her for part of the evening, let alone the whole of it. It was bad enough having her twist Mr. Davies around, as she had done at the garden party, but when one considered what she had encouraged with Simon Delaney before that…

Eliza could make this evening nothing but torment, and Prue couldn't have that.

She was already ill at ease for not having Camden escorting her. He'd offered, had sent a missive to her with a plan, but her mother had intercepted it and forced her to reply that they would go to the Hawkins' party together as a family, and he could meet her there.

Prue didn't know the Hawkinses well at all, but she knew they had a son in search of a wife, and she strongly suspected that was why they were invited at all. As they were wont to do, her cousin, aunt, and uncle had insisted on joining them, despite no official invitation themselves.

Her mother had agreed, claiming it was the only way to help her poor cousin, now that she was wealthy and sought after.

She didn't want to meet Mr. Hawkins. She'd rather beg off this whole affair with a vile headache and remain in bed. Up until an hour ago, she had fully intended to do just that.

Then, a secret note from Camden had arrived, and he'd asked for the first two dances.

Bessie had been called up at once and begun preparing Prue for the evening.

And really, she had outdone herself. Her hair was piled up elegantly, curled and twisted with lace ribbons, dotted with small white rosebuds, and quite secure, she was told, despite the looser appearance. Prue's gown was new, commissioned only weeks ago, and it was one of her favorites. Fairly simple as far as embellishments went, but the layers of folded muslin gave it a very light, flowing look, and the pale blue fabric seemed to imitate waves of water. A ruched bodice of the same folds enhanced what Prue did not have, giving her a finer figure than she possessed, and the sleeves seemed almost draped upon her shoulders.

She fingered the thin layer atop her skirts now, running the sheer material across her fingertips. She hoped she looked as beautiful as she felt, hoped he would notice, that he would approve...

The cool metal of the locket about her neck pressed against her skin, contrasting the sudden heat in her cheeks and beneath her chest. Her father's likeness was within the locket, and she'd grabbed the trinket as a last-minute addition, feeling anxious and wistful, desperate for any connection to him now.

You're as pretty as a picture, little lamb, his voice replayed in her mind, making her smile fondly. He'd been the first to call her a little lamb, with all the endearment in the world. The Spinsters had taken it up with the same sort of love.

Eliza found use in it as a mockery, twisting it as she did everything else.

Her father would have been pleased to see her tonight, and he would have borne her on his arm proudly to greet the Hawkinses and to face the room of guests.

She prayed his spirit and grace would be with her tonight as she managed the task alone.

The carriage rolled up, and the door was flung open by a smartly-dressed footman in gilded livery, who waited without expression for their disembarking.

"Remind me to try for the Hawkins heir," Eliza chortled as she got out. "This is very fine indeed."

Prue blushed on behalf of the footman now being openly appraised by her brazen cousin.

They were shown into the house, their cloaks were taken, and they greeted the Hawkins family along with the rest of the guests.

The knowing glint in Mrs. Hawkins' eye told Prue her suspicions were correct.

"Daniel," she chirped in a stiff tone, "take Miss Westfall and her cousin into the ball. You don't need to stand here any longer."

He smirked superiorly and offered his arm to Prue, who flushed, of course, and took it, lowering her eyes.

"Forgive my cousin, Mr. Hawkins," Eliza simpered. "She's so very shy. I am sure once she gets more comfortable with you, she will be right as rain."

"In that case, I look forward to making Miss Westfall more comfortable," Mr. Hawkins purred, his tone suggesting the opposite.

Prue shivered, her ears flaming at once.

Mr. Hawkins chuckled knowingly. "Poor Miss Westfall. Shall I set you to rights?"

"Oh, do try, Mr. Hawkins," Eliza teased, nudging him. "She would be so very grateful for your efforts."

Prue closed her eyes as another shiver racked her frame.

"Ah, Miss Westfall, there you are!"

Hearing Camden's voice, she nearly gasped with relief, and her eyes sprang open eagerly.

He was perfection embodied as he came to them, freshly shaved and groomed, appearing more a perfect, polite gentleman than half of the men in the room. He bowed with precision to their trio and even smiled at Eliza, then looked somewhat apologetic as he met Mr.

Hawkins' eyes, extending his hand to Prue.

"I'm so sorry to rid your arm of one of its fine adornments, Hawkins, but I have reserved the first two dances with Miss Westfall." He tsked as if this was all quite awkward, but he showed no sign of superiority or rancor. "Perhaps you may secure one yourself later?"

Prue put her hand in Camden's immediately, and he swept her away before Hawkins could do anything of the sort.

"I don't w-want to dance with h-him," Prue insisted harshly as Camden led her to the dance floor.

"And I'll be damned if I'd let you," he replied, losing the gentlemanly manner he'd just employed. "Not a chance in hell."

Prue coughed a relieved laugh and grinned up at him. "I'm glad to hear it."

He returned her smile. "Don't take this as flattery, Prue, but you are a vision this evening. Lovely and bright. I'll be beating the men away."

She blushed immediately. "Only because you like beating them," she replied stubbornly, her pulse thudding in her ears almost pleasantly.

"Well, there is that," he allowed with a light laugh. "Shall we make the room envious of me by your smiles? I think we shall. Only the best of suitors for you, love. On we go."

He was too teasing, too facetious, and it worried Prue. Why would he need to draw other suitors to her? He was supposed to be her suitor at this moment, though it was all for show, and he shouldn't be encouraging it. He'd known enough to steal her from Mr. Hawkins, and to not have her dance with the man later, but did he mean that he would have others do so?

They took up the dance, thankfully not leading, and Prue forced her worries and cares to the back of her mind. Dancing was one of her lesser-known passions, and it was rare these days that she found true enjoyment in it. Only a handful of men could dance with her and not make her feel embarrassed or self-conscious.

Camden was far and away the best of them.

He smiled at her the entire time in varying degrees, but he also smiled at the other females he encountered in the course of the dance.

She could see the amused smiles they exchanged with him and each other, could see the expressions of those watching him. No one knew what to make of this particular version of Camden Vale, who smiled and danced with ease and grace, every inch a gentleman worthy of admiration.

And pursuit, she considered, as she saw a predatory gleam grow in the eyes of some.

She swallowed with difficulty and smiled helplessly as he was returned to her, dancing her pattern with him, yet feeling somehow disconnected from him.

What did smiles for her mean if there were similar smiles for everyone else?

Did they mean anything at all?

The first dance ended, and they applauded the musicians on the far side of the room. Prue exhaled through her nose, trying to look at Camden without looking like she was looking.

He looked back at her, eyes crinkling at the corners with his smile.

She smiled back.

But she wasn't sure she felt it.

Camden didn't seem to notice, and when the music began once more, he took her hand just as warmly as before, smiling with much of the same.

He might have been dancing with any other woman at this moment. He was delighted to be dancing, it seemed, and any capable woman would have given that to him. He'd rescued her from Hawkins, but that was what he did with Prue.

He rescued her.

That's what this faux courtship of theirs was. A rescue. He was rescuing her from the pressures of too much attention, too many suitors, too many expectations. He was exerting himself to see her comfortable, but to what end?

This would all end at some point, once he'd decided he'd had enough of playing the suitor. He'd need to spend some time looking to his own prospects and future instead of dallying in the middle of Prue's. Those friends of his that he'd so recently reconnected with would undoubtedly like to further their friendships without the complication of her as additional baggage.

Any of these women could make Camden smile as she was now.

He wasn't smiling for her.

He was just smiling.

Generally, Prue didn't take anything that Eliza said as fact, knowing only too well that the truth was a fluid concept for her. But in this case, could there be enough accuracy in her words for it to be true?

Could Camden's interest and investment in Prue be nothing more than boredom on his side? A way to pass the time until his life was more settled? Could he be using this time with Prue to forge connections he would need later?

He wasn't at all villainous, she was assured of that much. He truly was helping her, and she would be grateful for it. She did not believe he would ever intentionally wound her, nor did she think his reputation was indicative of the man he was.

But when a girl like her had a connection with a man like him, much ought to be questioned.

Why would he want her?

What would happen when he left?

Prue inhaled sharply, amazed that, somehow, she was still smiling as she moved into the final pattern of the dance. Camden smiled at her, unaware of the torrent of misery currently encroaching on her state of mind. She took his hand and proceeded up the line of dancers, counting the number of ladies who watched Camden pass.

Fourteen.

Make that fifteen.

Mary Wilton stood just on the outskirts of the dance and watched him move, as well.

Courting Prue for show was giving Camden Vale a status he hadn't had before, and she could see the effects of that.

She couldn't stand in the way of that. She wouldn't. He shouldn't be courting her for show. He should be free and available for any of the women in this room. Any of them could be suitable; far more than she was.

He was her friend, and she wished him well.

Biting the inside of her lip, she forced herself to curtsey to him, though her knees trembled dangerously as she rose.

"There now," Camden said as he took her hand and led her away, letting the smile fade and working his jaw a little. "That was well done. My face is out of practice, that hurt quite a lot."

Prue smiled at the return of the Camden she knew. "You were very convincing."

"Well, my budding career on the stage will be gratified to hear that." He exhaled and scanned the room. "Right, where are the allies?"

She snickered a little and gestured towards the windows. "Lady Hetty always sits by the windows. She likes the sky."

Camden shrugged at that. "She's of an age where she can like whatever she wants. Works for me." He smiled to himself as he caught sight of them. "Ah, and Miranda is with her. Perfection."

"She is, isn't she?" Prue smiled at them both. "Good evening," she greeted as they approached the women.

Miranda was radiant in cream and gold, and she rose with a delighted squeal. "Prue! You are a goddess of the seas! What a vision you are!" She kissed Prue's cheeks warmly. "Oh, what I wouldn't give to have your figure, child, it is divinity itself."

Prue flushed in embarrassed pleasure, though she smiled at Miranda's effusiveness.

Miranda winked and pinched at Prue's cheeks gently. "Darling, I overstepped, didn't I? Sit here by Lady Hetty, she'll find a fault straight away to take the blush back."

"I will not!" Lady Hetty barked, smiling in spite of her refusal. "There's nothing to fault in Prudence but her lack of proper family, which is not her fault at all!"

Camden chuckled and released Prue's hand. "Well, will you try to come up with one while I take a dance with the lovely Mrs. Sterling?"

Miranda brightened considerably. "Oh, Mr. Vale, you are too charming! Surely you'd rather dance with a younger woman."

He winked at her. "What younger women?"

Lady Hetty cackled and waved them on. "Go on, the silly pair of you. The dance will be over before you've flattered each other enough."

Miranda placed her hand on top of Camden's and let him lead her on, beaming for all the world.

Camden had that effect on women.

Prue swallowed as her smile faded, watching as her mother eyed Camden with distaste, huffing and turning her back as she continued to talk with the other ladies around her, waving her hands wildly.

"It really is a pity that she's only a prospect for her money," she heard her mother warble. "Such a useless girl, always has been. Her cousin, however…"

As if directed to do so, Prue's gaze slid over to her cousin, dressed in the colors of a pale rose and looking as fresh as one. She had Mr. Hawkins by her side still, and Mr. Davies stood nearby, smiling at whatever she was saying. Her eyes met Prue's, and she gave her a smug smile. Then she slid her hand from Mr. Hawkins' arm and pulled Mr. Davies into the dance, though he was obviously willing enough to go.

Prue didn't care about Mr. Davies being taken in by Eliza, as she'd never had an interest in him herself. She did, however, care very much that Eliza only took him on to take him from Prue. That all of this was simply a way to remove things from Prue's life that could potentially bring her joy. That she found such pleasure in hurting her, and always had.

Say baa for me, lamb. Go on. Baa-aa-aa-aa…

Prue's cheeks colored as the sound of mocking bleating suddenly rang rampant in her mind, almost making it to her ears.

Laughter joined it, and she could not discern if it were in her mind or actually happening. It all blended together in a cacophony that threatened to deafen her.

"Prue, darling, why does your mother look like an actual blizzard? Snow drifts and giant flakes, and all?" Charlotte's voice broke in, laughing to herself. "And with the way she's flailing, it may actually snow in a moment."

"What in the world is she doing?" Grace's voice wondered, probably looking very pretty with the worry knitting her fair brow. "How embarrassing."

Embarrassing. Dreadful. Horrifying. Her family was an absolute nightmare to deal with, to even associate with. No one who had any sense wanted them about, not even her friends. Prue didn't want them around if she could help it, but she had little choice in the matter.

They were a trial to everyone, and no one would feel that more keenly than Camden. He'd suffered the effrontery of interrogation and degradation in his interaction with them, all for a connection that did not actually exist. He had endured their belittlement of Prue and the aggravation of their conversation more times than Prue could recall at present. They ought not to be such a burden for him.

Not when this all meant nothing.

Would any man want to deal with them for want of Prue?

Alas for love matches, no one would have accepted you as a relation for convenience alone...

Camden's words to Hugh Sterling came into mind, the same taunting accent in them, but now they were directed at Prue.

Her relations that no one would want.

Or was she the relation no one would want?

Her mind began to cloud, to thicken with the laughter, the bleating, the rumbling insults flitting about, and she looked around faintly for any sort of reprieve.

Hugh Sterling leaned against a wall, looking listless and wasteful as he drank deeply from the glass he held. His eyes cast around and settled on Prue for a moment. He seemed to laugh to himself, his expression morphing into a sneer, and he gave her a mocking toast of whatever he held before drinking the rest of it.

Prue's breath hitched in her chest, and her cheeks burned.

She was a mockery. This was all a mockery. She didn't deserve to be an heiress, she didn't have anything to offer anyone but her fortune, and even that would be a waste.

"Oh, Prue, you don't look well at all," Eliza taunted as she and Mr. Davies swept past. "Can you give a greeting to Mr. Davies? You remember him, don't you?"

She leaned closer as if examining Prue with concern.

Prue met her eyes, though her vision began to blur a little.

Eliza smirked. "You'll never get there, lamb. Simple ones never do." She bleated weakly, her ratafia-laced breath wafting over Prue's burning cheeks. She straightened and turned to Mr. Davies. "Poor thing, she's not even really here. We'll have to come back. Come along, Davies."

Prue exhaled on a whimper, tears beginning to sear their way down her cheeks.

"Don't pay any attention to that…"

"Prue, it's all right, you don't…"

Their voices faded into a buzzing as her entire body began to tingle, from the roots of her hair to her temples and down her spine.

Camden would leave her when he was tired of this mess of her life, this pretend courtship for no reason at all, and she'd be left all alone again.

Alone with the fortune she didn't want.

Alone with the fortune hunters who would not rest.

Alone with her family who refused to love her.

Alone…

A horrible, catching, wheezing whimper met her ears, and she wanted to beg whomever it was to stop, to leave her be, to let her have peace.

And then it occurred to her.

It was her.

She staggered to her feet and stumbled towards where she thought the door was, needing air and quiet and calm. The music from the orchestra suddenly overwhelmed every one of her senses, driving the tingling of her frame into a frenzy.

She couldn't breathe, couldn't see, couldn't stop the roaring of her own panic as it consumed her so completely.

Her arms were seized just as she felt her legs crumpling, and she felt herself being dragged, though her feet still moved, tingling to a painful extreme. Her chest ached with the breath she could not find, panicking further at the lack of air, quickening the pulse now pounding in her head.

She was going to die. She was honestly and absolutely going to die in this numbing, tingling, senseless state, and she would forever be tied to such an embarrassing end.

Her breath hitched loudly, and her knees were suddenly swept up, her body slamming limply into a much larger, warmer object.

"The door, Georgie. Charlotte, distractions."

Prue's head dropped back as her strength gave out completely, and rough sobs now ripped from somewhere in her chest. Waves of tingling, burning sensations cascaded through her.

"Oh, Prue…"

Was that Izzy? Grace? She couldn't tell, couldn't make out the differences.

Who held her? Whose voice had she heard directing the others?

"Come on, sweetheart, give me a second…"

She knew that voice, and her lungs seemed to quiver on their heaving sobs at hearing it.

Suddenly, she was positioned upright on a bench, flanked on either side by bodies, and her head was taken in hand.

"Breathe in, breathe out. Fear in, fear out."

Obediently, she inhaled deeply, the command registering on some deep, tormented part of her.

"Look at me, love. Eyes on me."

Wearily, she lifted the lids she hadn't known were closed and tried to focus on the dark ones before her. They were steady and strong. Warm. But… her father had blue eyes like hers.

Camden.

"Breathe in," Camden murmured, his hands pressing against her skin, "breathe out. Fear in, fear out."

Breathe in, breathe out. Fear in, fear out.

Somehow, she listened, obeyed, breathed with him, with both of them as her father's voice rang in chorus with Camden's in her mind. Over and over, the words repeated, from Camden's lips and in her mind, giving her focus, direction, purpose…

Camden nodded slowly as he breathed with her, seeing her clearly as she found the ability to focus again. "There you are. There's my girl. Breathe in, breathe out…"

"F-fear in, f-fear out," she whispered weakly.

He nodded again, smiling. "Almost there?"

She closed her eyes briefly in an almost nod.

Breathe in, breathe out. Fear in, fear out.

"That's right, love. That's right."

Prue felt herself nodding in his hold. She inhaled a shaking breath that sent tremors through her, then released it with the sort of stuttering she spoke with.

Someone wiped tears from her face, brushed her dampened curls from her brow, and someone else rubbed her upper arms gently.

"Oh, Prue…"

That was definitely Izzy, she could tell now.

"All right, ladies, would you give us a moment? Just guard the windows."

The girls beside her moved, and Prue was scooped up again, then settled against Camden's chest.

She blushed and shook her head, but arms clamped firmly around her.

"No, no," Camden soothed, brushing her hair back again. "Don't fight, sweetheart. You're calm, but you're not better. We can wait."

Prue whimpered as a fresh wash of tears appeared. She curled into Camden, loving how he collected her against himself as if to shield her from anyone and anything

"Shh," he murmured, his lips against her hair. "It's all right. Whatever it is, whatever it was, it's all right."

She nodded against him, grateful he didn't press her for details. How could she have voiced any of it? He was so central to what had set her off, and confessing all of that… She did not have that much strength within her.

But he was here now, and he had remembered every detail of the pattern her father had set for her, down to this last part. He hadn't balked at any of it or told anyone else what to do. He'd done it himself.

Breathe in, breathe out. Fear in…

"Fear out," he whispered against her hair, rubbing her arm.

She sighed heavily against him, weary in the aftermath. For several long moments, there was no sound but her breathing, and that slowly began to steady as well. When her heart resumed a normal, painless rhythm and her body no longer shook, she raised her head and looked into his face. He smiled gently at her, no sign of regret or disdain, no shame or embarrassment.

Nothing but warmth.

"There you are," he said fondly, his mouth lifting in a crooked smile. "We missed you."

Prue managed a smile at that.

His eyes searched hers carefully. "Better?"

She nodded again.

He raised a doubting brow. "Really?"

She wet her lips and gave another small nod. "Really."

A flash of pleasure lit his eyes at the lack of stammer, and he returned her nod, rising and setting her back down on the bench.

"Good. I'll take you home."

Prue shook her head quickly, collecting her thoughts in the sudden chill of the night. "No, I want to stay."

That surprised him. "Do you?" He put his hands on his hips, his brow furrowing. "Why?"

She looked up at him, seeming to see him in all his essence for the first time. "I want to dance. With you."

Slowly, Camden grinned at her, a tempting, attractive, earnest grin that warmed her more than her shame ever had. "Sweetheart, I will dance with you all night if that's what you want."

He reached for her hand and drew it to his lips, the fabric of her gloves doing absolutely nothing to deaden the shock of heat and lightning his lips created.

Prue laughed a breathless half laugh, and Camden heard it, his lips quirking at the sound. He winked, then lowered her hand back to her lap with the gentleness of a whisper.

"Cam, could you teach me how to punch properly?" Charlotte asked, effectively breaking the tension Prue felt rising between them. "I have a fiendish desire to hit Lizard Liza Howard."

Prue choked on another laugh, as did the others, and Camden threw a sardonic look at the outspoken spinster.

"I have someone you need to meet, Charlotte Wright," he said with admiration. "She could help you far more than I could." He returned his eyes to Prue, and they softened noticeably. "I'll be inside waiting for you, whenever you're ready. I expect marvelous dancing and nothing less."

"No promises," she replied in a low tone, smiling in spite of herself.

He returned it, nodded, and turned for the doors, offering an arm to Izzy, who took it with a merry laugh.

Charlotte followed, and seized his other arm, plaguing him with questions.

Prue watched them go, then sighed heavily as she looked around the terrace.

Georgie stood there still, eyes fixed on Prue, expression unreadable.

Prue blinked unsteadily, and she swallowed fresh nerves. "Georgie?"

Her friend's lips pursed as her eyes shifted to the ballroom, then moved back to Prue on an exhale. She smiled a small, knowing smile.

"If I were you, Prudence Westfall," she said at last, her voice laced with amusement, "I would kiss that man properly before too much time has passed."

Prue's heart suddenly lodged itself in her throat, and she squeaked in distress. She swallowed no less than four times, then whispered, "I... d-don't know how."

Georgie's smile spread. "That's all right. I'm fairly certain he does."

Chapter Sixteen

Sometimes, a girl must do as she's told. Sometimes, it's quite delightful to do so.

-The Spinster Chronicles, 8 July 1816

"Cam, where *is* she?"

"If I knew, I would tell you."

"But you did tell her to come, yes?"

"You sent her an invitation, Lydia. And yes, I told her. At least three times. She will come."

"Are you sure? She wasn't put off by you or by me?"

Camden stared at his sister in surprise. "Why in the world would she be put off by me?"

Lydia gave him the sort of look only older sisters can. "Because it's you?"

He frowned and looked over at Chadwick, feeling a bit disgruntled. "Do you see what sort of woman you married?"

Chadwick smiled and shrugged his broad shoulders. "Aren't I a fortunate man?"

Camden snorted and shook his head in disgust. "Hopeless."

"Oh, do be kind to yourself," Lydia scolded, patting his arm. "You're not entirely hopeless, just dense."

"Are you two *still* squawking at each other? I'd thought you'd matured long past it. But then, the Vales never were very mature."

Camden looked up with a frown as Dart and Julia entered,

looking the picture of a perfect London couple, all refinement and elegance, and were it not for the decidedly mischievous glint in both of their eyes, one would have expected them to behave in an equally perfect manner.

"Dart!" Lydia squealed, never one to behave as a perfect London lady.

He grinned at her and released his wife's arm to forgo any sort of propriety by hugging Lydia rather than greeting her formally. "You haven't changed at all, Lydia."

She pulled back, grinning up at him. "Neither have you, whelp, except in inches." She reached up and ruffled his hair as though he were twelve again, making them all chuckle.

Dart shook his head and stepped back, smoothing his hair down. "Lydia Chadwick, may I present my wife, Julia?"

"Oh, she's far prettier than you should have managed, Dart" Lydia beamed and rushed forward to hug her as well. "I never thought there would *ever* be a Mrs. Dartmouth! I love you already!"

Julia laughed and gave Dart and Camden a bewildered look. "Why shouldn't there be? Was Dart that hopeless?"

"Don't answer that," Dart said at once, giving his wife a severe look.

Julia returned it, then smiled at Lydia fondly. "I can see we have much to discuss, Mrs. Chadwick."

"Now you've done it," Camden muttered, shaking his head. "Excellent work, Dart."

Dart grumbled under his breath. "I presume that is your husband, Lydia?"

She glanced behind her at Chadwick, who seemed amused by the whole spectacle. "Oh, yes. Chadwick, darling, this is Trevor Dartmouth and his wife."

"So I gathered," Chadwick mused, bowing to them both. "I'd apologize for my wife, but I don't find that particularly necessary."

"I do," Camden told them all.

"Nobody cares," Lydia retorted. "You and Dart go away. I want Mrs. Dart all to myself. Clearly, she is the best of you."

Julia smirked, her full lips spreading just a touch. "I like you, Mrs. Chadwick."

"Lydia," his sister insisted. "Formality shouldn't exist amongst friends."

Camden rolled his eyes, shaking his head. "I can't go away, Lydia. You asked me to wait here for Prue. And you can't leave, you're the hostess."

Lydia scowled. "I'm so sorry, Julia, but my infernal and *younger* brother is insisting on politeness for the first time in his life."

"That's all right," Julia replied, tossing her head a little. "I'll go on in and make the rounds. Come and find me when you've been polite enough."

Camden looked at Dart in disbelief. "What in the world have you done?"

Dart shrugged, heaving a dramatic sigh. "I wonder that all the time, but every time I second guess, I find myself smitten all over again."

"Sounds painful."

Dart raised a dark brow at him. "It is. I wonder you don't know that by now yourself."

"As do I!" Lydia mused loudly, rounding on Camden.

"It does seem curious," Julia added as she eyed Camden in assessment.

Camden looked at his brother-in-law, apparently the only sensible being in this room besides him.

Chadwick twisted his mouth in thought, then winced sympathetically. "He does make an excellent point."

Camden glowered.

Never mind, he thought. No one sensible here but me.

Dart chuckled and clapped him on the back, then swept away with his elegant and impudent wife.

"I like them together," Lydia sighed, watching them retreat.

"You would," Camden grunted as he returned his attention to the door.

Prue should have been here by now. Everyone else that Lydia had invited was here, though she only seemed to care about Prue.

It was odd, but he felt exactly the same way.

Ever since her attack the other night, he found himself thinking of Prue constantly. Wondering if she was well, wondering what had set her off, wondering if it was normal to think of one woman so frequently…

He'd stayed by her the rest of the evening after settling her on the terrace, and while she hadn't been entirely herself, she'd improved significantly as time went on. She'd smiled and laughed a little, but her cheeks never fully lost their blush, and she seemed to look at Camden almost nervously for the rest of the time.

He'd assumed it was her anxious state after panicking so much, seeking him as a sort of security measure. It would make sense to look at him that way, particularly when they'd shared such a vulnerable moment for her. And her inclination towards reserve there could have been an embarrassment. He had seen her in a most distressed state, after all.

He wasn't embarrassed. He was glad of it. Not glad she had suffered so, of course, but glad he had been able to get to her. Glad he knew just how to calm her, to find her when she was so lost, to guide her back out of it. He'd felt as though he had formed a deeper bond with her because of it.

A connection. Something not entirely defined by words but framed by emotions not easily identified. They were forging their own path, it seemed, and the direction in which they were heading seemed rather unclear at present.

Her friends no longer had any reservations about him as far as he could tell. In fact, Charlotte had accepted him so completely that she began pestering him for information on Mariah Turner, whom he had yet to introduce her to, despite his promise. That was an act of self-preservation, and the only noble thing he'd ever done for the good of England and Society. According to Prue, Izzy, and Georgie, he was wise to wait until it was absolutely necessary to make those introductions.

He admired how the Spinsters looked after one another, how they loved one another, despite being so very different in situation and temper. They managed their own lives with dignity and strength, offering insight, wisdom, and wit with their Chronicles, and, aside from young Elinor Asheley, seemed to have no inclination towards bitterness or anger at their state.

Rare women, the lot of them, and though he would probably

never admit it, he felt strangely flattered by being included in their circles. But, according to Charlotte and Elinor, he was still not an approved candidate for matrimony, only for their friendship.

Apparently, the clarification was important.

He didn't care. He only wanted Prue.

He frowned at that. Wanted? What did he want? What did that even mean? Prue was his friend, growing dearer to him than anyone he'd ever known. His feelings for her were not anything remotely resembling a brotherly affection or defensiveness, nor were they restricted to simple friendship and protection.

She was a beautiful woman, anyone should have noticed that, and he certainly had. Her beauty was not the obvious sort that engendered flourished admiration, but a rarer type; a natural beauty that took time and exploration to properly appreciate. Yet once it was brought to light, it was impossible to forget or ignore.

And somehow, her beauty improved with every exposure to it.

Camden swallowed now as he imagined it, imagined how she might look coming in tonight, imagined those blue eyes meeting his and seeing the sweet innocence and insecurities swirling there, though she had nothing to fear. Seeking approval and permission, though she held all the power. Daring to reveal that impish, mischievous side of her that so few knew about.

Her lips growing into a smile, parting slightly when she listened, tugging at each other when she was lost in thought…

Saints above, he was standing here in his sister's house dwelling on the suddenly tempting lips of Prudence Westfall.

Madness. Absolute madness.

"She's here!" Lydia cried, nearly dancing in her place.

Chadwick put a hand to his wife's back. "Gently, love. Miss Westfall will likely be anxious. Mustn't overwhelm her."

Camden shot him a grateful look, loving his sister's enthusiasm, but having the exact fears that Chadwick described.

Lydia nodded rapidly, folding her fingers together. "Right. Of course, you're right." She exhaled slowly, closing her eyes, and a wave of serenity seemed to fall over her. "Poise, calm, gentleness…"

Camden watched her, bemused. "Does that work?"

Lydia cracked an eye open and speared him with a look. "If it doesn't, I'll beat you over the head with a vase. That will help immeasurably."

He grinned at her and nodded, turning his attention to the door where Prue was now entering.

"Not one of the expensive vases, please," Chadwick murmured. "I'm quite fond of those."

Lydia snorted a surprised burst of giggles, and Camden swallowed the laughter rising in him with an awkward cough. Chadwick only smiled very politely.

"I'm s-so sorry," Prue told them all as she approached, her expression worried. "My mother would not s-stop talking, and I couldn't get away."

"It's all right," Camden replied with a smile, still coughing a little from his laughter. "Really, it's fine."

"Yes," Lydia giggled, "it is. We're just so glad you're here." She squeezed her eyes shut and clamped her lips together as she laughed further.

Prue's brow furrowed, a curious smile forming, and she looked at Chadwick, who sighed heavily. "I can't explain them, Miss Westfall. I can only apologize."

"No n-need," she assured him, looking at Camden once more.

He was still smiling at her, and it had nothing to do with laughing at Lydia or Chadwick.

Prue just made him smile.

"Shall we go in?" Lydia asked, looking between Camden and Prue with too much interest.

Camden offered Prue his arm, and she took it at once. "What was your mother blabbering on about?" he whispered, leaning close.

Prue smiled a little, though her neck and arms suddenly were riddled with gooseflesh. "Mr. Davies," she whispered back. "Apparently, I am not paying him enough attention."

Davies? Camden could have groaned but settled for shaking his head. Davies would never have done for Prue at all, and if her mother had any sense, she would have seen that straight away. If there was a desperation to have Prue married off, which he did not understand, surely there were better options.

"We're to have dinner with Mr. Davies and his mother next

week," Prue went on, "and I already have my instructions for what I am to wear."

"Oh?" he asked, only feeling a cursory interest. If her mother wanted her to look her best, she could have done no better than what Prue was wearing this evening. Had a white and blue sprigged muslin ever looked so perfect on anyone? It complimented her eyes and complexion so attractively, and her hair was so elegantly plaited and pinned…

Get it together, his more sensible side scolded.

Prue huffed a little and looked up at him with a smile. "I cannot tell you how pleased I am to be here."

Never mind.

He returned her smile. "Me, too." He stared a little too long, then cleared his throat. "Right, well, we can certainly do better than Mr. Davies. Lieutenant Henshaw is here, you know him. He'd suit you well. And Mr. Andrews, as well. I wasn't aware, but he knows Chadwick, so he is here tonight. That's two potential suitors already better than anyone who has tried for you, and you are already comfortable with them. What luck! We'll find you more suitable suitors in no time."

"What luck," Prue echoed faintly, averting her eyes, but smiling still.

She sounded as enthusiastic about them as he felt.

But she was nervous with suitors, so that was to be expected.

"Prue, darling," Lydia suddenly said, turning to them, "would you mind very much if I introduce you to a few people? If it's too much to ask, just say so. I don't want you to be uncomfortable."

Camden felt Prue stiffen, but then she smiled and seemed to relax. "Of c-course," she replied.

Without thinking, Camden covered Prue's hand and rubbed it gently.

Lydia wouldn't know how Prue's stammer indicated her nerves, but he did. The fact that Prue was willing to do this even with her nerves was something significant indeed.

Prue left Camden's side and went with Lydia, not even looking back at him once.

He watched her go, brow furrowed, mind jumbled. Away from

him, she was vulnerable. Anything could happen. There was no telling what might make her panic, and if he wasn't there…

He cleared his throat and moved off, heading straight for the beverages, grateful his sister and Chadwick had not scrimped on the food for this soirée of theirs.

He was going to need it.

Taking up position on that side of the room, he watched as Lydia introduced Prue to some of her friends, including Julia and Dart whom she already knew, and then let Prue wander away from her. Prue situated herself in a chair near the window, not looking in any way flustered, and smiled up at Lieutenant Henshaw as he came over.

Henshaw was a fine fellow, Camden actually rather enjoyed his company, but when Prue laughed, and Camden could hear the musical sound dancing across the room, he thought the man's face would have been an excellent target for punching.

As unreasonable as it was, he hoped Prue stammered in Henshaw's presence. He hoped it was a trial for him to endure her conversation. He hoped…

"I know that look. Who are we killing, and where are we hiding the body?"

Camden took a long drink of claret to avoid revealing anything to Dart as he came up next to him.

Dart looked where Camden's attention was focused and grunted softly. "Ah ha. The lieutenant would make a fine opponent for you. Excellent height, proper physique… You would have your work cut out for you."

"Shove off," Camden told him, now eyeing Andrews as he also went to Prue.

"Now, Andrews presents a different problem," Dart continued, settling in against the wall. "He doesn't have Henshaw's stature, but I'd wager he has speed."

Camden's hold on his drink tightened, seeing how Prue sat there between two viable candidates for her hand with only the faintest blush on her cheeks. "I'm fast, too," he muttered to his friend.

Dart chuckled. "You are, yes. But you rely on your instincts more than skill. It serves you well, but I have no problem imagining Andrews as being particularly well-trained. Works for the Foreign

to bind herself to me, but there is nothing to be done about it now."

"I trust she had her reasons."

Prue found herself looking over at Julia Dartmouth, whose deep auburn hair seemed to glisten in the light of the room as she spoke with animation to those around her. She was filled with confidence and energy, someone who attracted people to her with minimal effort. Her smile was warm and infectious, and it enabled anyone to feel as though they had known her for a lifetime.

What would it be like to have such power?

"Miss Westfall."

She looked up at Mr. Dartmouth, arranging her smile into something more believable.

"Yes?"

Mr. Dartmouth returned her smile with a gentle one of his own. "I'll have you know my wife likes you immensely, as well. And that was before Vale told us anything about you."

"What did he s-say?" she whispered, swallowing hard as her eyes went wide.

Mr. Dartmouth opened his mouth, then paused as his eyes rose a little. He smiled curiously, then gestured. "I think he's about to tell you."

Prue looked behind her to see Camden there, looking at her with an inscrutable expression.

"Take a turn with me?" he suggested, his voice low.

She nodded quickly and rose, turning to excuse herself, but Mr. Dartmouth had already left. She frowned after him, then turned back to Camden.

He smiled a little, then gestured the way, strolling in the opposite direction from where the others had gone. "I've been thinking, Prue," he mused.

She matched his pace and looked up at him. "About?"

"You," he said simply, his tone light. "I don't see any need for you to marry."

Prue bit the inside of her lip as her heart skipped a beat. "No?"

Camden shook his head. "Truly, there is no need. You have a fortune regardless of your marital state, and it is entirely probable that with your marriage, your husband would gain that fortune himself.

The property would be yours, but what is the property without the funds to manage it? Unmarried, you are independent and free, able to retain control of your assets."

She listened carefully, trying not to let the words feel like a lash upon her soul. It was all so business-like, so cold and impersonal. As if the only reason anyone should marry was for security or convenience. As if matters of the heart had little significance. As if he had no personal interest in any of it.

He was advising her rather like a solicitor would.

"It's all so much work," Camden went on. "This courting business, I mean. Too many suitors who just want that fortune and have little respect for you. And if we found you decent suitors, you would still lose the fortune to them, and what if their affections changed? Not a fair prospect for a sweet girl like you."

Why was he doing this? Why was he talking to her in this distant, formal tone? It was nothing like the gentle, caring man who had held her in his arms after an attack until she was better. Her Camden was not here, and a stranger was in his place.

And yet, she felt the warmth of him, the vibrancy in his step, the heady pull of his essence beside her.

Her throat burned with unspoken emotion.

"But I want to be married," she heard herself whisper.

Camden's step stuttered, shuffling a bit. "Do you?"

Prue nodded, her cheeks flushing. "Not for security, or for any sort of status, but because I would love to run my own household. I would love to have children and take tea with the other married ladies. And how much better would it be to marry a man I was fond of, someone who wouldn't find my difficulties so trying, someone to grow old with, raise our children together..." Her voice faded out, and she swallowed twice. "I don't imagine finding love, but a lifetime of companionship in that way would be... most pleasant, I think."

Camden said nothing as he walked beside her, his brow slightly furrowed.

She had said too much; she had gone too far. He didn't want to hear about her fancies, he was only trying to do right by her for the sake of duty and honor. There was nothing...

"You should have that."

Now, it was Prue whose steps stuttered, and she looked at him in surprise. "What?"

He nodded to himself. "You should have it. Everything you just said, it's the perfect ideal. And you should have it." He suddenly shook his head, stopping. "I can't do this."

Prue's heart slammed against several ribs, and her breath caught. "What?"

His eyes met hers, and she saw a strange sort of turmoil in them. "I can't do this. Any of it."

Her bruised heart threatened to crumble into pieces, and she prayed she could remain composed somehow.

"Prue, I want to court you for real. Not for show."

She blinked slowly, unaware of any heart or thought at all. "Why?" she breathed, unsure if she meant why or what or how. He couldn't be serious, he couldn't mean…

He reached out and stroked her cheek gently, his eyes dark and intense and filled with emotion. "Because this isn't something I can pretend any longer. Not when it's real."

Prue looked around quickly, stunned that they seemed to have walked out of the room and into a quiet corridor. She looked back up at Camden, her breath hitching as his thumb stroked her jaw. "W-when what's real?"

"My feelings," he murmured, seeming unaware of the effect his fingers had against her skin. "For you."

Her knees started to quiver as his touch created a heat that began to spread across the terrain of her body. "Oh…"

"May I court you, Prudence Westfall?" he asked as his hand cradled her face. "Just to see what happens when it's real?"

She nodded the most pathetic, jerky sort of nod. "N-no promises, th-though."

He chuckled softly, the sound sending more ripples across her skin. "What am I going to do with you, Prue?" he murmured, his fingers wandering to her ear, her jaw, very gentle and light, and stoking a fire within her.

"I… I… I d-don't kn-know w-what you m-mean," she managed, the stammer worse than it had ever been with him as her breath and sense struggled to keep up.

He noticed and cupped her face gently with both hands. "Nervous, sweetheart? Why?"

Prue tried to think of a reason, but all she could say was, "Y-you."

Camden smiled a warm and tender smile. "That's more like it."

He bent his head and pressed his lips to hers, slow and lingering and tender, caressing her untutored lips until they relaxed against his. Prue's fingers wandered to his coat, flailing weakly for balance, and then grasping the fabric as she felt herself responding, somehow finding her way amidst the deluge of sensation.

Camden nibbled at her lips with steady patience, drawing her closer and closer, sending her senses reeling as they swirled under his influence. She could only hold onto him, trembling in a sea she did not understand, wishing for more yet fearing the same. But he was there, steadying her, guiding her, kissing her with reverence, her own lips eager but untrained.

There was so much… *so much…*

She sighed weakly against him, and he pulled back with one final, grazing kiss.

Dreamily, Prue opened her eyes and stared into his dark ones, wondering that she could breathe at all after that.

Camden smiled, seeming a bit breathless himself. "What shy creature?" he whispered.

Prue laughed once, and, finding that impish side, tugged on his coat once more.

And Camden kissed her again.

Chapter Seventeen

Truth will out, they say. Well, out with the truth, I say, and let the gossip commence!

-The Spinster Chronicles, 2 January 1818

The true courtship of one Prudence Westfall by one Camden Vale was far more enjoyable than the pretend one had been, which surprised Camden to no end.

Who would have thought that he would have enjoyed courting in earnest?

It didn't occur to him tell anyone that their courtship was not for show any longer, for the people that knew of that arrangement would find out for themselves soon enough, given the familiarity they now embraced with each other. The public had never known about the pretend nature of the first, so they would not know any differently.

Only he and Prue knew that there was no game any longer.

This was real.

Terrifying, nerve-wracking, and delightfully real.

They'd only been at it for a week, and already he was feeling far and away lighter, happier, more fulfilled. It was impossible for him to do anything but smile when he was around Prue, to look anywhere else, to think of anything else...

And she was somehow more remarkable than he'd ever imagined.

She was playful, even flirtatious with him at times, and he felt more knocked about by it each and every time. She looked at him from across the room, her eyes a mixture of amusement and understanding, which mystified him, as he wasn't quite sure what they were understanding. They both felt it, whatever it was, but its definition was lost amidst the melee of everything else.

It didn't matter; not now.

He was just going to enjoy this time with her, this shockingly alive sensation he felt all the time, and ride it out for as long as he could.

And tonight, he was going to introduce her to his friends. Properly.

Oh, she'd met them, certainly, but in company. Other people had taken away from the time they could have spent getting to know each other well, and he wanted something more intimate and enjoyable for all of them.

Another night at the theater.

Prue adored the theater, for whatever reason, and it was easy enough to arrange a box. He'd invited the Turners, the Dartmouths, and Lady Edith as a comfort measure for Prue, but Lady Edith had declined with all politeness.

He'd gotten to know the rest of the Spinsters remarkably well for such a short period of time, but Lady Edith was another matter. She was almost never seen in Society, and so Camden never saw her unless she had chosen to attend a small event. She was the same spirited woman he'd met that day at Prue's home, which did not account for her lack of presence elsewhere.

He'd have asked Prue about it, but he tended to forget a great deal when he was with her.

At the moment, she was on her way to the theater in the company of his sister and Chadwick. He'd have gone to get her himself, but Lydia had assured him that it was absolutely improper for him to do so, and she, as chaperone, would see to it.

Camden wasn't entirely sure how effective his sister would be as a chaperone on any given day, but there was no arguing with her.

He only wanted to be the one to greet Prue, to see her face, to catch the telltale glimpses that all was not well. She might be too collected to give those away when she arrived, and he would never know.

Mrs. Westfall was growing more and more anxious about Prue's chances with Mr. Davies and had sent her to the modiste this week for more gowns, more finery, more anything that she could get. Prue had dutifully gone, taking Amelia Perry with her, and Camden had happened upon them both there. It was a painstaking process, and one that he would undoubtedly avoid in the future, but he and Amelia had managed to turn it into a more comedic opportunity for Prue. He had no idea what she had actually come away with, nor did it actually matter.

What mattered was Prue's state of mind and state of being.

Eliza Howard had been remarkably reserved of late, and they all wondered at it. There were no indications that she was in any way acting against Prue, and she certainly did not consider Camden a viable suitor, which was undoubtedly why she had never tried to turn him against her.

She would have had a devil of a time managing that.

Prue was an angel, and no one would ever be able to convince him otherwise.

And she kissed with an enthusiasm that weakened him.

He'd never kissed anyone as innocent as Prue before, but it seemed the greatest misfortune of his life now. Not that any woman would have managed it with the same sweetness that she had, and it would have made him the cad that everybody presumed he was, but it was a very revealing experience. He'd taken great care not to overwhelm her, knowing how new this all would be for her, but the truth of the matter was that this was all very new for him, as well.

No kiss had ever tasted that way. No woman had ever distracted him this much. No dreams had ever been so poignant as the dreams he had of Prue.

He'd wanted to kiss her every minute of every day since that night at his sister's, but he'd only managed two since then.

Patience was a virtue, but it was also a torment.

If kisses had been food, he would be starving by now.

He paced in the theater now, his mouth dry, his head throbbing. He'd seen Prue this morning, for heaven's sake, as they had taken a morning walk together, and yet he felt as though it had been a lifetime.

"Is he creating a furrow for planting?" the bemused, lilting voice of Mariah Turner asked. "I don't know what would grow in carpets."

"Cornflowers?" Julia Dartmouth suggested.

A tsking sound answered her. "Those are hardy plants, to be sure, but I doubt they could grow in the London climate." Phillip's voice chuckled a little. "Any more and he'll have dug himself under the Thames."

"I'll sink you in it in a moment," Camden growled, turning to face the elegant ensemble behind him.

The ladies both wore shades of blue, Mariah's vibrant and bold, Julia's muted and elegant. Their husbands were perfect counterparts in their eveningwear, but no one would pay attention to them when the ladies provided such a picture.

Camden bowed to the group. "Glad you could make it. Thank you for coming."

Dart and Phillip exchanged stunned looks. "He just thanked us," Phillip pointed out.

"And was polite," Dart added.

"He's ill."

"Dying, probably."

"Oh, stop," Julia chided, rapping her husband in the chest. "He's fine."

Mariah scoffed softly, smirking at Camden. "Not at all. He's nervous."

Everyone looked at him, and he scowled at her. "Must you be so perceptive, Mariah?"

"I say that all the time," Phillip sighed.

"Don't be nervous," Julia soothed with a kind smile. "Miss Westfall will be charming, no need to fear for her anxieties."

"I don't think it's her anxieties he's concerned about," Dart murmured in a tone Camden barely caught.

Camden clasped his hands behind his back, exhaling slowly. "Breathe in, breathe out…" he sighed.

Phillip cocked his head. "What was that?"

"Nothing." Camden shook his head and started to pace again.

"…and *then* he decided it was an opportune moment to tell Molly he could out-climb her in the trees behind the house. I've never seen him fall so hard in my life, and he used to fall quite a lot."

Camden turned to face the traitorous sound of his sister's voice, eyes wide.

Lydia had Prue by the arm and was waving with great enthusiasm as she told the story that would have her killed shortly. Pity, his sister looked rather well in her new, green silk.

Chadwick followed the ladies, trying very hard not to smile, and failing. He might have to die, too, as he would try to avenge Lydia once Camden had wrung her neck.

Camden looked at Prue then, and the beating of his heart faded into a faint cadence in his head.

He'd said she was an angel; now she was dressed as one. A muslin of pure white, flowing like the clouds on a breeze, and the barest hint of gold detailing enhanced everything that ought to have been enhanced, taking her appearance from ethereal to absolutely celestial. She wore a simple gold chain around her slender throat. White and gold ribbons in her hair completed the look, elegant adornments an angel might have borne on earth. And the smile on her lips…

Well, it would have given unholy temptation to any saint, before or after sainthood.

"Breathe, Vale," Dart muttered as he came to one side. "She'd not enjoy being courted by a corpse."

Camden released an embarrassingly loud gust of air, but no one paid any attention to him.

How could they? There was an angel among them.

Prue looked up at him then, and the twinkle in her eyes dissolved whatever remained of his knees. Her smile spread, and she dipped her chin at him.

He swallowed and did the same.

"Here we are at last," Lydia said on a heavy sigh. "So sorry for the tardiness. Miranda Sterling's carriage took up half the way, and then she just *had* to flutter all over Prue."

Camden and Prue both smiled. "She does that," they said together, then laughed at their unison.

"Well, that was adorable," Chadwick said with a look at both of them.

Lydia elbowed him sharply, but he didn't seem to feel it.

Odd. Camden seemed to recall Lydia being in possession of some very sharp elbows.

"Do you know everyone, Prue?" Lydia asked, her attack on her husband forgotten.

Prue shook her head, revealing her shyness at last.

"I know you know the Dartmouths," Lydia said, waving her fan at them. They bowed and curtseyed accordingly. "This is Mr. Phillip Turner and his wife, Mariah. Very old friends, though not as old as Dart."

"I'm not that old," Dart protested plaintively, earning himself a sharp look from his wife.

Lydia rolled her eyes dramatically. "You don't have to be acquainted with Dart, my dear. His wife is much better. Mr. Turner, on the other hand, you should know."

Phillip bowed with a broad smile. "I'm flattered, Lydia."

Mariah scoffed again. "I'd say she should know you to be forewarned, not for any sort of privilege."

Camden eyed Prue as she watched the couples interact, and her smile seemed to be quivering at the edges, as though she wanted to laugh but did not.

That was a good sign.

"It's a p-pleasure to meet you," she told the Turners, curtseying. She turned to Dart and Julia. "And very n-nice to see you again."

Her stammer had been there, but it was hardly noticeable. A surge of pride swelled within Camden, and he tried to tamp it down with as much cynicism as he could muster.

Today, that was not much.

"Shall we go up?" Chadwick asked the group. "At this rate, they'll start without us, and Lydia cannot bear missing anything."

They all laughed, even Lydia, and proceeded towards the seats, Lydia taking her husband's arm at last.

Prue waited for them to pass, and Camden came to her, his eyes raking over her.

"Good evening," he managed, his voice rough.

She blushed, and it made him smile. "Good evening."

He offered her his arm, and she took it, her eyes lowering to his cravat.

His shy little thing. It was adorable and sweet, and it tickled somewhere in the center of his chest every time it was brought out.

"How are you?" he asked, grateful to be alone with her for a few moments.

Prue exhaled slowly. "Exceedingly glad to be away from home."

He winced a little. "Your mother?"

She nodded once. "It's getting worse. There are rumors that Charles Davies is courting Hope Charteress."

"That wouldn't be wise," Camden commented as they walked on. "She can't recite the alphabet without help."

Prue snickered into her gloved hand, her eyes squeezing shut.

"They'd have children who would have to be taught how to sneeze," he went on as if it were a great concern, "and might not be able to walk in a straight line without direction, guidance, and someone to follow."

"Stop," Prue wheezed, laughing harder. "Oh, Cam, stop…"

He grinned down at her. "Too far?"

She clamped down on her lips. "Probably," she eventually managed. "I should feel guilty."

"But you don't."

She gave him a sly look. "But I don't."

Lord, the things she could do to him with a look. He suddenly felt as though he were the one who stammered, and she the one to steady him.

"Four things, Cam," Prue murmured, still smiling in that way that drove him mad.

"Four things?" he repeated. "Are you nervous?"

She shook her head. "Curious."

Curious, was she? Well then…

Four things. Four things… At the moment, it would be four things about her, and that wouldn't have done at all.

He cleared his throat and looked around quickly, taking in the tapestry covered alcove they walked past on their path to the boxes. "You see those alcoves?"

She looked, and nodded, her brow knitting in confusion.

"Some people," he murmured, lowering his voice, "find ways to sneak into one. Usually intrepid couples, mind you. If I were so inclined, I might venture there with you. Then I would kiss those sweet lips of yours over and over and over. And then I'd kiss your cheeks, your eyes, and your throat… All while the opera played on, and no one would know. Four things to kiss, and such a length of time to do so."

Prue's cheeks were scarlet now, and her breathing was as ragged as if she had run a great distance. She swallowed hard, her eyes going wide, and she put her hand to her throat, looking away.

"That was simply four things I thought you ought to know," he said, feeling a trifle ashamed of himself for making her embarrassed. It had been a stupid idea, telling her exactly what he'd been thinking, what he was imagining… She didn't need any further reason to believe he was not right for her, but he'd just given her several.

Prue swallowed again, her hand still at her throat.

Camden scrambled for anything to say, any thought to put her at ease, any new topic. He couldn't take it back. That would be a great perjury, and he refused to let her believe he didn't feel that drawn to her. But what to say…?

"It's for the best that we're in company," he settled on, his pulse racing anxiously.

She looked over at him, her eyes not quite reaching his. "Oh?"

He nodded sagely, relieved that she was at least speaking to him. "It's not wise to be alone with me. I've been told I'm no gentleman."

"Nobody told me that," she told him, her color beginning to recede.

He snorted. "They should have."

Out of the corner of his eyes, he saw Prue smile a little. "That would require them to tell me anything."

He chuckled at that, and then the realization struck him that Prue hadn't stammered after his outrageous comments.

Not once.

"Now I wish we were alone," Prue whispered beside him, sighing softly.

Camden lifted his eyes to the painted ceiling and prayed for the strength to endure.

Prue couldn't believe what she had said, now that she was seated in their box and waiting for the opera to start.

Of course, she couldn't believe what Camden had said either, but the picture he had painted in her mind was now permanently etched there.

And she wanted it.

Her cheeks flushed with heat at her admission. It was not proper, and it was not right, and it was not something one admitted out loud. She ought to have kept her mouth shut. She couldn't encourage him, or this, or her own wild imaginations.

Still, if he wanted to sneak her away to kiss in an alcove…

She shook her head firmly. No, that was enough. She was a spinster, she reminded herself, and men like him did not actually want to take spinsters into alcoves, particularly if they were shy and stammering and didn't even know how to kiss properly.

Camden did not seem the sort of man who said things he did not mean, but she didn't know for sure. He had been truthful with her from the start, she thought, and he'd given her no reason to suspect anything otherwise.

The fact that she was living in a sort of dream world these days, with his attentions and looks and kisses, muddled all of that.

Who was Camden Vale really?

Who had he been?

Would he actually want her?

Could he?

"May I sit beside you, Miss Westfall?" Mrs. Turner asked gently, coming around to the front of Prue's seat.

Prue smiled weakly and nodded. "Please."

She sat and smiled at the stage. "I've always loved the theater. I can't even say why, as I've only lived in London as a married woman. But I imagined great theatricals at home, and I would be a grand star of the stage."

Prue smiled at the thought. "Where are you from?"

"Sussex," came the soft reply. She turned to glance at Prue ruefully. "My father was a ship captain. I was raised by him and my four brothers, so you can only imagine how ladylike I was."

"I've never been to Sussex," Prue murmured aloud, her gaze turning distant.

Mrs. Turner covered her hand gently, and Prue brought her attention back to her. Mrs. Turner smiled warmly. "We'll go for a visit." She winked and sat back. "You can see my very first stage."

"I never had a stage," Prue admitted, looking at the one before them. "I would be terrified to even pretend at anything like that."

Mrs. Turner chuckled, and it was a warm, gentle sound. "Oh, I pretended all sorts of things. I would have been dreadful, though. I cannot bear criticism. Which is why I clashed with my husband so furiously when we first met."

Prue looked at her in surprise. Mrs. Turner caught it and laughed again. "I was a right ruffian, make no mistake," she told her. "Not as far gone as I could have been, thank goodness, but certainly not the proper woman I am now."

A soft snort behind them made them both turn, and Mr. Turner was staring at his wife with a sardonic look, smirking to himself.

She narrowed her eyes at him, then blew him a kiss, which made him smile. Then she turned back to Prue. "It was all very serendipitous, and I won't get into details, but we came to London with my brothers, and I went to my very first real theatrical…" She sighed fondly, meeting Prue's eyes. "That's how I met Camden, actually."

Now Prue's interest was piqued. "Indeed?"

Mrs. Turner nodded quickly, her smile turning wry. "We met all of Phillip's friends. All three of them."

"I beg your pardon?" her husband protested.

"Beg away," she quipped, keeping her eyes on Prue.

Prue smiled at the easy banter, finding she ached for such ease, warmth, and fun herself.

"Camden is a rascal," Mrs. Turner said bluntly, keeping her voice down, "but the sort of rascal one loves rather than abhors. He's not nearly as wicked as anybody says, you know."

Prue glanced over at Camden, who was conversing with Mr.

Dartmouth and Mr. Chadwick. "I wondered about that."

"Oh, no one would be friends with him if he was that bad," Mrs. Turner scoffed, waving a hand. "He's difficult, to be sure, but only because he is a complicated man. I had a trying time of it with him once."

"Mariah," her husband warned softly.

She turned a little and smiled at him. "It's all right. I've asked Camden, and he said I could share this."

Mr. Turner nodded and sat back, folding his arms.

Prue looked at Mrs. Turner with interest, wondering what she could possibly have to share.

"I had made a friend in my short time in London," Mrs. Turner told Prue in a low tone. "Anne Bennett. Charming girl, very pretty and quite accomplished, but without any of the airs one like her usually had. After Phillip and I married and returned from our wedding trip, I returned to London to hear that she had been compromised by Camden Vale, ruined beyond any hope of repair, and that he would not marry her."

Prue's eyes went wide. Such a rumor, even if it were not true, could easily ruin anyone. It was astonishing that Camden had not been forced to marry her.

Mrs. Turner smiled a little. "I was irate, as you can probably imagine. I didn't know Camden well at all, and I knew Anne would never have done something so foolish without certain promises. So, I marched myself down to Camden's house, where Phillip already was, and I punched Camden right across the face." She grinned briefly. "My brothers taught me well."

Prue returned her smile, but hesitantly.

"Phillip was aghast," Mrs. Turner added with a laugh. "He said, 'Mariah! We'd already settled things!' And I replied, 'I hadn't.' And Camden looked up at me from the ground, not even put out, and said, 'Are you settled now?'" Mrs. Turner laughed to herself now, shaking her head. "I told him 'Only a little'." She sobered and gave Prue a very earnest look. "He had nothing to do with Anne's situation. He wasn't involved in any way. Not even close. But revealing the truth of the situation was not going to help anything, and Camden knew that. So, he let the rumors press on, knowing that he was not at fault, and that Anne was being taken care of as best as she could be, under the circumstances. It was better, in his mind, that he be painted as a villain than make matters worse."

Prue's throat tightened, and she fought to swallow, wishing she was brave enough to ask what really happened. But it was not her place to ask, nor was it Mrs. Turner's to tell. It was not their story.

But Camden...

"I've loved Camden dearly ever since," Mrs. Turner finished, looking over at him with a fond smile. "He tries my patience, and everyone else's, as evidenced by the rift between him and Phillip, and he and Dart, before this. He will always choose distance when emotions are too high for him to manage. When he fought with them, he chose distance. And when he was ready, he came back."

Prue watched Camden as he laughed at something Mr. Chadwick said, seeming so much more at ease than he had been when she'd first met him. He was a complicated, confusing, captivating man, and she couldn't fathom such a man wanting to be with her in any way. There was so much to him. So much depth and feeling and heart, so much humor and wit, so much...

So very much.

And she wanted it. She wanted him.

She swallowed uneasily and brought her suddenly misty eyes back to Mrs. Turner, who was smiling at her. "He's one of the good ones, isn't he?"

Mr. Turner leaned forward and put a hand on his wife's shoulder. "My dear Miss Westfall, take it from me. He is one of the best." His smile turned crooked. "But don't tell him I said that."

She shook her head quickly. "Never."

Mrs. Turner laughed and looked over her shoulder. "Julia, come over here and help me regale Miss Westfall with stories of our husbands and Camden and their misspent youth!"

"Coming!" Julia laughed, moving towards them.

"Me too!" Lydia cried. "I've got plenty!"

The men groaned in chorus, and the women laughed.

Mrs. Turner giggled and covered Prue's hand with her own. "First things first, call me Mariah."

Prue nodded and glanced over at Camden, who was watching

her, smiling her very favorite smile.

Her breath caught, and then, very slowly, she returned it.

Chapter Eighteen

How we react to challenges and situations is indicative of our very nature. Take care, therefore, to respond in a manner befitting you. Overreaction is not wise, no reaction is not helpful, but a perfect reaction is rare, indeed.

-The Spinster Chronicles, 27 March 1818

Prue heard the frantic steps in the hall before she normally would have. Sprawled out as she was on her bed, reading upside down, she paused, listening closer.

No one was supposed to be home. Her mother was on a rare outing with her sister, and Camden had walked with her already that morning.

That was one of the main reasons she had been spending this time in her room and on her bed. He'd found a secluded spot in the garden away from her mother's view and stolen a kiss, which Prue had been only too happy to allow. Even now, her lips tingled with the memory of his on hers, and her heart skipped in delight.

He held her hand as they walked, entwining their fingers, sometimes taking her gloves off to hold her bare hand with his own, and the heat that swirled between them on those occasions was almost unbearable. He was adoring, sweet, kind, teasing, and encouraging, everything she had never expected to find in any man, let alone in one like him.

And when they were with his friends, he was droll, sarcastic, engaging, and sometimes scowling, always finding a way to make the others laugh. In those times, he never forgot Prue, whether it be frequent looks and smiles, a hand at her back, holding her hand under the table, or even sending her little notes via footman, as he had done last night at his sister's dinner.

She'd never felt this giddy anticipation, this helpless smile that was a near-constant accessory, and this deep, strong connection to another soul. She felt confident with him, safe and strong, and was growing less and less fearful, though she still had her moments. The Spinsters had noticed Prue's change, but they weren't talking about it. They only smiled or giggled, which made her blush, which made them giggle more, and the cycle repeated.

The only one not pleased with all of this was her mother, who had not barred Camden's courtship, but her criticisms of Prue had come back in full force.

They hadn't seen Eliza in some time, which had been a blessed relief, but it concerned her mother a great deal. Perhaps she had been listening to the malicious lies Eliza had been spreading about Prue's being simple and unable to properly communicate with anyone, or whatever it was that Eliza had turned it all into. Prue had lost track. With Camden courting her, the throng of potential admirers had decreased significantly, and she was ever so grateful.

Still, the footsteps reaching her ears sounded harsh and strident, and if the sound of shaking beads were any indication, it was her mother, returned early from her errand with her sister.

Prue sat up quickly, snapping shut her book and setting it on the nightstand. She brushed her fingers through her unbound hair and waited, hoping her mother would pass by.

The door to her bedchamber swung open, crashing against the wall with a loud thump.

Her mother stood in the doorway, eyes large and wild, breathing unsteady, face as colored as Prue's had ever been. Her feathered hat was awry, the knot of the ribbons tight and decidedly askew, while strands of her graying hair dangled out of their pins. She trembled with rage, the beads around her neck and sewn into her bodice rattling anxiously.

Her dark eyes took in Prue on her bed, her glower increasing.

"Mother...?" Prue asked hesitantly, sliding from the bed.

"Don't speak," her mother clipped, her voice thin. "Don't."

Prue swallowed, nodding once.

"Just listen," her mother added, her tone rising in pitch as though Prue had dared to reply.

Prue waited, her hands balling up nervously at her sides.

Her mother inhaled briefly, but very audibly. "Do you know where I have just been?"

Prue nodded.

"With your aunt. In Bond Street. She said she needed a new gown."

Oh dear. Had Aunt Howard gone down in measurements while her mother had increased? It had happened before, and always put her in a foul temper. Nothing quite this severe, but perhaps it had been a trying day.

Her mother's lip curled into an almost smile, though her widened, crazed eyes negated any warmth in it. "Do you know what the gown was being commissioned for, Prudence?"

"N-no," Prue stammered, mentally wincing at the sound.

As she feared, her mother inhaled sharply again. "Don't stammer! And don't answer!"

She knew that. She knew better, but she couldn't help it.

"The dress my sister needed," her mother went on, her voice growing even more reedy, "was for a wedding. Whose wedding?"

Oh no… Oh *no*…

Her mother nodded slowly, her wild eyes fixed on Prue with too much intensity. "Your cousin, Eliza."

As Prue only had one cousin, that was not a necessary clarification. But she was not about to do anything to further agitate her mother.

"And to whom," her mother went on, practically spitting her words now, "do you think that your cousin Eliza, your beautiful, kind, accomplished, perfect cousin is going to be wed?"

Prue stood there, frozen, terrified to suggest anyone at all.

Her mother sneered slowly, dangerously. "Mr. Charles Davies, Prudence. Mr. Charles Davies. The man who at one time was very particularly keen on marrying you."

Prue's jaw dropped, and she sank onto the foot of her bed, her mind whirling.

Eliza had taken the man who had been pursuing Prue, the only one with any potential at all, in anyone's eyes but Prue's, and not only twisted him against courting Prue in any way but had also managed to turn him towards herself.

It was the perfect manipulation.

If Prue had had any interest in Mr. Davies at all, it would have been crushing.

"Do you know, Prudence," her mother continued, her hands tightening, "how many people have congratulated me on the prospect of Mr. Davies for a son-in-law? How many people thought he would make you a fine husband? Do you know how many people I have discussed your attachment to him with?"

She'd done *what?* There was no attachment with Prue and Mr. Davies! There had never been anything but a short acquaintance and the shared experience of Tinley House! He had never made any comments or suggestions about pursuing a courtship, and her mother had been spreading that around? Prue was courting Camden! *He* was her suitor!

If people thought that Mr. Davies had an interest in Prue and that she had some hope of an engagement, the news of Eliza's betrothal to him would reflect shamefully on Prue. She would be pitied for her disappointment. She would be an embarrassment in Society.

No one would believe that she had never wanted him. Why shouldn't she? He was moderately wealthy and respectable, with good connections, a fine house, and she was a spinster with a fortune she had no business inheriting. She ought to have been grateful for his attentions.

Would they look at her with Camden now and find something wanting?

"Prudence, you have shamed me," her mother said, quaking where she stood. "You have shamed me, and you have shamed this family. He was yours for the taking! He was there, in the palm of your worthless hand! His mother and I spent hours discussing your future, all the things you and he could accomplish with your fortune and his intellect. He. Wanted. You."

Prue winced as the words fell upon her like a lash, stinging her skin, turning her embarrassment into complete humiliation. "I'm s-sorry…" she whispered, her throat clogging.

Her mother released a screeching growl. "Stop stammering! Stand up. Stand up, you stupid, simple, worthless girl!"

A weak sob escaped Prue, her chest aching with its cry, and she stood, holding onto her bedpost.

"Come here!"

Shaking, steeling herself, Prue took the three steps towards her mother.

"Look at me."

She opened her eyes and met her mother's livid countenance, her eyes filled with hatred, disgust, and shame.

Her mother shook her head very slowly. "You are worthless, Prudence. A waste of fortune and effort. No one will want you now."

The cold, flat tone of the words did not make them any less painful, and Prue found herself trembling, nearly swaying with the effort of remaining upright.

"No one," her mother insisted, her voice rising in volume and timbre. "No one will want you now. Do you see what you have done? Do you see?"

A hand cracked against Prue's cheek, jolting her and making her stumble back. "M-m-mother!" she protested.

"Don't stammer!" her mother screeched, backhanding her with the same hand, the rings on her fingers cutting into Prue's skin, the force sending her into the chest of drawers. "I wish to God that I'd had a mute child instead of a bleating goat of a daughter! I wash my hands of you."

Prue whimpered, hands coming to her stinging, burning face, cradling her cheeks as tears began to fall upon the tender skin.

"Stand before me, child," her mother snapped.

Once more, she moved before her mother, her lower lip and jaw quivering.

Her mother shook her head slowly. "Your father would be ashamed of you, Prudence Westfall. Ashamed." She slapped her one more time, then turned on her heel and stomped out of the room.

Prue waited for the footsteps to fade in the distance, and then let her knees give way as she crumpled to the floor, covering her face with her hands and sobbing. She stifled the sounds as best she could, not wanting to give her mother any additional reason to punish her, but she couldn't contain them completely.

She curled up on the floor and cried. She cried for her mother, who had never been happy with Prue; for Camden, who had no idea what he was caught up in; for Mr. Davies, who would be married to a vindictive wife who did not feel anything for him. She cried for the shame her family would feel, for her inability to stand up to her mother, for her shyness, her stammer, the inheritance that had ruined her life…

And then she cried for her father, who wasn't here to hold her until she was better.

Eventually, her tears had all dried up, and an overwhelming weariness set in. She was supposed to go to Izzy's and meet the other Spinsters, but she could not bear to see them like this. She couldn't tell them, couldn't show them…

She pulled herself up and sat at her toilette, looking into the glass.

The cuts on her cheek were not deep, but they were visible and were beginning to bruise. Her other cheek would bruise a little, but not nearly as bad. The blood was sluggish now, and a small bit trickled down her cheek, echoing the tracks of her tears.

Prue reached for the bowl and pitcher of water she used at night, poured a small amount, and dabbed a cloth in it. She winced as she sponged the blood away, the cuts stinging in protest.

Her eyes burned, but she refused to cry more. She reached up and rang for a servant, and a maid was there rather swiftly. Prue looked up at her and saw the pitying expression.

"I need you to send three notes," she told the maid. "One to Isabella Lambert, one to Miranda Sterling, and one to Mr. Camden Vale."

Camden was pacing again. It was beginning to worry him how frequently he was doing this now; how familiar pacing had become for him.

But at this moment, there was nothing else to do.

A missive had come to him hours ago from Prue, but not in her hand. Why she shouldn't write in her own hand, he couldn't know, but a feeling of dread had welled up within him.

I must see you tonight in private at Miranda Sterling's ball. I will meet you there. Do not come here.

Recalling the words now sent a chill down his spine. He knew the moment he had entered Miranda's home that something was not right. While the other guests proceeded into the ballroom, a servant had nodded at him and beckoned for him to follow, though Miranda was nowhere in sight.

Now, he paced in a study, his thoughts veering into terrible, tremulous places.

He'd almost ridden to Prue's home a dozen times earlier, but her warning to not come kept him there. He wished to God he hadn't waited. He should have gone, he should have ignored it, should have saved her from whatever this was.

Whoever said ignorance was bliss was clearly out of their mind. Ignorance was madness.

The door to the study opened, and Miranda entered, dressed for the evening's entertainment.

"Miranda," Camden said with relief, striding over to her. "Thank God. What…?"

Miranda held up a hand, her expression somber. "I received a note a few hours ago from Prue. She asked if she might prevail upon me to invite her to my home early before the ball, and that once she was here, she would need my help. Of course, I accepted, but… Camden, darling, you need to prepare yourself. You need to be steady. Can you?"

"Good lord, Miranda," he breathed. "You're terrifying me."

She smiled sadly. "It's not as bad as you are imagining, I assure you. But it is bad enough. She wanted you to see her in private before the ball, just in case."

Camden swallowed with some difficulty. "In case what?"

Miranda watched him for a moment, then sighed and turned for the door, cracking it enough to reach a hand out. "Come here, love."

Camden watched as she gently led Prue into the room, and for a moment, he was distracted by the pure white dress, free of embellishment or finery, tied with only a thick white ribbon under the bodice. A matching ribbon was in her hair, accentuating its shade, a pale chestnut color that he had never quite seen anywhere else. She was lovely and fresh, her wide blue eyes paler than usual, and more striking.

He didn't see…

Prue saw the moment he noticed the color of her complexion and her eyes lowered.

Camden stepped forward slowly, his eyes trained on her face. She was pale, paler than she should have been, paler than natural for her. And yet her cheeks bore some color. A rosy shade, expertly applied, but again, not natural for Prue. No one would know with a cursory look, but he, who could have drawn her face from memory, and had done time and time again in the privacy of his home, knew better.

Why would she have need for cosmetics?

Her right cheek caught his attention first. Along her cheekbone was a thin mark, not hidden at all by the cosmetics, and when he looked carefully, he could see darker colors around it.

Bruising.

He reached two fingers up to touch the mark, and Prue winced silently with the faint pressure. The discoloration spread across the entire cheek, nearly to her eye, and while not enough to make anyone gasp in horror or recoil, it was certainly enough.

Camden's lungs constricted, his chest aching, his stomach in knots as he took Prue's chin gently in hand and turned her face towards the light.

Bruising on the other cheek, though not to the same degree as the first.

It was a masterful job of disguising the injuries. Cosmetics were not quite the thing anymore, but one still occasionally saw them. And anything as well done as this would certainly not draw comment.

All these rather logical thoughts passed through Camden's mind rapidly as his emotions took a moment to fully engage.

He had been in enough fights to recognize injuries sustained by blows when he saw them.

And Prue had them.

Anger roared to life within him, and his hold on her chin tightened, her eyes widening at the pressure. He dropped his hand quickly and turned away with a hoarse growl. He shoved his hands into his hair, gripping the strands tightly. The tide of rage and fury surged, giving him the desire to tear the room to shreds, to roar with indignation, to rip off the garb of a proper gentleman and take to the streets to fight whomever he could get his hands on. Anything to relieve this pain, this clawing need to lash out, to protect and defend…

"Cam…" Prue whispered, the sound breaking, soft as it was.

He gasped as though he had never breathed in his life, his lungs wracking in their efforts to breathe and find calm.

"Cam," Prue said again, a little stronger.

He exhaled slowly, then turned to face her, his hands on his neck, his expression tortured.

Miranda was gone, and only Prue stood there. A tear fell down her painted cheek, smearing the work, revealing more of the truth.

Camden shook his head, his eyes burning. He came to Prue, pulling her into his arms, cradling her gingerly. He couldn't even speak, couldn't bear to vocalize anything at all.

He just held her, burying his face against her, sweeping his hands gently up and down her back. She curled into him, burrowing against his chest, her frame trembling.

"Tell me," he finally whispered into her hair. "I don't know if I can bear it, but if I'm holding you, I might… I might…"

Prue held him tighter, silencing him without a word. Softly, she related the entire story, relived the experience anew, how her mother raged at her about Eliza, about Davies, about Prue herself, before striking her.

She told him about begging off of her Spinster meeting, claiming a headache rather than admitting the truth, reaching out to Miranda for help, telling him to meet her there…

"I don't care what anyone else thinks," she admitted quietly, leaning against him. "They already say enough about me, what's a bit of cosmetics? But I… I didn't want to pretend with you. I wanted you to know."

Camden released a heavy breath, churning inside with questions and simmering rage. It killed him that he couldn't do anything, couldn't take her away, couldn't thrash her mother as he would have done if she was a man, couldn't defend Prue properly…

He couldn't do anything.

He kissed Prue's hair and moved them both to the desk nearby, leaning against the edge and holding Prue close. "Does this happen regularly?" he forced himself to ask.

Prue shook her head. "No. Almost never."

He leaned back and gave her a look. "Almost," he repeated.

She swallowed once. "It's been years since she struck me."

"And that's supposed to make me feel better?" he cried, his voice rising.

"No!" she replied, her voice breaking again as she stepped out of his hold, pacing a little before facing him again. "I just… don't w-want you to see me as a v-victim."

It was as though he could feel his heart cracking in his chest. "Oh, love…"

Prue's face crumpled slightly. "This is my life, Cam. I can n-never please her. I never have. This is my l-life."

"It should not be your life," he said hoarsely, moving to take her hand in his. "You deserve so much more than this, Prue. You deserve a family who loves you and treats you well. You deserve to have your inheritance without any consideration to anyone else. You deserve…" He shook his head and kissed her hand tenderly. "You deserve the best."

"What if she's right?" Prue whispered, her eyes luminous. "What if no one will want me? What if my shyness and stammering and everything else are too much for any man to bear?"

Camden shook his head, wondering how much his heart and soul could take. "It isn't," he insisted, feeling that she needed truth rather than embraces at this moment. "Your shyness isn't anything insurmountable. Once you are comfortable, it fades almost entirely. And even if you aren't comfortable, it only takes patience and understanding."

She laughed once, a hard laugh, despite the soft timbre and

watery nature. "You've not seen the way men act around me. Before I had a fortune. It was hardly encouraging. And now… after this? How will anyone want to endure the trial of my nature and my life?"

Camden closed his eyes, gathering what strength and gentleness he could, and then pulled Prue back to him until he could take her face in hand, taking care not to press the tender flesh.

"You listen to me, Prudence Westfall," he told her, not bothering to hide the rawness in his voice, nor the emotion behind it. "The only trial about you is that your level of perfection is the most intimidating thing in the world. You are beautiful, you are sweet, and you have a wicked sense of humor that is breathtaking with its cleverness. If a man wanted to truly make you his, there would be nothing in heaven or earth to keep him from you. Your shyness is the only slightly less than perfect thing about you, and all it does is make you real, and that is the most fascinating, tempting thing of all."

Her eyes widened, filling with tears as she stared back at him.

"Do you hear me, sweetheart?" he asked, needing her to understand, to see what he saw.

At her nod, he swore under his breath, his emotions too much to bear anymore. He shook his head and stroked the bruised skin with gentle fingers. He bent and kissed the skin there, his lips dusting the discoloration and mark as though they could heal it. He turned her face and did the same to the other side, and then his lips were on hers.

She sighed, sliding her hand up to his neck, pressing him closer.

He resisted the temptation, could not bring himself to give in to his own desires, to kiss her madly, deeply, until he lost sense of himself and forgot his anger and madness. Until he was immune to all else in this world but her touch, her kisses, her sighs. Until he forgot where he ended, and she began. He could have pulled her more tightly against him, poured the very breath of his life into her, let her sweetness heal every ache in his heart.

But this wasn't about him.

It couldn't be.

Very gently, sweetly, tenderly he kissed her, caressing her lips with his own, desperate to soothe her pains, relieve her fears, quiet her anxieties. To let her know with this what his words could not say.

That she was cherished. Beloved. Adored.

His heart suddenly felt as though it caught fire within him as the truth of the matter came to light.

He loved her.

He kissed her again, breathless with the sensation of it all.

Love.

He pulled back and looked up at the ceiling, swallowing hard. "I need to protect you," he whispered, kissing her brow and leaving his lips there. "I don't know how, but I need to. I can't bear this, Prue. I can't."

Prue shook her head a little and reached up to take his face in her hands, forcing him to look at her. "Cam," she said in a tone he was terrified to understand, "I don't want to think about it anymore. Can you take me to the ballroom and dance with me? I just want to smile and laugh. With you."

Camden swallowed hard, stroking her cheek again. "Will you smile? Will you laugh? Can you?"

"No promises," she replied in a low voice, trying for a smile.

For once, he hated that answer. His brow furrowed, and he shook his head. "Why do you always say that? You should feel safe enough to promise, and you should expect promises in return. Promises should be fulfilled, not cast aside. You should have promises, and expectations, and vows, and hopes, and dreams…" He shook his head, unable to properly express what was now weighing heavily upon him. He tucked Prue against him closely, love, anger, confusion, and need filling him. "You should have so much, Prue." He exhaled slowly, kissing her hair again.

Prue held him, somehow comforting him while he attempted to comfort her. "Dance with me, Cam."

He nodded against her. "I will, sweetheart. But I need to hold you for a while first."

"And then Miranda will have to fix my face," Prue whispered, and he could hear her smile.

He chuckled roughly. "Nothing about you needs fixing, love. But if you like, we'll call Miranda back in."

That seemed to settle the conversation, but Camden was far from being settled.

Something would need to be done. He suspected he already

knew what it was, and it was the one thing he would hate most of all. But tonight, he would dance.

Chapter Nineteen

A little heartbreak is good for a soul. But only a little.

-The Spinster Chronicles, 14 September 1815

"Prue, do you want to write the main article this time?"

"Yes! It's been so long since you've put your delightful perspective in there."

"Not that any of your other articles were anything less."

"Not at all. Your Quirks and Quotes section was so engaging last time!"

Prue sat in silence on the sofa, staring off at nothing, aware of what her friends were saying but not paying any attention.

Izzy took her hand and squeezed it. "Prue?"

Prue swallowed and glanced at her.

Izzy smiled gently, her blue-green eyes searching. "Do you want to write anything at all this time?"

"Don't ask her that!" Charlotte protested hotly. "Of course she doesn't want to write anything this time, but we need her to!"

"Charlotte," Grace sighed, "do please pretend to have a heart, and kindly remember there are other people worth thinking about."

Charlotte squawked in dismay, but Prue couldn't bring herself to laugh at the obvious jab.

She couldn't laugh at anything.

"Everyone!" Elinor gasped as she ran into the room. "You'll never guess!"

"Undoubtedly," Charlotte replied, recovered already from her offended airs. "I never guess anything where you are concerned."

Elinor didn't react to Charlotte's comment, continuing further into the room, her eyes wide. "I was on Bond Street just now…"

"Just now?" Charlotte echoed. "You must have had a long run."

Now Elinor glared at her, albeit briefly. "I saw Eliza Howard procuring her wedding trousseau! She's going to be married next week, and she was just telling everybody with ears how fortunate she was, how blessed and delighted, and she *smiled* at me. It was awful, and *then...*"

Prue's head dropped, her eyes burned, she tried to block out everything else Elinor was going to say. She didn't need to hear it. She didn't *want* to hear it.

Her mother hadn't spoken to her again since that day she struck her unless it was to remind her of what she'd lost or to inform her of the details of Eliza's upcoming nuptials. Her mother had completely given up on her, giving her the neglect Prue had always wanted, but with a coldness that took away any relief from it. Prue was less than nothing to her now.

Eliza should have been her daughter. Everything would have been better if she were.

Everyone would have been happier.

Prue suddenly felt her hand being taken from Izzy's and tugged, and she looked up to see Georgie standing before her.

"Come on," Georgie murmured, smiling with an understanding Prue didn't comprehend. "We're going for a walk."

Prue let Georgie pull her from the sofa and lead her out of the room, the rest of the Spinsters surprisingly quiet as they left.

They collected their bonnets and gloves, and Tony, who had been taking his leisure in a nearby room, joined them as they departed the house. He smiled warmly at Prue, but said nothing, clearly letting his wife do as she pleased here.

Silently, they walked on, Georgie keeping her arm linked through Prue's, Tony walking a few paces behind.

Prue let Georgie lead, unsure where they were going and not particularly caring. There was too much to feel, too much to think, too much to consume her for such cares. It was so much easier to not think or feel anything at all rather than live in the despair that had been her constant companion for two weeks.

Two weeks.

Ever since that night at Miranda Sterling's ball when she had shown her bruises to Camden, when he had been so exquisitely tender with her, torn by what she had suffered, things had been different. He'd kept his promise to her of dancing with her, and had done so time and time again, making her smile and laugh, but there had been something else there. A hard edge. A false energy.

He had been pretending the entire night.

Pretending at what, she couldn't say. The look in his eyes had been enough to soothe her, to drive away her anxieties…

To make her hope…

He had worshipped her with gentle kisses in the study, and when he had taken her home, at Miranda's insistence, he had kissed her once more.

Just once.

That kiss had terrified her. The same hard edge he'd been trying to hide that night was alive and well in that kiss, though the aching sweetness of it had not been lessened. Prue thought at the time that she had imagined it, but it had felt very much as though he were bidding her farewell in the only manner he could have borne.

Now she knew better.

He had been.

She had not seen Camden for two weeks. He had not been at any of the events she had gone to. He had not responded to the messages she sent, though none of them had been returned. No morning walks, no unbearable interviews with her mother as chaperone, no flirtatious looks across rooms.

Nothing.

And people were beginning to talk.

Eliza was getting married next week, and she took every opportunity to lord over Prue with that fact.

"I told you, lamb," she'd sneered only the other night. "I told you Vale was nothing but trouble and nothing serious. You should have minded your surroundings and situation. Now, I have the perfect match, and you can go back to sitting in corners. Waiting."

She'd bleated mockingly before sweeping away to talk to her intended once more, who had been very kind to Prue since the engagement, treating her as if she were a younger sister, though still believing that Prue was suffering some great affliction and needed special care.

He deserved more pity than she did. He would be married to Eliza and have to endure her for the rest of his life. He would have to give her children and raise them with her as their mother. He would realize only too quickly what a gross error of judgment he had made, and how Eliza had manipulated him. Bitterness would rise, and they would be miserable for the rest of their natural existences.

Meanwhile, Prue would have her estate and her fortune, free to do as she pleased at any given time.

Alone.

Her mother was now speaking of leaving Prue without chaperone or guidance and moving in with her sister, leaving London with them at the end of the Season. She would close up the London house, and Prue would have to take herself off to the Hertfordshire estate and manage on her own, "as she is apparently so capable of doing".

Hertfordshire would be a blessed reprieve from London.

Lonely, but better.

"Lord bless you, Prudence Westfall," Georgie sighed from beside her. "I don't know how you're managing any of this."

Prue forced a small smile. "Same as you would have done, I expect. One f-foot in front of the other."

Georgie rubbed her arm. "Yes, but I would have made a lot more noise about it."

Tony snorted softly behind them in agreement.

"I'm not particularly noisy," Prue reminded her. "Nothing I do is loud."

Georgie pulled her across the street and into Hyde Park, and it seemed that all of the people walking by stared at the three of them, and at Prue in particular.

"I can't bear this," Prue hissed, her voice catching. "They all s-stare, they all kn-know…"

"Hush," Georgie murmured rubbing her arm again. "It'll pass."

It wouldn't pass. It would always hang around her neck, become part of who she was, draw attention and comment…

"I miss Cam," Prue found herself gasping, a hand going to her suddenly throbbing chest.

Georgie made a pained noise beside her and pulled Prue closer to her. "Oh, lamb, I know. I know you do."

Prue's lip quivered dangerously. "Why has he left me? Why won't he see me? Have I… have I been mistaken in him?"

"No," Georgie told her firmly. "No. Absolutely not. Camden Vale is a good man, and he cares for you very much. Anybody could see that."

"But he's not here." Prue shook her head, exhaling roughly. "He's not here. He said he would be here to s-save me, and yet…"

"Then you might need to save yourself, love. And you might need to save him."

Prue paused a step, looking over at her friend. "Save him? From what?"

Georgie looked over her shoulder at her husband. "Tony, come and help me."

Obediently, he came to Georgie's side and took her hand, starting them all walking again. "A man like Vale has likely never known anyone like you," Tony told Prue with a kind smile. "He's so used to going through his life without reference to anyone, and his temper, nature, and emotions were his own to contend with."

Prue nodded slowly, considering his words. "Distance," she murmured.

"What was that?" Georgie asked, her brow knitting.

"Distance," Prue said again with a clearing of her throat. "Mariah Turner, she told me that when Cam gets too overcome, too extended beyond his comforts, he opts for distance. Safety in distance until he is settled."

Tony reared back a little, surprised. "Does he?" He inclined his head in thought. "I can see the benefit in that. Wreaks havoc on those in his life, but in reality, it's a healthy act of self-preservation." He glanced at Prue again with a sheepish smile. "Men are more complicated than we should be, and not always the most logical of creatures."

Georgie scoffed a little but leaned into her husband all the same.

"I wonder," Prue said softly, looking out over the park, "if it was all too much. My mother, my cousin, my situation… me… Was it all too much to endure?"

"No," Georgie and Tony said together.

Prue smiled at them. "You are very kind friends, but you'll forgive me if I doubt you."

"Then listen to this, Prue," Tony responded, rather fervent in his expression. "With the right woman, any man worth his salt would jump at a chance with her, no matter what unpleasant complications would come with it. You might not have seen it, but everyone else could see the difference in Vale when he was with you, and after spending time with you. You changed him, and very much for the better. If he is choosing distance now, then he may be overwhelmed with whatever it is that you make him feel. In that way, perhaps, he is not so unlike you."

"Me?" Prue shook her head, bewildered and lost. "How?"

Georgie was nodding to herself, smiling a little. "When you feel too much, you panic. You cannot manage your anxieties and emotions and everything pressing in on you. Perhaps Camden has the same difficulty, but his distance is the way he recovers. The way he gathers himself. The way he finds his way out."

Prue blinked unsteadily, wondering at this revelation. Could it be possible that the problem was not that Camden did not care, but that he cared too much?

Could his distance be a sign of this?

He was finding his own way through the haze and mist of his own demons and emotions, and she knew only too well how difficult it was to endure such chaos without assistance. Without someone who knew the way and could guide them.

Without someone who loved them enough to wade into it together.

"I love him," Prue breathed as a wave of warmth washed over her, sending ripples of pleasure and pain across her skin. "I… I love him."

Georgie smiled at her, and Tony chuckled. "I already knew that, Prue," Georgie told her, tugging on her arm a little. "I was just waiting for you to realize it."

Prue laughed in breathless disbelief as wonder filled her. Then it all plummeted again as agony clutched at her heart. "Oh, Lord, I miss him so much," she whispered. "How can I bear it?"

Tony stepped back again, letting Georgie have this moment with Prue.

Georgie sighed and moved her arm to encircle Prue's shoulders. "You bear it the same way you bear everything else, Prue. One foot in front of the other. One day at a time. I don't know how you'll manage everything, but I do know that you will. Do you have any idea how strong you are? How brave?"

Prue shook her head. It was impossible, she wasn't any of those things.

"Oh, that's just not going to do at all," Georgie groaned. "I can see you're going to need to spend more time with me until you do. Things will be hell for you until Eliza leaves. Why don't you come stay with us? Your mother shouldn't mind, I'm a respectable and married woman now."

"I would love to," Prue murmured as tears welled up.

Georgie nodded, smiling. "Excellent. Because if you said no, I was going to have to resort to sending Miranda to fetch you, and that might have gotten out of hand."

Prue laughed, the tightness in her chest easing slightly. "Oh, Georgie… what would I do without you?"

"Haven't the faintest," Georgie quipped lightly. "After all, it was me who told you to kiss Camden properly, and I daresay he was worth that effort."

"You did *what?*" Tony cried from behind them.

Prue and Georgie giggled and walked on, Tony shaking his head as he followed.

She loved Camden Vale.

The fact didn't solve anything, didn't take away the ache of his absence or the pain of her family's contempt, but it did make the day a little brighter.

And for now, that was enough.

"I hope you know what you're doing."

Camden looked up from his fourth reading of the latest issue of The Spinster Chronicles to find his sister in the doorway. "How did you get in here?"

Lydia gave him an utterly derisive look, which was probably where he had learned to do it. "I knocked. Butler answered. I walked in."

He glowered at her. "I don't recall inviting you."

"I don't recall needing an invitation."

He scowled and returned his attention to the paper. "Did you bring Chadwick?"

"Not this time. He's busy with Mr. Andrews and some others at the Foreign Office." Lydia swept into the room and sat herself down in the armchair near him.

Camden looked up at her again. "Foreign Office? Why do they want Chadwick?"

Lydia raised a brow. "I don't know if you know this, darling, but my husband is brilliant. Quite remarkable. Many people seek him out. And you know he doesn't have the body of a scholar, so…"

"And now you should go," Camden interrupted, widening his eyes as he stared back down at the newssheet.

His sister scoffed loudly. "Oh, really, as if I would go so quickly when I have so much to say."

"Oh, good."

"Are you going to listen?"

"Probably not."

"Very well. I'll wait."

An uneasy silence stretched on, the only sound the ticking of the clock on the mantle. Camden tried to read the Fashion Forum, though he did not care about its contents at all. He only wanted to figure out, if he could, which segment Prue had written. There was never any regularity with authors and particular segments, as far as he knew, and she rarely told him which one hers was. But this was all he had of her now, and he was desperate for any glimpse into her state.

It was the most horrendous, poignant, unbearable torment he

could ever have devised for himself, keeping himself away from her. He had attended very few events in the last two weeks, preferring to either go to his club or remain at home instead. He'd declined to attend a dinner party at the Sterlings, which could have been disastrous, as he genuinely liked both of them, and were it not for seeing Henshaw at the club two days after, he would never have known that Prue had declined as well, thereby negating his lack of attendance somewhat.

Henshaw hadn't told him anything else, but he was not particularly close with Prue any more than he was any of the Spinsters, apart from Georgie.

No one could tell him anything.

Dart and Phillip told him their wives had seen Prue at various functions and spoken to her, and that Prue had not looked well at all. She had stammered a little, but they had learned not to mind that.

Camden minded. He should have been there to help her, to see that she was comfortable and safe, to diffuse that anxiety that made her stammer. He didn't mind the stammer; he minded what it meant.

Prue was unwell. And he had done that.

"Cam, you look like death."

He looked at Lydia, having momentarily forgotten that she was there. She looked at him with some concern, yet her expression held a good deal of scolding.

"Do I?" he asked, also forgetting to be indignant.

She gestured at his face. "You have not one, but two black eyes. Yes, you look like death."

He touched the still-sensitive skin and winced. "Yes, well, I wasn't entirely prepared for Mr. Gallagher's blows. But I thrashed him well and won the bout."

Lydia rolled her eyes. "You always win."

"True."

"Were you fighting with more than just your pride to motivate you?"

He did not feel the need to reply, though the memory of the fight still played in his mind. Yes, he had been fighting harder than usual, nearly outside of his head with rage and guilt, fury and anguish, everything he had pent up and left unsaid. Gallagher hadn't entirely deserved the brutality of the fight, but there was nothing for it.

Lydia didn't need to know that.

She made a loud tsking sound and turned in her chair, curling her legs under her as she had done when they were children. "What are you doing, Camelot?"

The sound of her pet name for him almost undid him, made him confess everything, but he bit back the impulse and bit his tongue as well. "Reading."

Lydia's mouth drew up on one side. "No, you're not. Your eyes weren't moving at all." She cocked her head and propped it on a hand, resting her elbow on the armrest. "Tell me, Cam."

"Tell you what?" he inquired blandly.

"Tell me why you are letting everyone in London believe that you have tossed Prue over," Lydia snapped. She quirked her brows in suggestion. "Her vile cousin is getting married soon, and everybody is talking about how Davies was supposed to marry Prue, but you were too distracting, and now you've done with her. She's been left for the vultures of Society, and she'll be picked over by anybody in search of a fortune."

Camden's jaw tightened, and the paper crinkled in his hands. "I didn't throw her over."

"No?" Lydia seemed to doubt that very much, and she drummed her fingers against her cheek. "Because I haven't seen the pair of you together in almost three weeks, and neither has anybody else."

Camden swallowed, wishing he didn't feel a surge of guilt. "I'm only maintaining distance. Until the fuss over her cousin is over."

"Does Prue know that?"

He shook his head, looking back at the paper, pretending to read again. "I thought it best to let it proceed naturally."

"Naturally?" Lydia cried. "Breaking a girl's heart is somehow natural to you?"

"I did not break her heart!" he exclaimed as he tossed the paper aside. He ran his fingers through his hair and rose, pacing the room. "I couldn't do that, not to Prue."

Lydia watched him pace incredulously. "What do you think happens when a girl forms an attachment, and the man in question abandons her?"

He glared at her quickly. "I have not abandoned her."

His sister barked a callous laugh. "You are more naïve than I ever, ever thought you would be. You have abandoned her, Cam. She is dealing with the fallout of her cousin's choices without you. She is bearing the brunt of Society's pity for not only not securing a husband, but losing a prime suitor as well, again without you. She is managing to put on a brave face, knowing she is being gossiped about like never before. Without you. Because you left her there. In her hour of need, you left her."

Camden snarled at his sister. "I should call you out."

Lydia's lip curled as she snarled back. "Do it. I'll win."

Unfortunately, that might have been true.

Camden stopped his pacing and drove the heels of his hands into his eyes. "I'm not abandoning her, Lydia. I'm trying to save her."

"You're trying to… what?" She shook her head and straightened up. "Explain that to me, if you please."

He exhaled slowly and folded his arms. "Did you know her mother struck her?"

Lydia's eyes widened, and her lips parted. "What?"

Camden nodded. "Because her cousin secured Davies and not Prue. She struck her across the face. Repeatedly. Prue had bruises from it. She was told that she was worthless, a disgrace to the family, and that no one would want her after this."

Lydia didn't move for a moment, then shot to her feet with a snarl and marched towards the door.

"Where are you going?" he demanded.

"To beat the tar out of that good-for-nothing, worthless excuse of a woman," she snapped. "You can't thrash her, it's not proper, but I certainly can, and when I'm through…"

Camden grabbed Lydia by the arms and pulled her back. "No," he told her in a surprisingly calm voice. "No."

She paused, then nodded once. "You're right. Mariah, then. She would do a much better job."

With a laugh, Camden hugged his sister. "No, not Mariah, either. We're not thrashing Mrs. Westfall, though it makes me glad you want to."

Lydia reluctantly hugged him back, then moved to the chair once more. "Fine," she grumbled, "but I don't like it." She shook her head, snorting rather like a horse, and looked up at him. "What does Prue's mistreatment have to do with you?"

That brought a wince to Camden's face. "It's my fault," he admitted, stunned at the swift vulnerability he felt lancing through him.

"How, pray tell?" his sister asked dubiously.

He shook his head. "If I hadn't gotten in the way, she might have secured Davies. Then her mother wouldn't have lashed out at her, and there might be some peace and contentment in her life."

Lydia stared him as though he had quacked like a duck. "You cannot be serious. Why in the world would she want Charles Davies?"

Camden scowled, rubbing at his aching chest. "You don't understand."

"Don't I?" she retorted. "Of the two of us, which one has had the experience of being a woman in search of a husband? Oh, that would be me." She raised her hand as if he needed further indication. "I am well aware of the intricacies of that matter, I can assure you, though I did not have Prue's fortune, nor her timidity. And even with that timidity, I can promise you that if she had wanted Mr. Davies, she would have secured Mr. Davies."

"But I was in the way!" he protested, ignoring the sense in her words. "I was a distraction!"

"You are not that distracting, love," she assured him sympathetically. "Andrews is a more attractive man, and more interesting. And what exactly were you in the way of? Did Prue have a man in mind for herself?"

Camden scowled. "No."

"Ah ha."

"But with me always being around," he added, waving a finger at her, "I kept her from meeting other suitable candidates."

"I'm assuming you're not counting yourself as a suitable candidate," Lydia said with another raised brow.

Again, he glared at her. "Obviously."

She nodded. "Right. Continue with your rant."

"Because of me, because of my reputation," he went on, turning towards the window, "she didn't have the chance to enjoy the prospect of any others. I pushed myself into her view, into her life, and when I should have been helping her find worthy men to have her, I spent the time indulging myself in flirtation. I was selfish. I didn't think about Prue and how it would affect her. And now she has to cope with Eliza's betrayal, and the speculation over her ties with me, given who I am and who I am rumored to be." He shook his head, his throat constricting. "It's so much worse for her because of me than it would have been otherwise."

"Cam…"

"No," he said quickly, cutting her off. "I am keeping my distance. I am forcing myself to stay away for her own good. For her sake. The sooner she can be rid of my influence, the sooner someone else can have a chance. Someone she deserves. Someone that will not give her the grief that I have given her. Distance, Lydia, to sever the ties between us without doing something unforgivable."

Lydia said nothing behind him, and when he turned to see why, he saw her smiling rather peculiarly at him. A small, bemused, almost sad smile.

"What?" he prodded, no force at all behind the word.

Lydia shook her head slowly. "You're in love. You love Prudence Westfall."

He opened his mouth to deny it but found no desire to. He exhaled slowly through his nose and nodded once.

His sister's smile grew, and she tilted her head at him. "Don't you think *that* is what she deserves?"

She pushed up out of her chair and came to him, still shaking her head, and laid a hand alongside his cheek, looking deeply into his eyes.

"Look at that," she murmured.

"What?" he asked after too much difficulty.

Lydia patted his cheek. "I've found a suitable candidate." She dropped her hand and kissed his cheek, then left the room without another word.

Camden stared after his sister, more confused than ever.

She was wrong. He wasn't suitable for Prue at all, and they would all see it soon. Once enough time had passed, it would be quite clear.

She was wrong.

She had to be.

Chapter Twenty

A woman in love is capable of remarkable things. Having never been such a woman, this writer isn't quite sure what things, but it seems a fair thing to say.

-The Spinster Chronicles, 11 March 1816

"I can't thank you enough for coming. It means a very great deal."

"Well, I can't sit at home all the time and be antisocial. Besides, keeping you company is no hardship."

Prue smiled at Edith, delighted that she had accepted Georgie's invitation to accompany them to the theater. It was the first time she could recall Edith doing anything so public, and while the woman did not look exactly at ease, her discomfort was not obvious.

She was a beautiful woman, and her reserved gown did nothing to hide that fact. Dark hair and green eyes, a full smile, and a figure beyond reproach… Lady Edith Leveson would make many heads turn if she decided to take on Society in her own right.

But for now, she was Prue's comfort, and that seemed to be enough for her.

"So sorry to be late," Amelia gushed as she hurried into the box. "Such a crush! It was amazing that Frederick and I managed to get in. If not for Mr. Morton, we would have been lost, I swear!"

"Not so lost, Amelia," her brother replied in a droll tone. "I am fully aware of the location of the boxes."

She waved that off and sat down next to Prue excitedly. "You'll never guess what I heard about Mr. Andrews."

Prue smiled a little. "What did you hear?"

Amelia's eyes danced. "I've heard that he is musical."

"No," Prue said, trying to match the enthusiasm and dramatics that engulfed her friend.

Edith snickered behind her.

Apparently, she was not acting very well.

"Yes!" Amelia squealed, missing Prue's horrendous acting attempts. "He plays the violin!"

"Better than playing the villain," Edith muttered with a wry grin.

"And do you like the violin, Amelia?" Prue asked patiently.

"I don't know," Amelia admitted, eyes wide. Her smile spread. "But I think I could." She sobered a little. "But it is Mr. Andrews, and Lord knows what that means."

"Indeed." Prue quickly made the introductions for Amelia and Edith, and they chatted together for a bit, waiting for the opera to commence.

Being surrounded by friends did wonders for her, as had living with Georgie and Tony for the last two weeks. She was not whole, nor was she particularly happy, but she was healing. Camden had still not seen her, but she hadn't tried to get him to. She always looked for him everywhere she went, but she was not brave enough to call upon him. She wished she was that brave, that bold, that sure of herself, but she was not. She still wanted him to save her.

But not because she was a damsel in distress, as all the fairytales said. She wanted him to save her because there was such great delight in being saved. In knowing she was not alone. In having someone else to rely on.

She'd never had that before him, except for her father.

He'd given her hope and strength, and now that was gone.

And yet somehow, it wasn't. She felt changed from the woman she was before he entered her life. She felt a certain sense of awareness that she'd never had, a clarity of thought and of self. She still stammered, of course, but her occasion for nerves had lessened somewhat. She felt a comfort in being herself, in not worrying so much about what her mother or anyone else thought.

It was easier to do so when her mother was not about.

After Eliza's wedding, her mother had asked if Georgie and Tony would mind hosting Prue a little longer, as it would 'undoubtedly do her good' to spend some time with a proper couple of such estimation.

Georgie had shrieked for a good twenty minutes on the indignity of having gained approval from Mrs. Westfall, but there was nothing to be done about it now.

Prue was better and getting better, but in one regard, she was as weak as ever.

She missed Camden.

Every night, without fail, she dreamed of him. Last night they had walked the grounds of her estate, though she had never seen it, and both of them were easy and carefree, warm and affectionate. The night before that had been a grand masquerade ball in London where he had taken her to a secluded garden and kissed her until they were both breathless and dizzy. The night before that…

More and more of the same. Sometimes romantic, sometimes friendly, sometimes a painful illustration of their current distance.

But always Camden.

Always.

Had he loved her? Could he have come to love her? Would this imposed distance ever end, or would her heart forever cry out for him to an emptiness with no response?

It was a disheartening thought, but at some point, she had to stop wanting him.

Didn't she?

Georgie didn't talk about it unless Prue did, preferring to let Prue do whatever she wished. The Spinsters hadn't spoken of Camden or Eliza or anything else that might affect Prue, but she knew they were curious. More than that, she knew they missed Camden. He might not have been in their association for long, but he had made an impact.

Even Elinor had made a comment about wishing Camden had been around, according to Georgie.

Thankfully, the friends she had made through Camden had not neglected her for his distance. Mariah and Julia greeted her as warmly as ever when they saw her, and Lydia refused to be satisfied with anything less than a tight hug when she saw Prue. None of them ever spoke of Camden unless he was brought up, and Prue was grateful for that.

She did not need any further reminders that he was absent, and no reason to hurt more than she already did.

She sent him notes from time to time, which went unanswered. Nothing of significance, just details of her day, along with a brief admission of her missing him. Letters to Cam were becoming almost an entry in her diary with her thoughts, feelings, and impressions…

She didn't know if he wanted to hear any of it. But she wanted to tell him.

After Eliza's wedding, which he had not attended despite being invited, she had written him a three-page letter with all the details. Everything from her mother's attempt at tears outstripping Aunt Howard's real ones, down to the lace-choked gown Eliza had worn, which was so overdone it was unflattering. She told him about Eliza's superior looks at Prue, her sheep impersonation every time she passed her, and the way Mrs. Davies looked at Prue as though she had committed a gross sin.

But that was all over now, and she was only grateful that Eliza and Mr. Davies had retreated to Tinley House for a time.

Prue could breathe in London whenever Eliza was removed from it.

"Prue?"

She turned in her seat quickly to see Georgie standing at the box entrance, looking a trifle bemused. "Would you come here, please?" Georgie asked, waving at her.

Prue smiled at Amelia and Edith, rising and moving to the back of the box. "What is it?" she asked when she reached Georgie.

Georgie tilted her head to indicate outside the box, and Prue turned, at a loss as to what was happening.

Lydia Chadwick stood just outside the box, wringing her hands a little.

"Lydia?" Prue shook her head, worry knitting at her chest. "What's wrong? Are you well?"

Lydia smiled quickly. "Oh, very well, dear. Only a trifle anxious."

She giggled at that. "I supposed you of all people would understand that sensation. It is rather overpowering."

That was an understatement, but Prue smiled all the same.

"I've done something rather unforgivable," Lydia confessed, biting her lip. "I should probably be ashamed of myself, but I can't quite manage it."

"What have you done?" Prue asked, her curiosity unwittingly piqued.

Lydia twisted her lips, then reached into her reticule. "I called upon my brother several days ago, and during a flight of fancy, I picked up something of his and took it home with me. It wasn't until some time later I managed to open it and examine its contents, as a studious and caring elder sister would." She pulled out a small, black, leather-bound book and looked at it for a moment. She exhaled quickly and held it out to Prue, meeting her eyes. "You need to see it."

Prue looked at the outstretched book, hesitation raging within her. "Wh-what is it?" she managed to ask.

Lydia smiled at her. "Take it, Prue. Open it. You'll understand."

She reached out with shaking fingers and took the book from Lydia, tracing the rough edges of the book lovingly.

"Is this…?" Prue began, unsure if she could get the words out.

"Open it," Lydia murmured gently.

Prue pried open a few pages, then gaped.

Her likeness was on the page.

A very good likeness.

An impossibly skilled likeness.

"Go back two pages," Lydia suggested, putting a hand on Prue's arm.

Prue did so and found a rough sketch of a woman at an easel, a small plant before her.

"But it's… it's…" She shook her head and looked up at Lydia. "It's that day in the orangery. At Tinley. He… he said he drew on occasion and he would do so while I sketched."

"On occasion?" Lydia echoed. She laughed to herself. "Dear girl, drawing happens to be one of Camden's greatest skills. He was always sketching things as a boy. People and plants and buildings…

Whatever captured his attention."

She reached out and flipped a few pages slowly, showing the contents to Prue.

Every page had an image of Prue on it. A somber expression, a secretly pleased one, laughing, contemplative, even one of her scowling. There was a sketch of her coming down the stairs that first night they went to the theater together, the style of her dress captured in near-perfect detail.

"You captured his attention, Prue," Lydia told her in a very gentle tone. "For quite some time."

She turned to a page towards the end, though not the last one.

"This is the last drawing before I took it. Look, he dated it."

The date was a full two weeks after Miranda's ball and would have been done without much reference, as they had not seen each other since that night.

It was the most detailed sketch in the book.

Prue couldn't breathe for a moment, though it had nothing to do with panic or anxiety. She stared at her own likeness, at the smooth lines drawn to capture her, wondering at the undertaking such a meticulous sketch would have been. How long it must have taken. How patient the artist must have been. How invested.

Lydia squeezed her arm again. "You needed to know, Prue."

Prue looked up at her, searching her eyes for a long moment. "Thank you," she replied softly, somehow managing to avoid stammering.

Lydia winked at her and turned away, the tall form of Mr. Chadwick appearing beside her only a few paces down.

Prue watched them go, belatedly realizing that she still held the book in her hands.

She turned back into the box, trembling and unsettled, reeling with the revelations. Camden hadn't forgotten her. Hadn't been bored by her. Hadn't strung her along, as Eliza had accused. Prue had never believed her, but the proof was here in her hands. He would not have planted this for his sister to find, this was something personal.

She ought to feel guilty or ashamed for seeing it, but she could not.

She only felt love, and an overabundance of it.

Georgie smiled at her, glancing down at the book, and then back up to Prue with wide eyes. "Goodness, Prue. I think the man is besotted."

Prue's cheeks colored, but she met her friend's gaze squarely. "I hope so."

That earned her a wink, and Georgie gently pushed her back towards her seat. "So do I."

Prue sat again as the music for the opera began, though she was barely paying any attention to it.

She missed Camden so fiercely at this moment that she could taste the bitterness. A raw, aching need filled her, and she suspected it always would be there. Part of her. As he was.

As he always would be.

Dazed by her emotions and by the book in her hands, she looked around the theater slowly, unable to focus on the performances at all.

Every other guest was riveted on the stage, enjoying what had to be exquisite performances, nothing disrupting their enjoyment of the evening. No life-altering revelations, no trouble finding coherent thoughts, no gaping void within that may never properly heal…

Up in a box across the theater, two couples and another man appeared, quickly and quietly taking their seats. Prue watched them, smiling at the way both ladies turned to shush their husbands, at their elegance, their ease…

One of them sat forward a little, her auburn hair catching a hint of candlelight.

Prue gasped silently as she got a good look at the woman.

Mariah Turner.

She ran her gaze down the line. Phillip sat just behind Mariah. Julia was next to Mariah. Dart was behind her. And then…

Her heart sprang into her throat.

Camden.

She drank in the sight of him, wishing she could fly from this box to his side. He looked dark and brooding, yet every inch of him pristine and perfect. Time away from him had only made him a dearer sight, and far more attractive than even her dreams had painted him to be.

Prue stared without reservation, without any of the timidity she was known for. While he was there, living and breathing in the same space she was, she could look nowhere else.

Why had he left her alone? Abandoned her to the bleak nature of her situation after telling her such sweet things? And when he clearly thought of her a great deal, had drawn her face over and over again? How could he then pretend to be so indifferent?

Her heart seemed to be breaking all over again for love of him, and for wondering.

At long last, he looked over, and their eyes met. He stiffened, and he stared as boldly as Prue, as blatantly as they had done in this very theater after returning from Tinley. Even from this distance, his eyes held her captive, and the look in them told Prue that he was not indifferent.

Not in the least.

His gaze was intense and mesmerizing, steady on her, and while he looked, she had hope.

Prue watched as he swallowed, and then he dipped his chin just slightly, the barest hint of a nod. Then he returned his gaze to the stage.

She continued to watch him, but he never looked back. He was fully aware of her, yet his gaze never moved in her direction again.

Why? She didn't understand, could not comprehend why this distance was between them now. Why, when they had shared so much, was this to be the end?

She needed him. She needed the strength he provided, the gentleness he possessed, the intensity he lived with, the wit in every syllable he uttered…

She loved him with a depth and breadth and pain that she did not know she was capable of. For a woman who had spent her entire life being overwhelmed by emotions and sensations, this was new and foreign territory. Nothing she had ever endured compared to this.

Breathe in, breathe out. Fear in, fear out.

Prue's breath caught in her chest. For the first time in her entire life, the voice calming her in her mind, reciting the pattern that saved her, did not belong to her father.

It was Cam.

Tears sprang into her eyes, and she bit down on her lip to keep from making a sound. His was the voice she wanted to hear when she needed to find her way, when all else was lost, when she could not manage on her own. His was the voice she wanted calling out to her, calling her back, and leading her home.

His was the voice that could save her.

I'll save you, Prue. All night, I'll save you.

He had saved her. Over and over again, he had saved her. Now, he was further from her than he had ever been, leaving her alone.

What was it Georgie had said? She just might have to save herself.

Could she? Could she save herself from what she currently suffered?

Prue looked at Camden for a long moment, her heart pounding hard, but not particularly fast.

Yes. But it wouldn't be herself alone she would save. She would save them both. Camden needed her to lead him out of his turmoil, to show him the way, to save him…

But what could she do? What would she say? She'd never done a bold or determined thing in her life, and now she was supposed to take charge with the man who meant everything to her?

She ground her teeth together. "What shy creature?" she muttered to herself.

The moment the interval struck, Prue moved from her seat, not even bothering to applaud for the stirring aria that had ended the first act.

"Where are you going?" Georgie demanded, eyes wide.

"Out," Prue managed, knowing if she stopped, she would never start again.

"Not alone!" Tony insisted.

Prue didn't stop, sweeping out of the box.

A man suddenly appearing at her side made her gasp and jump, but the kind expression of Mr. Morton looked back at her. "Lead the way, Miss Westfall," he urged, nodding in encouragement.

Prue flashed him a grateful smile and moved on, pleased that he was keeping pace and not asking questions. She wouldn't have been able to answer, and if she thought about this too much…

All too soon, they approached the boxes near where Camden had been.

Prue swallowed harshly, hesitant and fearful.

"Do you want me to go in?" Mr. Morton asked gently.

She nodded frantically. "F-fetch Mr. Vale, if you please."

"I gathered that," he chuckled with a surprising degree of warmth. "Don't move."

She watched as his form entered the box, waited while he was within, feeling as though everything inside her was quivering.

I'll save you...

Moments later, Camden appeared, his expression carefully blank. "Miss Westfall," he greeted stiffly, bowing to her. "Are you enjoying the opera?"

Prue bit down on the inside of her lip sharply, steeling herself. "Might I have a word?"

He looked mildly surprised but nodded and gestured down the corridor.

They walked for just a few paces, and then Prue caught sight of one of the tapestry-enclosed alcoves Camden had teased her about only weeks ago.

Perfect.

She looked around quickly, then shoved him with all her might, forcing him to enter the alcove, the tapestry effectively hiding them from the eyes of everyone else.

Camden stared at her in shock. "Miss Westfall..."

"Don't," Prue snapped, starting towards him.

He backed up until the wall met him, his eyes wide.

Prue took his face in her hands, seizing any and all courage she had ever wished to possess, and kissed him.

He broke off almost at once. "Miss Westfall..."

"D-don't!" Prue said again, not nearly as strongly. "I'm going to do everything you s-said in here. Every single thing. Because I don't kn-know what else to do."

Camden shook his head at her. "What?"

Prue's strength dissolved, and she fisted her hands into his coat. "I've had enough, Cam. I can't bear this anymore. I don't know why you've put this distance between us, but I w-won't have it anymore!"

Tears began to roll down her cheeks, and she shook her head. "I miss you, Cam. All the t-time. So, I'm s-saving myself now. Right now. And I'll save you, too, if I can."

His hands slid to her upper arms. "Oh, Prue…"

"I l-love you." She hiccupped and swiped at her tears. "And I wish I didn't s-stammer when I said that," she added in a whisper, pained that she could not even confess herself without difficulty.

Camden cupped her face in both hands and forced her to meet his eyes. "I love your stammer," he said fiercely. "It makes every word more precious to hear."

She whimpered a weak cry, gripping his jacket more tightly. "Why did you leave me?"

He held her steady, his hands returning to her arms, and tried to meet her gaze. "Prue, I've been keeping my distance, trying to give you the opportunity for someone better. Someone worthy of you."

"I don't want distance or opportunity," she complained weakly. "I hate it. I just want you."

He groaned and at last pulled her into his embrace. "So do I. It's tearing my heart out to be away from you."

Prue nuzzled against him, her heart finally calming. "Don't make me do it anymore, Cam. I can't bear it."

He kissed her hair and buried his face in it. "No, love. No more." He exhaled and put a hand under her chin, lifting her eyes to his gaze once more. He held them steady and stroked the underside of her chin. "I love you, Prue. I've loved you from the first, and it terrifies me to my core." He leaned in and kissed her tenderly, his lips wringing exquisite pleasure from her.

Prue leaned into him, into this kiss, terrified that it could all end once more, that it wouldn't last.

Cam groaned against her lips, his kiss turning hungry for only a moment before he broke off, shaking his head. "God help me, I know you deserve better, but I can't give you up."

"You don't have to," Prue whispered, taking his face in hand, bringing his brow to hers. "I'm not going anywhere."

He kissed her again, his arms encircling her tightly. "No," he rasped, "you're not. And if I recall, there's a list of things to get through while we have this alcove before either of us are missed, so we'd better get started."

Prue blushed, giggled, and complied eagerly.

When the second act opened, there were still five figures in the far box, though one had not been there originally. But one dark-haired man was as good as another, surely.

In the Sterling's box, a man and a woman returned, just as had departed, though the gentleman was not an original occupant.

They were five minutes late into the act, but nobody seemed to mind very much.

Chapter Twenty-One

But in the end, dear friends, it is gossip that will take the day and keep us all on this side of heaven.

-The Spinster Chronicles, 1 November 1817

"And *then* I was told that Mr. Ferguson was coming back into London, but I knew that could not be correct, given that he was practically chased out last year what with his gambling debts."

"Indeed."

"Mr. Morton has some excellent statistics, you know."

"Does he?"

"Yes, he already has an estate in Bedford. And he's still in possession of his commission, though he is not currently with his regiment."

"Lovely."

Prue couldn't muster up the energy to be as enthusiastic about Elinor's research as she ought to have been. It had never been of particular interest to her what the men in London and Society were like as far as prospects. It all seemed rather analytical and formal, which was what she realized they were trying to get girls away from focusing on. It ought to be considered, certainly, but she, of all people, understood just how much more there ought to have been in considering a candidate for marriage properly.

Most of the men who had tried for her would have never done for her at all, and she would have been a dreadful wife for them. But no one was pursuing her now, so it was all behind her.

Camden had seen to that.

Ever since the theater last week, he had been the most attentive suitor anybody had ever seen. He was with Prue nearly all the time, calling at the Sterling's regularly, accompanying Georgie and Prue to their Spinster gatherings, escorting Prue and Miranda on an outing to Bond Street… He endured every activity a gentleman ought to have dreaded without a single expression of dismay.

The Spinsters were beyond delighted to have him back, frequently asking him for advice and input on their columns, which made Tony furious, as he had never been permitted such access. Elinor, in particular, found Camden to be a valuable resource, as he knew more about the truth of gossip than she did. Somehow, he handled her inquisitions with patience, which was more than any of the Spinsters themselves could have said.

They'd gone to Almack's and danced too many times for the stodgier ladies, though Lady Hetty found it perfectly acceptable that a woman not dancing should dance with a man who asks, even if it would be more times than was usually permitted. They'd attended Chadwick's gathering of scholars, and, oddly enough, found it interesting, which Camden begged her to keep quiet. They'd gone for carriage rides, a card party, a musical evening wherein Mr. Andrews *did* play his violin, and very well, and they'd taken to walking Hyde Park every morning.

For all the distance there had been of late between Camden and Prue, there was nothing of the sort now. One or both of them were always confessing their love, neither took care to hide their expressions of delight, and they laughed so often that people began to disapprove.

Prue did not recognize herself these days. She'd never imagined that she would have a love match, and yet she found herself in the middle of a whirlwind one. She'd thought about writing a commentary on it for the Chronicles, but that was too much.

Some of her thoughts and feelings would remain her own.

Some things ought to be discovered by experience rather than education.

And some things could not be described.

"What are you talking about, Miss Asheley?" Amelia asked from Prue's other side. "I've gotten a bit lost."

Prue smiled at that. Emma Partlowe, one-time Spinster and Elinor's older sister, had heard from Georgie and Izzy about Amelia and begged them to try to get the two girls to be friends, as they were of a similar age. The outing this morning was one of the first engagements they had arranged for the two to associate on a more intimate level than one of Society's events, and Prue had been designated as the sponsor of it.

She did not mind, but with the pair of them together, she felt very aged indeed.

"My position," Elinor informed Amelia with some superiority, "requires me to have copious notes and research on all of the eligible men in London. Their financial situation, holdings, profession, history, rumors, any ties to particular females, and the like. It is very taxing, but proves most useful when trying to find appropriate marriage candidates for any young ladies that may ask."

Amelia's eyes were wide, and she toyed with her bonnet ribbons absently. "Heavens. I will have to consult you and your information when I find a gentleman of particular interest to me."

Elinor beamed, nodding in encouragement. "Oh, please do! It is such a simple thing to check the facts on one's interest to be sure it will be a wise use of time. And it is no trouble at all. If you ever have a man in mind, Miss Perry, make me aware of it, and I will find out everything available."

"You are too kind," Amelia gushed, beaming at her new friend. Then her smile turned rather impish. "Have you started collecting notes on my brother yet?"

Elinor gasped. "You have a brother?"

"Oh, Miss Asheley," Amelia drawled, now looking and sounding more mischievous than Prue had imagined she could be. "We have so much to talk about."

Prue would have to seriously consider telling the others that this friendship was a terrible idea.

"It was shocking, to be sure. I'd never thought Mr. Vale capable of such horrific behaviors."

Prue stopped on the path, her eyes going wide, her face starting to flush purely based on the voice that had spoken.

She turned very slowly, and, sure enough, only a few yards down a separate path was her cousin, the newly-returned and newly-minted Mrs. Davies. She had a gathering of a dozen or so around her, both men and women, and her husband was nowhere in sight.

And her gathered listeners were rapt on her.

Eliza shook her head, a lace-gloved hand on her chest. "I was so shocked, so very aghast. After all, the man was, and is, courting my dear cousin, Miss Westfall. I had been in his company many times as he engaged in a very proper, polite courtship with her, and so I had learned to trust him. I'd thought he was a gentleman." She seemed to fight for composure and looked away to gather herself.

And looked squarely at Prue.

Prue stared at her, unsure whether her complexion was losing its color or gaining it. She couldn't seem to feel anything but coldness seeping through her skin, her heartbeat fading into almost nothing.

Eliza's lips quirked, but she was quick to cover them in another display of dramatics. "He was so violent in his affections to me, the moment we were alone. On the very eve of my wedding, he made such… untoward attentions. He claimed that the courtship of my cousin was for show, all in an effort to draw closer to me."

The crowd murmured and muttered to themselves, an almost eerie rumbling to Prue's ears. Their expressions were confused, in some cases aghast, and none of it was for slander of Camden.

They believed Eliza.

They believed every word.

"I resisted his efforts," Eliza told her listeners, sliding her hand to her throat. "I vowed I could never betray my cousin in this way, nor my beloved. I am a lady of Society, I told him, and I will behave with the propriety instilled in me."

"What happened, Mrs. Davies?" a middle-aged lady begged, her eyes wide.

"Well," Eliza answered, tossing her head, "I confessed everything to my sweet husband. I could not condone marrying him under false pretenses. He is so good, he married me without hesitation." She heaved a heavy sigh. "But that was not the end of Mr. Vale's actions."

"No!" several people gasped.

Eliza nodded sadly. "Only a few nights ago, Mr. Davies and I returned to London, and at our very first event, Mr. Vale came to me. He begged me to be with him, though I was now a married woman. His attentions were just as wild and untamed as the man himself is, and I was appalled that he should suggest any such thing. Were it not for my husband's impeccable timing and physical strength, he might have overpowered me."

Prue gaped at her, practically gawking at this outrageous lie, at the damage she was inflicting on Camden's character and reputation, to say nothing of the impact it could have on Prue herself.

Which was undoubtedly Eliza's objective.

She didn't care about Camden one way or the other.

It was Prue she wanted to ruin.

Eliza sniffed loudly, fanning herself with a small fan one of her admirers had given her. "I just felt that it was my duty to share my experience so that Mr. Vale would never be able to inflict the same harm on someone else, or far worse. And my poor cousin…" She hitched an audible breath and reached a hand out towards Prue, drawing everyone's attention to her. "Oh, my sweet cousin, who might already be ruined and too ashamed to admit that he has ensnared her. Perhaps she doesn't know, and if I had only told her before I was wed…"

"Oh, for the love of…" Elinor muttered, trailing off into an expletive that would have made Charlotte blush.

Eliza hiccupped loudly and came over to Prue, who could not move, though Amelia and Elinor sidled out of the way.

"Oh, Prudence," Eliza wailed, draping herself on Prue with another cry, her body shuddering against Prue's unmoving one.

Prue swallowed hard, not seeing the crowd any longer, not seeing anything but the pond ahead, the blue above, the green beneath. She faintly heard Elinor muttering something about beating Eliza with a stick, but the words were not clear.

Then, all sounds disappeared as Eliza breathed menacingly, "Baa-aa-aa, little lamb. Baa-aa-aa…" She chuckled and pulled back, smirking and giving Prue a wink. "We should invite you for dinner soon, Davies and I. Perhaps not your suitor, as he has a shocking reputation and all." She grinned, and then pushed on past Prue, a lace handkerchief dabbing at her eyes as she moved away from the crowd. Amelia restrained a suddenly lunging Elinor, but Prue could only watch her cousin amble away.

One by one, that crowd dispersed, some coming past Prue, eyeing her with concern, others averting their eyes and their path until only the three of them remained there.

Prue began to shake then, her body trembling with embarrassment and shame, fury and indignation. She felt weak, almost slumberous, and the world seemed to spin in all of the wrong ways.

"We need to get her back to Georgie's," Elinor said brusquely, grabbing one of Prue's arms. "Is it too far to walk?"

"I think so," Amelia replied as she came to Prue's other side. "She'll never make it that far. Oh! It's Mr. Andrews in a phaeton!"

"And Mr. Morton and Lieutenant Henshaw!" Elinor gasped, hurrying Prue along. "They can hail us a hack, we won't all fit in Mr. Andrews' phaeton. Mr. Morton! Lieutenant Henshaw!"

Prue lost track of the conversations as she focused on regaining control of her breathing. She would never recover the shame of panicking into an attack out here in the open of London. She could manage, she could breathe, she could find her way. There was nothing to panic about, only a situation to handle.

Cam would help her. Cam would make it right.

Cam would…

Cam would…

Oh, lord, what would Cam say?

"She said *what?*"

Camden shot out of his chair, swearing colorfully, shoving his hands behind his head.

"Steady on," Andrews murmured, looking only mildly surprised.

Camden glanced at Amelia, who appeared a little impressed. "Apologies, Miss Perry."

She shook her head, smiling a little. "I have two brothers, Mr.

Vale. I do believe I've heard most things."

"I doubt that," Camden and Andrews said at the same time, sharing a rueful look.

Camden cleared his throat. "You're sure, Miss Perry? About what you heard Mrs. Davies say?"

She nodded. "Quite sure. And Miss Asheley heard it as well, you can verify the story with her."

"Elinor never lies," Camden muttered. "Lord, this family…" He ground his eyes with the heels of his hands. "How was Prue?"

"Mortified," Amelia said bluntly. "The crowd was so taken in with Mrs. Davies' claims, and Prue just stood there, shaking like a leaf, changing from pale to flushed and back again."

Camden groaned. "She didn't believe it, did she?"

Amelia said nothing.

He turned to look at her warily. "Amelia…"

Apology was written all over her face. "I don't know, Mr. Vale. She was saying things to herself while Mr. Morton and Lieutenant Henshaw helped her into a hack. Something like 'Cam wouldn't… Cam couldn't…' or the like. I begged Mr. Andrews to bring me to you, so I don't…" She looked up at Andrews for help.

He shook his head at her. "Hard to say, Vale. She was very distressed, to be sure."

Camden stared at them both, horror setting in. "I've got to go to her. I've got to go now."

Andrews nodded, stepping back. "Take the phaeton, Vale. We'll send a missive to Miss Perry's family to have her fetched home. Your housekeeper will stay with her until then, and I will remain on your premises until you return."

Camden nodded absently, only half hearing. "Thank you, Andrews." He raced out the door and down to the waiting phaeton, taking the reins from the footman. He snapped the reins sharply before the footman could mount his seat, calling out to the horses, who took off with a jolt that nearly unseated him. Now might not have been the best time to admit to Andrews that he hadn't driven a phaeton in ten years or more, and it certainly wouldn't do to destroy the phaeton when it had just been so generously loaned to him.

He pushed all that into the back of his mind. Prue was the

important one here. How could Eliza have embarrassed her so publicly like that? There was speculation of an engagement between Camden and Prue, which was undoubtedly what had set Eliza off, but to bend this far in her attempts to foil it…

There was a very particular circle of hell for people like her, and he would be only too glad to push her into it.

Prue had to believe him. She *had* to. She'd accepted everything about him up to this point, hadn't she? None of the other rumors had blown her off course, so he could only presume that…

But she hadn't heard all the rumors. She wouldn't have, not with her connections and acquaintances. Those rumors were for a very particular circle, but they remained, nonetheless.

Unless someone had told her those.

None of them were true, but he'd spent so long laughing off his reputation, pretending it had no effect on him and his life that rumors about him tended to be counted as fact. He'd told Prue himself that the bad she would hear about him was mostly true, never imagining that she'd hear anything truly wicked.

This rumor would stick for some time. The story would change and morph with every subsequent retelling unless someone could prove that Eliza was wrong.

He would deal with that later.

Right now, he needed to see Prue. To hold her. To tell her…

The Sterling's townhouse was before him, and he pulled the horses to a stop, throwing the reins to the side and racing up the stairs.

The butler let him in, and Camden heard him instruct a footman to tend to the phaeton, but he didn't bother checking on that.

Tony saw him first and changed direction to meet him.

"Where?" Camden panted, grabbing at his shoulders.

Tony pointed to a far parlor, and Camden thumped his shoulder in gratitude, moving as fast as he could to the room where his fate would await him.

The afternoon light streamed through one of the windows in the room, bathing Prue in beams of sunlight that ought to have brightened her to an angelic degree. But sitting as she was, slumped in a chair, elbows on her knees, hands clasped, head bowed…

She looked as though she had been defeated in battle.

He entered the room slowly, not wanting to startle her. She didn't move at his approach, but he saw her eyes lift enough to see his boots as he neared her.

"Prue?" he said gently, stopping before her.

She didn't respond, did not lift her head, made no indication that he was here.

A cold fear struck Camden's chest. She believed Eliza. Her insecurities about herself and his nature had given her enough doubt that she believed the malicious rumors.

He sunk down to his knees before her until he could see her eyes. She focused on him, her breathing slow and steady, her face pale, but devoid of expression.

"Prue…" he began roughly, reaching out a hand to cover her clasped fingers. "I swear on my life, I never had anything to do with your cousin or any other woman since I've met you. I never touched her. I never said a word to her beyond politeness, and I barely managed that. I never made any advances, untoward or otherwise. My reputation is not entirely unfounded, I told you that, but…" He tightened his hold on her hands. "I promise you, Prue. I *promise* I would never…" His voice faded with emotion, and he shook his head, helpless under the power of her eyes. "I love you more than life, and I would never betray you."

"I know."

Her soft words were nearly lost on him, though they were the only people in this room. Her lips had barely moved when she spoke them.

But he couldn't have heard her correctly.

He blinked at her. "You… you what?"

Prue inhaled softly. "I know. I know you didn't do this. I know you wouldn't do this. I know, Cam." She swallowed, and her eyes filled with tears. "I'm only sorry you had to be involved at all. I can't believe she would slander you this way."

Camden stared at her in disbelief, his heart beating in an unsteady, hesitant rhythm. He cleared his throat. "Your cousin is spreading malicious rumors designed to hurt you in a very particular way, and you are worried about me?"

Her lower lip trembled, and she nodded. "Yes." She exhaled a rough sob. "I'm so sorry, Camden. I don't know what to say."

Camden couldn't believe his ears and exhaled a feeble almost-chuckle. He rose a little and took Prue's dear face in his hands, tilting her head up to meet his gaze fully. He shook his head in wonder, his thumbs stroking her cheeks.

This woman… This remarkable, breathtaking, incomparable woman not only believed him in the face of adversity but thought more of him than she did herself.

She loved him far more than he deserved, and he felt weak in the face of it.

He did not deserve her. But he was not about to let that stop him.

"Prudence Westfall," he said roughly, emotion catching at his voice. "I didn't think I could love you more than I already did, but… will you marry me?"

Prue blinked at him once, twice, and then it dawned on her. "What?" she breathed.

He smiled and touched his brow to hers, nudging her nose with his. "I love you," he whispered. "And I will love you every day for the rest of our lives, and beyond, if I can find a way to arrange it. With every breath, I will love you, cherish you, save you, if it comes to it, and breathe in and out with you until every trace of fear is gone." He grazed his lips across hers, catching her faint gasp. "I promise you, love, I will live my entire life for love of you."

One of her shaking hands came to rest on his cheek, gently rubbing against the stubble. "Cam…"

He captured her mouth in a kiss, pouring every promise and every wish into the molding of their lips, every passionate thought, every fanciful whim, every daydream, night dream, and things yet to dream, all melding together as he kissed her.

"I love you," Prue whispered, her lower lip catching at his with the words. She shook her head against him. "I love you."

Camden smiled and gave her one more feather-light kiss. "Then marry me, my adorable, feisty, remarkable tangle-tongue. Marry me and save me from a life without you."

Prue pulled back a little, smiling dreamily at him, stroking his cheek. "I'll save you, my love. All my life, I'll save you."

He turned his face to kiss the palm of her hand twice, then leaned into her hold. "Promise?"

She smiled, nodding. "Promise," she vowed as she leaned in to kiss him again.

Epilogue

❦

I will never understand those who choose to spread poison to further their own agenda and use slander as a way to improve their opinion of themselves. To parade their self-importance for the world and trample whomever they can in their path. Does the arrogance of such individuals know no bounds? Does their malicious behavior fill some innate need to strike out and be heard? How does such a person look at himself or herself with any sense of dignity? When their honor and integrity lies in tatters on the ground beneath their trampling feet, will they even feel the gaping wounds that their words and actions will enact on their own person? Those who seek to hurt and degrade others rather than lift and support will find that the darkness they create will be their own end reward.

-The Spinster Chronicles, 7 June 1818

"A bit on the nose, isn't it, Izzy?"

"You didn't complain when you reviewed it."

"And I'm not complaining now, but really, right in the issue after we heard the full nature of Lizard Liza's filth?"

Izzy turned in her chair to look at Charlotte, who had come early for the Spinster gathering that day. "You know I had to do it then. I would have lost my nerve if we had waited."

Charlotte seemed to consider that, then nodded with a heavy sigh. "Yes, I suppose you're right. You're far too nice, Isabella."

Izzy grumped and turned back to her writing. "Tell me something I don't know."

Charlotte suddenly moaned with great dramatics. "I'm so bored. When is Prue coming back?"

"Next week," Izzy told her for what had to be the seventh time. "They left right after the wedding for Hertfordshire. That new estate needed to be examined."

"I doubt very much it's the estate they are going to be examining," Charlotte chortled.

Izzy coughed in surprise, her face turning as red as Prue's ever had as she whirled to face her. "Charlotte Wright!"

"What did they do with Mrs. Westfall?" her friend went on as though she had not said anything shocking, sitting forward on the sofa. "I know she's not in London anymore, which is a blessed relief."

Izzy fanned her still-flaming cheeks. "Camden bought her a dower house as a wedding present. It's near her sister's place in Somerset."

"Aww," Charlotte moaned, pouting for effect. "We'll likely not have the pleasure of seeing Mrs. Westfall looking like a caged gorilla at our London balls anymore."

Izzy shook her head and again returned to her writing. There was nothing to be done about Charlotte. She would know; she had tried. Charlotte said precisely what she thought, exactly how she felt, and did not apologize for it.

What freedom there must have been in being so true to one's self without consideration to anybody else. Izzy could never have done something like that. She was far too eager to please, to be liked, to be nice, as Charlotte had said, and she would feel so guilty that she would wind up apologizing for everything.

Then again, it was undoubtedly a very good thing that there were not more versions of Charlotte around.

One was quite enough.

"Good heavens, I love that line, Izzy," Charlotte gushed proudly. "'Those who seek to hurt and degrade others rather than lift and support will find that the darkness they create will be their own end reward.'" She applauded and moved to the window. "Such viciousness. Remind me not to make you angry."

Izzy looked at Charlotte's back with a sardonic look. "It is only because it's anonymous that I can say such things. You know I could never do it face to face."

Charlotte shrugged. "Then write a speech, and I'll say it for you. Ooh, I wish I could have seen Eliza's face when she read it. She had to know we meant her."

"Probably," Izzy allowed, dipping her pen in ink again. "But it could have worked for Mrs. Westfall, as well."

"Yes, but she cannot read, so she would never know."

Izzy chuckled and put a hand to her face. "Oh, Charlotte."

"What happened to the lizard anyway?" Charlotte asked, changing topics yet again. "I haven't seen her at the last three gatherings."

"That's because she's at Tinley for the foreseeable future," a familiar voice said from the door.

Izzy and Charlotte turned in surprise to see Prue standing there, grinning at them all, a lovely sapphire ring glinting on one hand.

"Prue!" they squealed in chorus, dashing over to her and hugging her close.

She laughed and grinned so easily, it was as if she were a different person. "This is a fine greeting. Had I known I would be so missed, I should have stayed away longer."

"Where's Camden?" Izzy asked, looking past her.

"Never mind the man," Charlotte scoffed with a wave of her hand. "What about the lizard?"

Prue looked a little pained, and her cheeks flushed, but she still smiled. "Mariah Turner took a dislike to w-what Eliza was saying about Cam and me, and Mariah is very protective. She paid Eliza a visit, and…" She trailed off, her smile turning rueful. "Well, Mariah can be very persuasive. Eliza and Davies will spend the rest of the Season at Tinley. Recovering."

Charlotte laughed loudly, clapping her hands. "And the rumors?"

"Aunt Howard knew they were false, and she was so embarrassed." Prue shook her head, sighing. "She went to Mrs. Davies, and they quietly went about to set things straight. We're to dine with Aunt and Uncle before they remove to Somerset. Camden is so looking forward to it." She rolled her eyes, making them all laugh.

Izzy was stunned by the change in Prue. She was entirely herself, but with a confidence and grace that she had never managed before. She seemed perfectly at ease and bore a healthy glow now that Izzy was envious of.

"How's the house, Prue?" Izzy asked, waving her into a seat while Charlotte sat in her chair again.

"Gableshead?" Prue smiled, folding her hands in her lap. "It's so perfect, Izzy. It's absolutely perfect. Come and stay with us in the autumn. We have apple orchards. Camden and I would love it if you came."

"I doubt very much Camden would agree," Charlotte laughed.

"Notice I didn't invite you, Charlotte," Prue shot back, which made Charlotte laugh harder.

Izzy turned back to her writing, desperate to get one line more. With the others coming, it would be impossible to complete what she wished, but if she could finish just this thought…

"Working on another article, Izzy?" Prue prodded gently.

Izzy scrambled quickly, shuffling papers atop one another, then shoving them all in a drawer. "No. Well, maybe. Ideas. Nothing really." She turned and smiled at Prue quickly.

Prue looked at her, clearly knowing better, but she did not pry.

"Where is Camden?" Charlotte demanded at last. "I'll make him invite me, and he still needs to introduce me to Mariah Turner. I am even more eager than before to make her acquaintance."

"He's fetching presents, Charlotte," Georgie answered as she entered the room herself, smiling smugly. "I've just seen him. And the other girls have just arrived." She turned her gaze to Prue, made a noise of content, and looked at the rest. "One down, four to go!"

Izzy and Charlotte groaned, and they heard accompanying groans down the corridor, signaling Grace and Edith's arrival, and possibly Elinor's as well.

Prue did not protest at all and smiled back at Georgie. "I fully support this endeavor."

"Traitor," Charlotte muttered.

Izzy said nothing but caught Prue's eye as she looked at her once more, still uncertain.

She couldn't tell her the truth. She couldn't tell any of them. It was her secret, even from Georgie, and what if nothing came of it? It was better left unsaid, especially since she had no promises.

She wasn't going to marry like the others might do. She wasn't the sort of girl that men married. She'd never minded being a spinster before, but now her closest friends were married, and her options were running out.

This secret might open a way for her.

Time would tell.

Coming Soon

Spinster AND Spice

The Spinster Chronicles

Book Three

"A Spinster like her is
everything nice…"

by

REBECCA CONNOLLY